NITTI

By

Edward
Licciardello

DEDICATION

I dedicated this to my grandparent. My grandparents
who left their homeland then past the lady with the torch.

FORWARD

Once upon a time, there was a little girl who waited for her mother and father to take her home. One day this young girl reads a book.

Once upon a time, it was girl meets boy.

Once upon a time, a woman and man ran away and had a child named Andy.

Once upon a time, a boy named Andy found an empty pine box.

Once upon a time, a woman and two children found a man named Andy who lived in a pine box.

Once upon a time, we had no fence on our borders.

CONTENTS

ACKNOWLEDGMENTS

I dedicate this to my grandparent. They had to leave there home land and pass the lady with the torch.

CHAPTER ONE

Borders

It is Thanksgiving Day, 1900. A child is born to a young married migrant couple. The boy is named Andy Nobel Johnson. The next day, a boy is born to an immigrant couple. That boy is named Nicholas Litti. The two boys grow up together and become lifelong friends.

Eighteen years later, one young man is stationed in England. His name is Nicholas. He is a driver for a general and his daughter. Nicholas is the one who sits with the young girl as her father spends hours in war meetings.

Springtime, early evening, in a part of a European country that is under siege, on a field that has scars from years of battles. The field looks like a razor has cut painful lines across its face of dirt.

A preacher gives a sermon the night before the last major battle of a long war. It's a cool night. The sun is about to set. The preacher stands on top of a trench looking down on a group of soldiers. The preacher was warned about snipers.

The sermon

For thousands of years, this dirt under your feet has given life to fields of daisies and flowers. The daisies and flowers gave life to the birds and the bees that feed of its nectar of life that has a sweet taste. Life flourished on this field of life with daisies, flowers, and butterflies before man could get up on his two legs and walk upon it.

One day, man managed to get on his two legs and walked upon this beautiful land that was cover with daises, flowers, and butterflies that had so much life on it. He looked out onto its endless expanse of beauty. Man, seeing no other men around, claimed this expanse of endless beauty *his* land.

As other men managed to walk and traveled past this land, they became envious of this man's land with its endless beauty and fields of daisies, flowers, and butterflies.

Then other men started to claim part of the endless beauty and fields of daisies and flowers. So many men came to this now small expanse of a land of beauty, a new word called 'borders' had to be made. They made the word borders into an understanding of separations.

They made borders into a way of life for man. They made borders into laws. The borders they made were often changed and adapted to fit the ever-growing population. Laws of separation of us and them.

To keep this land, men found the need to claim and put borders on and around his land. Man found the need to defend his claimed land. To defend this claimed land, man had to fight, kill, and die for it.

Man came together in groups to better protect his now claimed land. Man did this better in groups of men. They did this with a chosen leader. They did this with the pride of a self-given cause and justification.

This pride and self-given justification were often shown as a color or a shield. The color or shield was held up as a warning to outsiders not to cross the border that was protected by those who claimed the land under a given color or shield.

Lines were drawn. Borders were marked to claim what land belong to whom. Colors and shields were worn to identify those who belonged among the people inside a border.

Man, with it still-growing population, divided himself into nations. The shields and colors were transformed into flags of different colors. Different groups now became a nation as the population grew.

A nation that now occupied a land had a flag that was different from other nations. The flags of different colors and of different symbols were placed as a headstone on the borders of each nation.

Man had found the need to travel and wage war to protect their borders. They would raise an army of their young and place them under a flag for the homeland.

Some of these armies were built to defend the homeland. Some of the armies were built to capture and occupy land outside the border.

This land we stand on today.

Others have come to this land from other nations to capture and occupy it. They do this under the flag of their own nation.

They wish to put new scars on this dirt and call it their new borders. They wish to make the new borders their borders. They wish to tell who should live on this dirt inside their new borders.

They come to give this land with new borders laws not chosen by its own people. New laws written by those who sent the army of the other nations.

Tonight, as the sun goes down and the stars come out, we think of our own homeland. We dream of it, and the people we have come to know. Our loved ones. Far away from here our minds will be.

We find ourselves in this place we can't leave. We find ourselves with the past motivation of any propaganda long gone and forgotten. Liberty. The word was often heard back home. It is not found on anybody's lips here.

The cold reality of being here. The reality of here is a place to die. The reality that the dirt under us is where we will bleed when we die. That the dirt under us is the last place we will know.

For thousands of years, the dirt gave life to fields of daisies, flowers, and butterflies. The daisies and flowers gave life to the birds and the bees that feed of its sweet nectar. This dirt has been waiting for us to come along bleed and die on it.

I cannot make it any clearer to you. I can't make it any clearer than to tell all of you we are going to die.

Your sacrifice may one day be remembered. Your sacrifice that will be mourned by the loved one you think of tonight. The ones you wish to be with tonight.

Your sacrifice for what?

The nation that will have its flag over this dirt will never know the names of all those who have fallen before you. Or your names that are the soon-to-be fallen.

Tomorrow, after you have fallen, another nation will put a flag where you stand. They will mourn who they have lost. Then the flag will change again, then more will die, and more will be mourned.

The dirt our blood will bleed into? That dirt will not know whose flag flies over it. The blood of the fallen will just become the new dirt.

The night will end, and morning will come. With the morning sun, the earth will shake. The armies will march. The armies will cross borders they have died to take and defend. They will cross the borders of a no-man's-land looking for the next border, and many more will die.

The armies will cross and take this border we stand on, and all of you will die. Then they will try to defend this border, and many of them will die. They have no hope to keep this border.

A new mighty nation has stepped onto this dirt. It has the might greater than all the nations who have sent their young to die and bleed on this dirt.

You will hold a flag and a border on this dirt tonight. The flag and this border are just a trap that is meant to draw the last hope of a dying nation. That nation's army is on death's doorstep. They have lost too many of their young.

This war for the dirt you stand on has seen more people die than any other war. We have found new ways to kill any life that comes. We still kill face-to-face. We kill from miles away. We kill from the air and the sea. We kill with clouds of white mist.

When the killing is done, new borders are won and lost, when the last of the few are left, when the last of the young are old, the dirt you bled and died in will give life to fields of daisies, flowers, and butterflies. The daisies and flowers will give life to the birds and the bees that feed of its sweet nectar.

Life again will flourish on this field of dirt someday, long after man got up on his two legs and walked. I pray that we have no flag on this dirt that day. I pray that we have no borders on this dirt that day.

I pray that someday a little girl will come along and pick some daisies that have grown from the dirt that so many young people have bled into it.

I pray on that day that a young boy will come along trying to catch a butterfly that dances on its path of flight, eluding him.

There is nothing here for you but death on these days. I pray that your sacrifice will be so that the young can cross any borders. I pray that your sacrifice will not hold a child to any land because of a flag. I pray that a young child can cross any border to pick daisies and chase butterflies.

There is nothing here for you but death. You are bait in a trap. Someday here there will be a field of daisies with no borders.

Amen

In this trench that night and the following days, a young man named Andy Johnson loses his time as a young man.

Chicago, a city that has seen its share of young immigrants come to its cold, windy city. Some of these young immigrants have left their birthplace in hopes of finding a better life for themselves and their family. Some of these young immigrants are seeking the dream of a place where the streets are paved with gold.

Some of the young immigrants will find streets that are paved with broken dreams and the potholes of poverty, not gold. The days of unbearable hardship will be the days the once-young immigrant will know for years. The once-young immigrant may live just long enough to see their future generation walk the same street with broken dreams and poverty, not gold. For countless generations, the pain and hurt of a family who just fails in the city where the hard, cold street takes its toll on people's lives and dreams.

Some of the young immigrants will find the opportunity for a better life in the work they do. Some of the young Immigrants will find opportunity that an education can give to better their life and their family's life.

Some immigrants will find that the right helping hand, at the right time, by the right person—not work or education—will lead to that dream of a street of gold. Even if that hand is on the wrong side of that so-called dream of a street paved with gold.

On the south side of Chicago, a part of a city that was once a home for a well-run crime organization. That once had control or an influence on the lives and businesses in the city by the power of bribery, intimidation, greed, and violence.

Over the years, the crime organization that had once grown in power and ability to draw borders of separation on a city map, started to splinter and divide. This organization is now on death's doorstep. The power that was used by this organization is now killing itself.

The human acts of bribery, intimidation, greed, violence, and killing are now the uncontrollable human acts that topple all. Those acts are now destroying the organization from within.

CHAPTER TWO

Chicago

Once upon a time, around 1900, a poor Italian couple in Chicago was blessed with a son they named Nicholas. Nicholas grew into a good-looking, smart boy. At ten years old, he found a job sweeping floors for the local barber.

One day, Nicholas saw the barber, his boss, cutting up a man's face with a straight razor. The boy kept silent on what he saw when the police questioned him about it. The barber, who was grateful, took the boy under his wing. The boy proved to be very bright and loyal.

At the age of twenty, Nicholas married the barber's ugly, fat daughter. This act of loyalty to the barber was repaid by the acceptance to the barber's family. His crime family. Nicholas, a day after the wedding, purchased an old building that was once a telegraph building for the railroad with money from his new father-in-law.

Nicholas turned the old building to a restaurant, bar, and hotel. In 1921, during Prohibition, Nicholas turned the restaurant in to a money-making machine for his father-in-law and boss. He ran the restaurant as a front. The illegal booze, prostitution, and gambling made him and his father-in-law lots of money.

In 1922, the young man Nicholas gives his father in-law a grandson and was a model citizen in the city. He gave the local church thousands of dollars and was there every Sunday with his wife and young son. The church was where he baptized his son.

In January 1923, the twenty-three-year-old Nicholas met an eighteen-year-old beauty named Sadie. The two acted like old friends. He fell for this blonde, blue-eyed Irish girl. Sadie knew who Nicholas was and that he liked her. Within two days, she had him upstairs at his restaurant impregnating her. So, the rumor had to be started, so the stories had to be fabricated. September 1, 1923, Sadie had a baby girl.

Nicholas and Sadie worked out a large cash agreement. Sadie would not publicly name who the real father was. Sadie and the baby were given a large bodyguard.

The baby girl would stay at Nicholas's restaurant and hotel. Sadie's bodyguard parents were Irish immigrants who were brought in to watch over the child. Sadie named the girl Nitti. Just Nitti, after Nicolas Litti, to leave no doubt who the father was.

Sadie loved the party life so much she wouldn't give it up after she had Nitti. As the twenties turned to thirty's and Sadie got older, she would find herself with younger men who were just good-looking and small-time wannabe gangsters. Nicholas moved on from Sadie to other affairs with other pretty women.

In a small part of the big city of Chicago in 1935 there is a small restaurant at the corner of Railroad Avenue and Cemetery Road. To one side of the building is a cemetery. On the other side is a train yard.

The restaurant is a three-story building with a basement. Behind the restaurant, the railroad and the cemetery meet at a dead end. The trains pass with such noise so often that the local resident on this dead-end street didn't even notice the noise.

The restaurant is now run by Andy Johnson. Andy is the bodyguard for a twelve-year-old girl named Nitti. They never had to worry about the quality of the food they served in the restaurant. The owner, Nicholas Litti, just had them stay open and stay quiet about his business and some of his friends that frequented the restaurant.

Throughout the twenties the restaurant was a very busy place. During the day, money went out of this place to some connected people. At night, the money came into the restaurant. Illegal booze, prostitution, and gambling was the big income for the restaurant in the twenties. Food service was just a small percentage of the business for the restaurant.

Andy Johnson, the bodyguard, was wounded in WWI. Andy was in a trench that was overrun. An enemy soldier threw a hand grenade into the trench that killed everybody but him.

Andy laid under some dead soldiers for two days, bleeding from shrapnel wounds. When the Americans came and took the trench, Andy was almost dead. He lost some of his hearing and his body was pockmarked and scarred. Andy lost some of his parts from the hand grenade as well. He would only be able to relieve himself sitting down.

Nicholas picked Andy as Sadie and Nitti's bodyguard. They were boyhood friends. Andy, who was a onetime hitman was not capable of having sex ever again. When Andy came back from the war, he was such a mess with scars on his face and head, everybody called him Raggedy after the doll.

By 1935 Raggedy was now Nitti's full-time bodyguard and surrogate father. Raggedy would drive Nitti to the local all-girls school and pick her up after school. Nitti lived in one of the rooms above the now almost-legitimate restaurant.

Prohibition was over. The prostitution at the restaurant had gone on to more lucrative locations. Once a week, some of the crime family members and bagmen would come to this restaurant and play poker all night because of the small amount of people who still went to the restaurant. They had their own room to play cards in, with all they could drink and eat. The next day, the bagmen would leave to go to work.

On Sunday, September 1, nine-teen thirty-five Nitti turned twelve years old. Nicholas has taken his daughter out for her birthday.

Sadie would show up at the restaurant to dry out for a day. Sometimes, she was looking for some money. Sadie didn't show up for Nitti's birthday.

Raggedy has a mother who is called Rag, and his stepfather, who is called Conversation, was now running the numbers horse and sports betting in the restaurant. Rag was a surrogate mother to Nitti. Rag and Raggedy were being paid by Nicholas to watch over the girl and run the restaurant.

Nicholas was keeping the restaurant alive by paying all its legitimate bills. He did this just to give his daughter a roof over her head. Nicholas' wife knew of Nitti, the illegitimate child, and she would have little-to-nothing to do with her. She would not let Nitti stay at her home with her father.

At the restaurant, there are just two cooks and four-to-six waitresses, depending on who was going or coming. The waitresses were just a current girlfriend of a member of the crime family.

The restaurant had found an old homeless man they used as a busboy, cleaner, and gofer. The old man was caught with some stolen money in his coat at the card game and was shot by one of the bagmen.

The next day, Raggedy was told by Nicholas to take the old man out to the cemetery and throw him into a grave. Then Raggedy was told by Nicholas to go and find a homeless boy to take his place, because a homeless boy would be afraid to steal anything.

That day, Raggedy put the dead man's body in an empty grave and buried him. Then Raggedy went down to the orphanage and found a boy to take his place. The boy was fifteen with no family or history.

He was found on a chicken farm by the police looking for a bank robber. The people who ran the farm took the boy from the streets a year before the police found him.

The people on the farm found the boy in a haze from being beat up once and couldn't remember who he was. So, the people at the farm called him Hayes. The people on the farm used the boy to kill the chickens.

The police took Hayes from the chicken farm to an orphanage.

Raggedy was in the orphanage's president's office when Hayes first met Raggedy. Hayes saw a muscular-bound man over six-foot tall and well over 250 pounds. The large man had a white short-sleeve shirt on and black pants. The large man had a tattoo on each of his big forearms. The right forearm had a daisy on it. The left forearm had the words 'pushing up.' The man's face and bald head was pockmarked with scars. Raggedy puts his hand out to the boy and introduces himself. Hayes shakes Raggedys hand.

Raggedy takes the boy called Hayes back to the restaurant, after paying the orphanage's president some cash.

Hayes was given a room in the basement of the restaurant with the bugs, mice, rats, and roaches. The basement has a twenty-four-inch sewage pipe running through it. The sounds of sewage flowing in the pipes could constantly be heard running. Raggedy tells the boy what his jobs will be at the restaurant and he should never try to leave. He was also told if he stole anything or caught trying to run away, he would be buried alive.

It's late at night. Hayes is in his new basement room for the first time. He looks around and sees a treasure of different items. He sees several shelves with old books that are labeled 'Property of the Chicago Library.' He sees jewelry cases of watches. Different clothes racks with enough clothes to do a Broadway show. On one wall is an old city map that somebody has drawn lines of separation and borders of crime organizations' territories. In a corner sits a large car-racing trophy. A 500 winner's trophy from Indiana. New dishes, pots and pans in cases with the names of all the different restaurants in Chicago.

On the other side of the basement are racks of shotguns, rifles, and handguns. A dozen new radios are stacked on the floor. On a coatrack are several police and firefighter uniforms.

CHAPTER THREE

Restaurant

It is Monday, September 2, 1935. Raggedy is up at 5:00 AM and goes down to the basement and wakes up Hayes. Raggedy tells Hayes that he should go upstairs, brush his teeth, and wash his face before anybody in the building wakes up. Hayes gets up, makes his bed, and goes upstairs to use the restaurant's restroom. He washes his face and brushes his teeth.

Hayes goes to the bar in the restaurant where Raggedy told him to be. Raggedy shows Hayes the kitchen and what he should clean. Then he shows him the back of the building where all the garbage goes. Raggedy picks up the daily paper that was delivered. Raggedy tells Hayes all his morning jobs and that he'll be back soon. He also warns him not to leave and to keep working. The people who live or work here will be by to tell him who they are and what they want him to do.

Raggedy is talking to Hayes when Nitti comes into the restaurant to tell Raggedy, she is ready for her ride to school.

Nitti looks at Hayes standing by Raggedy and says hello to him.

Hayes looks at her and says good morning. In Nitti's hand is a book of *Romeo and Juliet*. Raggedy witnesses a case of girl meets boy. He takes his hand and puts it on the back of the boy's neck. He then asks Nitti to wait in the car for him. Nitti says okay and smiles at Hayes. Then Nitti does a girly wave to Hayes and walks outside to Raggedys car.

Raggedy waits for Nitti to leave, then, with his hand on the back of Hayes's neck, he squeezes and pushes the boy down to his knees. The boy falls to his knee from the pain. Raggedy grabs the boy's hair with his other hand and turns Hayes' face to his. Raggedy takes his hold of the boy's neck and uses the hand to pull out a gun.

Raggedy shows the gun to him and tells Hayes, "If you ever talk to the girl again, I will kill you."

Hayes looks back at Raggedy and tells him, "I already died. I don't fear dying anymore." Raggedy asks Hayes what he meant by that.

Hayes tells him a story of waking up on a railroad track as a freight train was passing over him. Some people beat him up and left him on the railroad track between the rails, so a train would run over him.

Raggedy thinks about what Hayes just said. He felt the same way after he recovered from the near-death experience of the hand grenade in the trench.

Raggedy puts his gun back and lets the boy go. He tells Hayes to start working and he'll be back soon. Raggedy has Nitti in the car with him as he drives her to school.

Nitti: "Raggedy, who is the boy I saw this morning?"

Raggedy: "He is our new worker. I had to take care of the old man. He was caught stealing."

Nitti: "Where did the boy come from?"

Raggedy: "I got him from the orphanage. You should stay away from him. I don't know much about him. If he says anything to you, let me know."

Nitti: "Raggedy. I can tell good people from bad people. I think he is a good person."

Raggedy: "You can do that at all of twelve years old?"

Nitti: "It's a woman thing, Raggedy. You wouldn't understand."

Raggedy: "Nitti, it's a man-thing to physically hurt other people. So stay away from him and he won't get hurt. I don't know if your father is going to approve of him."

Nitti: "I understand, Raggedy, but I think he is going to be a nice person. You may even get to like him."

Raggedy drops Nitti off at her school. Then Raggedy goes and tells Nicholas about the new boy.

Hayes had started to work when Raggedy left. Hayes goes and gets the papers that Raggedy took inside. He then goes up to the top two floors and drops a paper in front of each door. When he comes down to the first floor, he puts four copies of the paper on a dining table.

Raggedy told Hayes to put a paper by each door on both floors and pick up any papers at the door left from the day before. He was not to check if somebody was in the room. Just leave the paper and go on with his work. After he drops the papers off to the rooms, he goes down and empties the garbage.

The morning cook came in and asked Hayes who he was and where the old man was. Hayes told him he was the new busboy and house cleaner. The cook told Hayes to call him Randy.

Randy shows Hayes how to set up the bacon and eggs for him each morning. Randy was a black man who was about fifty years old. Randy shows Hayes the kitchen and tells him how he wants things done. Then he tells Hayes about a woman he will meet called Rag. Randy tells Hayes never to say anything about the outfit she wears, or she may shoot him.

A waitress comes into the restaurant by the backdoor. Randy introduce Hayes to her. The waitress is somebody's girlfriend who works in the local family. She shows Hayes how she wants her table set up in the morning.

Her name is Catherine. Catherine tells Hayes that he will not get any tip money. If he steals any of her tip money, her boyfriend will beat him up.

Back in the dining room, Raggedys mom and stepdad meet Hayes. Hayes see a woman in her sixties dressed up in a police uniform with a policeman's hat on.

She has a large men's Rolex watch on each wrist. She has a gold cross earring on her right ear. She has the Star of David earring in her left.

A man in his early forties is behind her. The woman introduces herself as Rag to Hayes. Then she points to the man in his forties and says, "This is my friend and his name is Conversation. I call him that because it's not what he says it is how he says it."

Rag and Conversation use a dining room table as a desk. They will spend the day there taking bets and running numbers. Rag sends Raggedy out to collect from people.

Rag has an old, worn-out rocking chair. At her side of the table, in front of her chair, is a white tea-stained coffee mug. On the side of the mug is a bottle of bourbon.

Rag tells Hayes how she wants her table set up every morning. She shows him how sharp she wants her number-two pencils. Rags tells him to have the deck of cards shuffled and the paper open to the crossword puzzle.

On the table are two phones with two phone books, several yellow folders with white paper inside them, two clocks on each side of the table, a large jar of aspirin, a large jar of paper clips, another large jar with rubber bands, two full bottles of gin, and an old six-by-nine picture of a young Raggedy in a baseball uniform.

Behind the table is a blackboard called Raggedys deliveries. There are places on it with names that tell who must pay and how much.

Rag pulls out a .38-calaber handgun and tells Hayes she will shoot him in his groin if he steals anything. Then Hayes returns to the kitchen.

Some people from the local neighborhood come in for breakfast this morning. It is a slow Monday morning, but Hayes is very busy, and the work is very hard. Raggedy comes back and talks to the people who worked at the restaurant about Hayes.

As more of the day passes, Hayes meets the local delivery people who delivered food and supplies.

At 11:00 AM, a new waitress names Stacy comes in. She also gives Hayes the same warning about stealing money. Then Stacy tells Hayes how she wants her tables set.

At 4:00 PM, Raggedy and Nitti return from Nitti's school. Nitti goes to the bar and takes a barstool to the far side of the bar with her books. This gives her a good view of the new boy.

Randy, the cook, comes out of the kitchen and gives her something to drink then asks her how her day was. Nitti talks to Randy about his kids and her summer. They talk for a while, then Randy goes back to the kitchen and makes her dinner.

The next cook comes in and introduces himself to Hayes. His name is Joe. Joe takes Hayes back into the kitchen and shows him how he wants his kitchen to be. Two more waitress come in till closing time. One is named Linda and one is named Sue, and they both give Hayes the same warning about tips and stealing.

Nitti sees Hayes running around the kitchen and the tables trying to help the waitresses and clearing the tables. The bartender comes in and is introduced to Hayes. His name is Gus. Gus tells Hayes that he is not to handle any cash that is on the bar. He tells Hayes how he wants his bar set up.

At 6:00 PM, Nitti has left the bar and has gone to her room for the night. Rag tells her son that Hayes won't last a week and he is going to have to get somebody older.

Raggedys stepfather doesn't say anything to him. He just walks to the bar for his alcohol. Raggedys mother leaves them and goes up to her room.

Its 12:00 AM. The restaurant is closed for the day. The only two people left are Raggedy and Hayes. Hayes is worn out from his long day. Raggedy tells him he'll wake him up at 5:00 AM to do it all again. Hayes walk down to the basement and falls asleep.

It's 5:00 AM, Tuesday morning. Raggedy wakes Hayes up. Hayes goes upstairs to the restroom and starts another long day. He goes outside and picks up the papers. After emptying the garbage, he brings the copies of the paper to the rooms on the top two floors.

He picks up the leftover papers that are in front of the doors from yesterday. On the third floor, he picks up a paper that is in front of a door. This paper is a little different than the others. It's open to the crossword puzzle and has a different smell to it. Hayes thinks it's perfume.

He is looking at the puzzle as he walks down the stairs. He notices his name written on the puzzle and the word 'hello' in front of it. Then he notices the name 'Nitti' written underneath it and the words 'let's be friends.'

As Hayes walks down the stairs, he reads more of the words: secret; I; gofer; put; him; money; killing; in; me; coat; and guilty. The rest of the puzzle just has some letters written in it. Hayes takes all the papers he collects and throws them out.

Raggedy is waiting for Nitti at the bar that morning. Hayes sees Nitti come downstairs. She says hi to Hayes and walks with Raggedy out the door and to the car. Hayes goes on with his day of cleaning and bussing tables. When Hayes gets the chance, he starts to wonder why the girl would leave him the note. He asked himself if she knows the trouble that would get him in.

Raggedys mother, Rag, is on Hayes' all day, how she wants her table set and getting her food and everything else. Conversation doesn't say a word. He just shakes his head all day as Rag yells at the boy.

Hayes' torcher of a day goes by slow. At 4:00 PM, Nitti comes home from school with Raggedy. She takes her seat at the end of the bar and does some homework and eats. She talks to the cook and the other people there but not to Hayes.

At 6:00 PM, Nitti goes upstairs for the night. Midnight comes slowly on this Tuesday. At 12:00 AM, Hayes goes downstairs to his room.

The next day, Hayes starts his day all over. He goes upstairs to bring the new papers and take the old ones away. At the same door as yesterday, he sees the paper open to the daily crossword puzzle. Again, he sees his name with Nitti's name under it. This time there are words on it that says 'Let's be friends please. Please reply.' Hayes reads it then takes it to the garbage and throws it out.

The same things with the paper go on in Hayes' week. Every morning, Nitti writes him a note in the puzzle. When Friday night comes, the restaurant, as far more people in it at night, Hayes must bring drinks up to the second floor where there is a card game going on. He works till 1:00 AM, then Raggedy tells him to stop working and go to bed.

The next day is Saturday. Raggedy lets Hayes sleep till 6:00 AM. When he wakes him up, Raggedy tells Hayes he likes the way he works. Hayes gets up and starts this Saturday later than a weekday. When he brings the papers up to the rooms, he finds no paper at Nitti's door. He collects the other papers, then takes them out to the trash.

An hour later, he sees Nitti at the bar talking to the cook about what she wants for breakfast. After she tells the cook what she wants, she turns to Hayes.

Nitti: "Hayes, good morning. Thank you for bringing the paper to me in the morning. I love reading the paper every day. You never know what you may find in it. Do you know what I mean, Hayes?"

Hayes: "I don't want to get in any trouble. Please just let me be. I don't want to go to the orphanage again or sleep on the street. Please."

Nitti: "I understand, Hayes. I won't be mean to you. I lost my paper you left me yesterday. If you find it, let me know."

Hayes: "Okay, but how will I know it's yours?"

Nitti: "You'll know, Hayes, when you see it."

Hayes: "I need to go back to work."

Nitti: "Bye, Hayes. Keep in touch."

Hayes goes back to work and spends the day avoiding Nitti. Later that night, he goes back to his bed in the basement. On his bed he finds a copy of yesterday's paper. It's open to the crossword puzzle. On the crossword puzzle is a letter from Nitti.

Hayes,

Please rescue me. I am as lonely as you. I live in a gilded cage. The bars are the people who are paid to watch over me. Like you, I have no real mother or father. Raggedy told me about you. You don't need to be afraid of him. He likes you, Hayes. You remind him of himself when he was young. I think I am the only person who understands Raggedy.

Maybe if I told you about myself, you would understand me. My mother is a drunk who can't stay away from a drink. She only comes and see me when my father pays her. My father is one of the most powerful men in Chicago. I only get to see him on some weekends.

He takes me out to eat and sometimes we see a movie. His fat wife wants him to spend time with his so-called real family.

The people here know I am their meal ticket. That's why they are so nice to me and not you. I don't want to be here anymore than you. I have no other place I can go. Nobody really wants me.

There is a dumbwaiter that I took to come down here and leave you this letter. Please don't tell anybody or they will close it. When I was little, I would hide down here and dream of running away. Please do not use it. You are two big and may break it.

I would like it if you would write me back. You can leave me letters in the crossword puzzles. No one will ever know. It could be a game that just us two can play.

Nitti

Hayes puts the letter into the furnace. He then finds the hidden dumbwaiter door and sticks a board against it, so it can't be open from the inside. Then he goes to sleep.

CHAPTER FOUR

Rag Time

The next day was Sunday. Hayes got to sleep till 7:00 AM before Raggedy woke him up. Hayes did the same things as the days prior. When he passed Nitti's room, he just left the paper. He didn't even bother to look for a note from her.

As the days and weeks passed, Hayes develop the ability to get himself up and start the day the same way. He does the same thing every day. After several weeks, no one had to ask Hayes anything. He was already doing everything that needed to be done.

Rag and Conversation come down to their table on this morning. They will spend the day there taking bets and running numbers. Rag has an old worn-out rocking chair. At her side of the table, in front of her chair, is a white tea-stained coffee mug. On the side of the mug is a bottle of bourbon.

Hayes knows how Rag wants her table set up every morning. He has her number-two pencil sharpened this morning. The deck of cards is shuffled, and the paper is open to the crossword puzzle. An old six-by-nine picture of a young Raggedy in a baseball uniform is on the table.

On the table Hayes has set up are two phones with two phone books, several yellow folders with white paper inside them, two clocks on each side of the table, a large jar of aspirin, a large jar of paperclips, another large jar with rubber bands, and two full bottles of gin. Behind the table, Hayes has cleaned the blackboard called Raggedy Deliveries.

Rag dresses in a taxi cab driver outfit with the hat on this morning. She has her gold cross in one ear and the Star of David in the other. Rag walks over to her table and looks at the placement of all the items on it. Then she turns and looks at the freshly washed blackboard. Rag calls across the room to Hayes. Hayes is washing some tables. He turns and looks toward Rag. "Nice job this morning, Hayes. If everybody could do what they are paid to do as good as you, I would be much happier." After saying that to Hayes, Rag looks toward Conversation.

Conversation just takes his seat and opens some yellow folders. Hayes goes back to work. Rag takes her seat. She takes her bottle of gin and puts some in her white tea-stained coffee mug. Rag looks at the crossword puzzle. She takes her number-two pencil and has six words done within a minute. Randy, the cook, brings out a teapot for Rag and a coffeepot for Conversation.

Randy fills their cups with the tea and coffee. Rag gives Randy her breakfast order. Randy looks at Conversation and says, "Two bacon, lettuce, and tomato on white bread, toasted, with mayonnaise, I know." Randy then walks back to the kitchen.

Conversation hands Rag a yellow folder. On the folder are the words Raggedy Collections. Then Conversation hands her single white paper that has 'last rights' written on the top of it. On that white paper are two names with the address.

Rag opens the yellow folder and starts writing names and addresses on the blackboard. Randy brings out two trays with Rag and Conversation's breakfast. He puts the trays down and goes back into the kitchen. Rag finishes putting the list of names on the blackboard.

On one side of the board are six names that Raggedy is to visit and get money from people who have made bets and lost. On the bottom of the board are the two names from the white paper.

She has written the words 'last rights' by each of them. Rag then sits at the table and eats her breakfast.

Hayes comes out from the kitchen with the pot of tea and coffee. He refills both cups up then walks back into the kitchen. Rag and Conversation eat their breakfast. Rag works on her crossword puzzle. Conversation is reading the paper.

Raggedy comes back from dropping Nitti off at school. He walks over to the delivery board. He looks at it and lets out a couple of four-letter words.

Raggedy: "That board is ridiculous. Why do I always have to go out on so many last rights? Nicholas' father-in -aw always gives me those. I hate those. He must have forgotten what it is like. It's not like I'm going to get any help with it. It's not just going there and turning around and coming back. Somebody's going to die. It's going to be me or them. And to give two of them in one day."

"These people are morons to owe that much money. If they don't have it, don't bet it. We all know what's going through their degenerate mind. I have a hunch.

It's my lucky number. A friend told me he had inside information. It's my last chance. I should just risk it all."

"Then the best is 'I had a dream that the horse would win. So, I bet everything and borrowed more.' I hate these people. I should go out and shoot every gambler I see. Just think of all the paperwork we would save. No, I can't do that. These people are our customers."

"And do you see where I must go? I must go outside our territory. If I have a problem, it could become a bigger problem. It's not like everybody drives a used green four-door 1928 Cadillac Model 341. You can see that car coming a mile away. Once I cross those tracks, everybody is calling everybody."

"Conversation what do you do around here? Why don't you go out and do my job for a day? What do you think I do? You think I just look for places to eat? It's not liked the old days. They would bring in somebody from the outside. But that costs too much, so they send me. I am tired of it."

Raggedy then goes off into the kitchen to eat his breakfast. Rag and Conversation look at each other as Raggedy storms away. The two go back to their breakfast and crossword puzzle.

Hayes turns the open sign around, and the restaurant opens its doors to the public. There is no waitress this morning, so Hayes must cover all the tables.

Two old people who frequented the restaurant show up this morning for breakfast. They would order very little but spend hours at a table. Hayes goes over to the table to take their order. Ten minutes later, he has an order for two cups of coffee.

Raggedy has finished his breakfast and goes out to Rag. Rag hands him a list of places and names. Raggedy takes the list without saying a word and walks out the door.

Hayes has the old couple's coffee and fills their cup. Ten minutes later, they give an order of four slices of toast and a bowl of hash. Hayes brings the order to Randy.

Three bagmen dressed in suits come into the restaurant. One of them walks up to Rag. He gives her a yellow folder. Rag talks to the bagman as the other two men take a seat at a table. Conversation leaves the table and goes back upstairs.

Conversation comes back from his room with a locked brown suitcase. Conversation hands the suitcase to the bagman who's talking to Rag. The bagman takes the case then walks over to the other man he came in with. The bagman puts the brown suitcase on his chair. Then he sits on it.

Hayes brings the food to the two old people. Hayes see the three men in suits. These three come in once a week. Most of the time there is a waitress here. The three of them will try to pick her up. After Hayes places the food for the old people, he walks over to the bagmen. Hayes takes their food and alcohol order, then goes into the kitchen and gives Randy their order and tells him he must get them some drinks.

Two men come into the restaurant and sit at the bar. A man and a woman come and take a table. Hayes is very busy taking orders and serving people.

Raggedy opens the yellow folder the bagman gave her. She reads it then hands it to Conversation. Rag picks up a phone and calls Nicholas' father-in-law at his barbershop. The two talk a couple of minutes about who owes money.

Rag tells him there is a big college game this weekend. She asks him if he could get an injury update on the quarterback. She tells him Conversation wants to change the line. Conversation thinks too much money is being bet because he may be hurt more than is in the paper. He tells her he'll see what he could do, but it may cost more than the information may be worth.

The two talk more about other betting lines. After the daily update on the betting lines are discussed, he changes the conversation.

Nicholas' father-in-law brings up the new boy, Hayes. He asks Rag what she thinks of him. Rag tells him that she likes the boy and he never stops working. The man asks Rags if he could be trusted with money. Rags tells him that she isn't sure yet. That last one was a surprise to her. He had better chances to steal more money and get away with it. Why he would take some poker money off a table and put it in his coat pocket was just so stupid. Then to leave the coat with the money sticking out of the pocket on the door handle to the room the card game was being played in was just dumb.

Then Nicholas' father in-law asks about having him around with Nitti there. Rag tells him that Hayes is nice to her. Rag tells him that Hayes tries to avoid her, but she thinks Nitti may have her first crush on him, but it will pass with the next crush.

Then he tells Rag if the boy does anything wrong to call him first before she tells Nicholas. Rag tells him she would. Rag and Nicholas' father in-law finish talking, and Rag hangs up the phone. Rag looks at Conversation and tells him that they may keep the boy.

Conversation opens a yellow folder. He pulls out some invoices from the restaurant, the barber shop, and some other places. Then he grabs a checkbook and stars writing some checks for the invoices.

Rag looks at Hayes working the tables and helping the customers. She picks up the phone again and starts her morning work of trying to collect money from people before she must send Raggedy to see them.

Rag makes a call to a better who owes a lot of money. A woman picks up the phone.

Rag: "Is John there?"

Woman: "No, this is his wife. What are you calling him for?"

Rag: "John owes some people some money and he needs to pay that money back."

Woman: "I'm his wife, Mrs. Terry Douglas. You can call me Terry. What money does he owe you?"

Rag: "I rather talk to John. Is he there? I need to talk to him."

Terry: "No you can talk to me. What money does my deadbeat husband who can't find a job owe you?"

Rag: "You should ask him. He owes $319. He needs to pay that money back today. Do you have the money? I can send somebody out to get it."

Terry: "Oh my god. I don't have a dollar to buy my kids food. We owe everybody we know. Let me guess, you're his girlfriend and you let him borrow some money. Well, you can forget that money and any other money you gave him. If you want that sorry excuse of a father, you can have him."

Rag: "I don't want him. I don't even know the loser. He made some bets and lost. Then he borrowed money to get even. Then he lost again. That is what they all do is lose. If we don't get the money, he owes us, somebody who is big and scary will be by. So, before you pay anybody else, pay us or you will get hurt, mommy."

Rag hangs the phone up and starts making other calls. About lunchtime, Rag and Conversation stop working. Conversation goes outside for his daily walk. Rag goes upstairs to use the restroom.

About 1:00 PM, Rag and Conversation are back at the table. Hayes and a waitress are working on about six customers. Hayes is taking some orders and bussing some tables.

Conversation turns the radio onto a radio soap opera. Rag picks up the phone and calls somebody else for money. This time, she calls the man at his work. His name is Larry Potter.

Larry: "Hello, my name is Larry, and this is the office of the Board of Education. How may help you."

Rag: "Hi, Mr. Larry. I am your conscience. You owe somebody a lot of money. You should pay back the money you owe before some bossy tattletale tells on you."

Larry: "Who is this? You can't call this office. Who do you think you are?"

Rag: "I am the person who wants the money you owe for betting on a horse race. The race that you bet too much money on. The race you had to have the money. We want our money now, Mr. Big Time."

Larry: "I will call the police if you call this number again and ask for me. Do you hear me?"

Rag: "Listen to me, Mr. Big Time. I am an old woman. How would you like me to show up at that Board of Education saying that you got me pregnant? I may just show up in my bra and big-boy boxers. I will be singing the praises of what a good lover you are. The things I did when you paid me and my mother to have sex with you. I will be talking a lot about us. I'll tell them the days that you called out sick was just excuse to have sex with me and my mother, you sick bastard."

Larry: "They would fire me. My wife would leave me. You can't do that. Please don't. Nobody would believe you."

Rag: "Okay, Mr. Big Time, pay me. If you must steal the kids' lunch money, pay me. If you must steal the kids' piggy bank money, pay me. If you must make your young, pretty wife walk the streets, pay me. Pay me, Mr. Big Time lover. Pay me or else."

Rag hangs up the phone. She looks at Conversation and tells him that phone call got her hot. She sees Hayes cleaning some tables. It's the early afternoon-slow time. Rag tells Conversation that she going to take Hayes into the basement and explain why they have what they have down there.

Then she tells Conversation if he doesn't come up, she'll kill him the old-fashioned way, but he will be a man if he survives it. Rag gets up and asks Hayes to follow her. They go down to the basement.

Rag: "Hayes, I like the way you work here. You're one of the best workers I've ever seen."

Hayes: "Thank you, Rag. I do try."

Rag: "We know, Hayes. That's not why I came down here with you. I hate it down here. I must explain the stuff down here. I don't know what Raggedy told you about this stuff.

"These items are not mine or anybody who lives here. Maybe Nitti is the exception. It belongs to Nicholas Nitti and his father-in-law. People who can't pay what they owe will sometimes have the chance to give something in exchange for the money they owe. Everything down here has value to the business of what we do.

"The uniforms are used when there is a need to have a policeman, fireman, or whoever. The radio we hope to sell someday. The guns...well, you can figure it out. The books somebody thought that we could sell them back to the library. That is still in the works.

"The trophy is a novelty. I think somebody drank too much that day to take that. It will never be worth anything. It lost its value when the second guy won the next race.

"Hayes, this is who we are. This is what we do. There are three places where a person can get money: a bank, a pawnshop, or us. We are somewhere between them. We don't go looking for them. They come looking for us. That's what we do."

Hayes: "I understand, Rag."

Rag: "That's good you understand, Hayes. You don't have to like it."

Hayes: "Are we done now? I have to get back to work."

Rag: "No, Hayes, not yet. I have something else to talk to you about."

Hayes: "Okay, Rag, what else do you want to show me?"

Rag: "It's Nitti. She likes you. It's her first crush on a boy. It's not a good thing for you that she likes you. Her father is our boss. Our boss isn't just any boss.

Our boss has people killed. He has that power to have somebody killed. You look at that girl the wrong way, it could be a problem. That problem will be your problem, or it could be our problem.

"The best way to avoid a problem is to avoid having a problem. It's avoiding having this problem the first time. All that is needed is to have Nitti tell her father anything. Hayes, avoid the problem and a void Nitti. The less said to her the better.

"I like the girl. I liked her mother. I tried to help her mother. Some people you can't help. All they want is to see the next drink in front of them. That's all her mother wants. I'm afraid that's all that woman is ever going to want.

"Her mother just loved Nicholas too much and couldn't keep him. She couldn't handle it. Then all the men and all the money they would spend on her. All the men went to her head. Then the drinking. Then the money, drinking, the men, the drinking, and the drinking. Then Nitti.

"She hoped that Nitti and her father's money would take her away from places like this. Nicholas had other ideas, then Sadie ideas. It is Nitti who ends up with the mess that is her mother.

Nicholas is the man who controls everything and everyone around her. Her father, the man with the money and power to do it.

"I like Nitti. If I had a daughter, I would like her to be like Nitti. So, Hayes, if I ever see you do something you shouldn't, I may not like it. You should be more afraid of Raggedy. He is paid to take care of her. So, avoid Nitti and you will avoid a problem that may cost you your life.

"Hayes, one last thing I think you must know. Raggedy and I don't have any other place to go. His father was killed a long time ago. I married Conversation to give Raggedy a father. At the time, it was a good idea. Raggedy never took to Conversation as a father. The two got along for me.

"Hayes, you can't make people make a family. It doesn't work that way. You are born into a family. That will be you true family and you can't change it.

"Raggedy and I are family. We both like the people here. Raggedy and I have closeness to Nitti, but Nitti needs her own family."

Hayes: "All right, Rag, I will avoid Nitti. Can I go back to work now? Randy is going to wonder where I went."

Rag: "Sure, Hayes. Go ahead. I'll tell him you were helping me fix my under-wear. Just kidding. Go ahead."

Hayes goes back to work. Rag goes back to her table with Conversation and her work

Rag and Conversation are at their table. Conversation is reading a book called *Gone with the Wind* and listening to his daytime radio soap opera. Rag makes another call. This one is to a woman who is home named Terry Lane.

Terry: "Hello."

Rag: "Hi, my name is You Owe Us Money. So, when are you going to pay us?"

Terry: "I think you have the wrong number."

Rag: "I think you have the wrong idea of who we are. You made a bet at a horse track last Tuesday. You were wearing a blue dress. You were holding your boyfriend's hand. His name is Sam. You lost that bet and then borrowed two hundred dollars. Then you and Sam went to the Main Street hotel. At 6:00 PM, you both went to the track again. You lost again. Should I go on or do you want to know how many times he was on top of you. Miss Lane, whose husband works in the local bank."

Terry: "Please don't. Somebody may be listening. I will get you the money. Just give me a couple of days, please."

Rag: "Your time was up when your husband couldn't get it up. But don't worry about that. I have a 300-pound brother who never had sex. I think you would be a good piece for him. He doesn't smell too much. He just can't wash in between all the folds of skin. So, what I am thinking, Miss Good Time To-Be, is I will send some big men down to get you and bring you to my brother.

"It wouldn't be like a rape because it would be just an exchange of service. He'll pay off your debt. And he will get to do to you what your husband couldn't do to you.

"An exchange of service... It sounds like the old barter system to me. So, go down to that bank your husband works at, find some guy who can't get a woman, who's counting the money. Then do whatever you have to do to him. We know where you live. You're going to know where my fat, smelly brother's bed room is, if you don't pay us, you soon-to-be-crushed whore."

Rag hangs up the phone.

Raggedy comes back about 3:00 PM. He walks up to Rag and Conversation and drops a pile of cash in front of Conversation. Then he tells the two, "Both last rights paid up. I didn't have to do anything to them. One of the last rights wanted to give me more, just to get on my good side."

Conversation starts to count the cash. Rag tells Raggedy tomorrow may be a lighter day. Raggedy tells her if it is, he is going to catch a game tomorrow. Raggedy asks Rag how Hayes was this morning, when the waitress didn't show. Rags tells him that it didn't faze him. He just kept working. "I found a good one this time," Raggedy tells Rag.

"The last one was okay. I just don't understand the why and how he did what he did," Rag answers back.

Raggedy goes up to his room. Rag and Conversation go on with their work and calls. At 3:30 PM, Raggedy comes down from his room and goes to get Nitti from school.

At 4:00 PM, Raggedy and Nitti return. Nitti goes to the bar and takes a stool to the far side of the bar with her books. This gives her a good look at Hayes. Randy the cook comes out of the kitchen and gives her something to drink then asks her how her day was. Nitti talks to Randy about his kids and asks how they're doing at school. They talk for a while, then Randy goes back to the kitchen and makes her dinner.

The next cook, Joe, comes to work. He talks to Randy about food stock and the old stoves. Then he finds Hayes. Hayes tells him who did and didn't show up for work.

Nitti sees Hayes running around the kitchen and the tables, cleaning and trying to help the waitress. The bartender comes in and talks to Hayes about what needs to be ordered.

At 6:00 PM, Nitti has left the bar and gone up to her room. Rag and Raggedy are talking about some of the stops Raggedy will have to do tomorrow. Conversation gets up and goes to the restaurant register and starts to count the cash for the day.

Conversation fills out an end-of-day report and takes the cash with him. Raggedy tells Rag he's going out for a while, then he leaves. Rag and Conversation close it up for the day.

Conversation takes all the cash Raggedy bought back from his day and what cash the restaurant had. The two go up to their different bedrooms on different floors.

Hayes walks over to the table and starts to clean it and set it up for tomorrow. Then he cleans the blackboard.

Its 12:00 AM. The restaurant is closed for the day. The only person left is Hayes. Hayes checks the locks on the doors. He opens the empty register then goes down to the basement and falls asleep.

CHAPTER FIVE

Good-night Nitti

Nitti and Hayes seldom talk or acknowledge each other. Thanksgiving 1935 comes, and the restaurant closes for regular business. Randy brings his family into the restaurant for the holiday meal. Rag wears a Texaco man with a star, gasman suit.

For lack of another place to go, a couple of bagmen who frequent the place showed up for the meal. A couple of the waitresses showed up with their boyfriend or somebody's husband. Some of the betters who are paid up and have no other place to go show up. It was a group of people who had nowhere else to go.

Nitti sat on one side of a long table and Hayes sat on the other side. After the dinner, Raggedy drove Randy and his family home to keep them safe after dark.

The next day, Raggedy took Nitti to meet with her father. Later that night, Raggedy bought her back home. Nitti had received bags of presents and some new dresses. The Friday passed into the weekend.

On the next Monday, the restaurant returns to its regular weekday schedule.

Christmas comes and the restaurant closes again. The restaurant had another big meal. A couple of new faces were at the dinner. Randy had his family there for the meal. Nitti and Hayes sit on the other side and other end of the table. After dinner, Raggedy took Randy and his family home again. The next day, Raggedy took Nitti to her father. She came back with lots of presents.

New Year's comes and the restaurant close early. All the waitresses had dates and went to the big parties. Raggedys parents went to bed early like old people do. Raggedy, Nitti, and Hayes found themselves alone at the bar that night, waiting for the new year. The radio was on as they listened to a radio New Year's show.

At 10:00 PM, Raggedy told Nitti and Hayes he will be upstairs for a while and he would be down later. Nitti and Hayes had never been in the same room alone. For the past four months, they hardly talked. It was never more than a hello and good-bye.

Nitti and Hayes both listen to the radio playing music, while waiting for Raggedy to come back down. After an hour, Nitti looks at Hayes.

Nitti: "I don't think he's coming back down, Hayes."

Hayes: "You should go upstairs now."

Nitti: "Why?"

Hayes: "It's late."

Nitti: "Yes, it's late. It was late before, and it will be late later."

Hayes: "Raggedy would want you upstairs."

Nitti: "If he wants me upstairs, he would have told me."

Hayes: "I should go downstairs now."

Nitti: "Why?"

Hayes: "It's late."

Nitti: Yes, it's late. It was late before, and it will be late later."

Hayes: "You said that before."

Nitti: "Yes, I know. I am the one who said it."

Hayes: "Yes."

Nitti: "Yes what?"

Hayes: "Yes, I know you said it."

Nitti looks at Hayes who is across the bar from her. They're looking back and forth at each other for a while, then Nitti ask Hayes a question.

Nitti: "Hayes, do I have a name?"

Hayes: "Yes."

Nitti: "Please tell me you know what it is. Please Hayes, please."

Hayes: "Yes, I know what it is."

Nitti: "WELL!"

Hayes: "Well, it's late, and you should go upstairs. And I should go downstairs."

Nitti: "If you say it's late again, I will punch you in the face."

Hayes: "Okay."

Nitti looks at Hayes. They're looking back and forth at each other for a while, then Nitti asks Hayes a question.

Nitti: "Please, Hayes, say my name. I want to hear you say it. It's not an ugly name, so please, Hayes, say it for me, please."

Hayes: "Why?"

Nitti looks at Hayes and gets up out of her chair, walks around the bar, and sits right next to him. She grabs his shoulders and turns his face to hers.

Nitti: "You're scared to say it. You're scared that Raggedy will come down here and hurt you. That's funny, Hayes."

Hayes: "Yes, I am."

Nitti: "Hayes, do you want to hurt me?"

Hayes: "No."

Nitti: "Hayes, then he wouldn't hurt you. He may hurt you, if you do something he doesn't like. He's my bodyguard, Hayes, and I think of him as my friend. He gets paid by my father to protect me. But he is my friend for free. He is the only person I get to talk to away from school. Hayes, I like Raggedy, but he's not much to talk to. I was hoping I could be friends with you, and I would have someone to talk to. Please be nice to me, Hayes."

Hayes: "I am sorry. I don't want to do anything wrong. I have nowhere to go. I don't want to live on the streets again. I am afraid."

Nitti: "How long did you live on the streets?"

Hayes: "I don't know. I was beat up bad. I woke up on a train track as a train passed over me. My face was beat black and blue. My ribs were all black and blue.

"I worked at a chicken farm. One day the police came in and raided the place. I couldn't tell them who I was or how old I was. So, they put me in an orphanage.

"I was there for five years, till four months ago when Raggedy took me out of there and bought me here."

Nitti: "I'm sorry to hear that, Hayes. Raggedy told me a little about you. He said I should keep away from you. He said my father would not be happy if I was to talk to you. Hayes, I would like it if you would be my friend."

Hayes: "I don't know how to be a friend. I don't ever remember having any friends. Even at the orphanage, I couldn't make a friend."

Nitti: "What will happen, Hayes, if you remember who you were, before you forgot who you were?"

Hayes: "I don't know. Something tells me I don't want to go back to where I was. There's something very bad back there. I think I saw somebody do something."

"Somebody may have thought they killed me and dumped me on the track. If they think I am dead, they may not try to find me. I hope I never remember."

Nitti: "Hayes, the only person you need to worry about now is Raggedy. Just do what he wants, and he'll protect you too. I think he does like you."

Hayes: "Raggedy told me all this is yours. You're very lucky."

Nitti: "It's not mine. My mother had an affair with a very powerful man. My mother had me and uses it for money. She dumped me here in his restaurant. My father hired Raggedy to protect me. His mother and stepfather are raising me. At the same time, they run the numbers and bets on horse racing. Raggedy is an old hitman, who now goes out and collects money on deadbeats. His mother sets up his delivery board after he drops me of at school. Someday, my father is going to get killed or thrown in jail. I will lose this place I sleep in, and the school I go to will kick me out because I will not be able to pay for it. Then, Hayes, I'll be in that orphanage you came from. Hayes, I have no illusions that I can live like this forever."

Hayes: "What about your mother?"

Nitti: "My mother is a drunk. The only time she sees me is when she wants money. She brings her drunk self in here threatening to take me away. If I leave, my father will close this dump down. So Raggedy and his mother buy my drunk leach of a mother off till the next time. It's so sad. I have pictures of my mother. She was so pretty. I have pictures of her when she was a singer for a band.

Then she found a bottle. Then my father found her. Now I find myself without a real father or mother. I just find my way back here every day."

Hayes: "We have that in common. We both found ourselves here."

Nitti: "It will end one day, Hayes. It's just a matter of time. Speaking of time, it's almost New Year's. You know what I would like to do, Hayes?"

Hayes: "What?"

Nitti: "Apple pie and vanilla ice cream. It's what I live for."

Hayes: "Is it good?"

Nitti: "What, you don't know what hot apple pie and ice cream tastes like?"

Hayes: "I don't know. I don't remember. I remember the words and what they mean but not what it tastes like."

Nitti: "Come with me into the kitchen. I will make you some hot apple pie and vanilla ice cream."

Hayes: "What if Raggedy comes back downstairs?"

Nitti: "Well, Hayes, I guess he is just going to shoot you, then bury you in the graveyard behind us with the other people he shot and buried."

Hayes: "I hope the apple pie and ice cream is worth it."

Nitti: "It will be, so get up. Let's go to the kitchen and I'll make you the best ice cream and apple pie you'll ever remember."

Nitti and Hayes get up and go into the kitchen.

Nitti turns the stove on to heat the oven. She asks Hayes to turn the radio on, so they can listen to the countdown till midnight. Hayes gets the radio and puts on some music. Nitti then asks Hayes to get a pie that was made today. Nitti then puts the pie in the oven, and then goes to an icebox and gets some ice cream.

She puts it in two bowls. She puts one bowl in front of Hayes and puts the second bowl across from him. She then goes to the oven and turns it off. She pulls the apple pie from the oven and puts it on the table between the two dishes of ice cream. She then gets two glasses and some milk and puts it on the table.

Nitti then takes a seat across from Hayes and puts some pie in his bowl and does the same for herself. Nitti then tells Hayes to try it.

Hayes looks at her and smiles. He takes his spoon and dives into the ice cream and tastes it. Hayes closes his eyes and smiles. He opens his eyes looks at Nitti.

Hayes: "If Raggedy is going to shoot me, I hope he waits till I finish this. I can't ever remember having anything so good."

Nitti: "I come down here to get some ice cream and apple pie when I am sad or having a bad day. This stuff has got to be better than any booze."

Hayes: "I would agree with that."

Nitti: "I am glad you like it, Hayes. When I feel sad, we can sneak in here and do it again."

Hayes: "I don't know about that. I am so tired after work that all I want to do is go to sleep."

Nitti: "I wish I could make it easier for you, Hayes, but I can't. Everybody here works or has a purpose. If anybody here loses their purpose, they disappear. That is just the way it is here."

Hayes: "I understand."

Nitti: "I can't run away. I am just a young girl. It would be too dangerous for me. Have you thought about running away?"

Hayes: "I don't want to. I am starting to feel like I belong here. Raggedy did tell me if I tried, he would find me and kill me. I don't want to."

Nitti: "Hayes, I am glad you like the ice cream. Let's clean these dishes and get back into the bar again."

Hayes: "Okay."

Nitti and Hayes clean up the dishes, then go back into the bar to wait for midnight and the New Year. They take a table by an old grandfather clock. They have two glasses of milk as they sit at a table facing the old clock.

The man on the radio starts the countdown from ten seconds. The man on the radio starts to play old "Auld Lang Syne" song as the clock strikes twelve. Nitti raises her glass of milk up to Hayes.

Hayes and Nitti push their glasses together and say Happy New Year. Then they down their milk. Hayes finishes his milk and looks at the clock.

Hayes: "It's a minute past twelve and the clock didn't go off."

Nitti: "I haven't heard that clock ring its bells in years. I think it broke and nobody ever fixed it."

Hayes walks over to the clock and opens the front door. He looks inside and sees two Thompson machine guns, two high-powered rifles, and one sawed-off shotgun. Under the guns was a bloodied police uniform. Hayes picks up the shotgun. Nitti walks over to Hayes and looks over his shoulder.

Nitti: "Hayes, you better close that door, put that gun back, and forget you saw any of that. That uniform was left here by a cop who couldn't pay his gambling debt. It was used in that massacre back in 29. I was about five and I saw them put the guns and the bloody uniform in there. Just close the door. Hayes, we should forget we saw this. We should go to our rooms. It's late, you know."

Hayes: "Okay, I understand. I'll put it back the way I found it."

Nitti turns away from Hayes. She starts to walk to the stairs to go up to her room. Nitti turns at the top of the stairs to look at Hayes at the bottom.

Nitti: "Good night, Hayes. I had fun."

Hayes: "Good night, Nitti."

Nitti smiles at the sound of her name and they both go back to their room-- Nitti to the third floor and Hayes in the cellar with the bugs and rodents.

The next day was New Year's 1937. Hayes gets up and starts his day. The restaurant is closed so no cooks or waitresses show up for work. Hayes goes outside on a cold Chicago morning and gets the papers. He drops the papers in front of all the same doors. When he gets to Nitti's door, he sees that her paper is open to the crossword puzzle. He picks it up.

The paper has a perfume smell to it. He sees that the puzzle is half-done. As he looks at it, Hayes can make out some of the words: fun, thank you, pie, good, friend. Hayes throws the other papers away but keeps Nitti's crossword puzzle. He takes it down to his room and stores it there. Hayes has come back from his room and is now sweeping the restaurant floor.

Rag and Conversation come down from their room and take the same table. Rag is dressed up in a fireman suit and sets up Raggedys delivery. Raggedy comes in and writes down his delivery schedule. Nitti comes down the stairs all dressed up. She is going to spend the day with her father. It's a day she will see him away from his family.

Nitti waves to Hayes and says, "Good morning, Hayes."

Hayes replies, "Hello, Nitti."

Raggedy, Rag and Conversation hear the exchange and look at Hayes. Hayes turns around and walks into the kitchen. Raggedy takes Nitti out to her father.

Hayes spends the day cleaning the restaurant and the kitchen. He has cleaned what needs to be clean and he just goes about his business and works all day. When night comes, Raggedy brings Nitti home. Hayes sees her come in with her arms filled with shopping bags. Nitti waves to Hayes and goes up to her room. The day ends, and Hayes finishes his work and goes to bed.

CHAPTER SIX

Haircut

The cold Chicago winter has now turned into the spring of '37. Hayes' basement room is not as cold anymore. He is now like everybody else at the restaurant. Except he never gets to leave. He gets to talk To Nitti after her day at school. They don't get a lot of time because Hayes has so much to do. On weekends, Nitti spends time with her father.

Nitti's school year ends. On a Tuesday morning, she is standing at the bottom of the stairs with her bags packed. She sees Hayes and calls him over. Nitti tells him she must go away to a summer camp and she will be gone all summer.

Raggedy comes over and takes her bags and starts to carry them out to his car. Nitti tells Hayes, "I will miss you. Be here when I come back."

Hayes answers her back, "Okay, Nitti, bye."

Nitti leaves for the summer. Hayes goes back to work.

July 4, 1937 comes to Chicago and the restaurant. Hayes gets up from his room in the basement and starts his long workday. After he puts the papers by the doors and throws the old ones out, Raggedy stops him and asks Hayes to have a seat at the bar. Raggedy takes a seat by Hayes.

Raggedy: "Hayes you been here for a while now and I think you're doing a good job. No one has to say anything to you now; you just do it."

Hayes: "Thank you, Raggedy. I do try to work hard."

Raggedy: "Rag, Conversation, and I have been talking that it's time we take you in. We feel that we can trust you. Trust is what we need from you, Hayes. We are going to give you a room on the second floor. You will have the room between Conversation and me. You will be able to use the shower and the bathroom at the end of the hall. You are still not allowed on the third floor unless you are getting the papers. If I catch you there when you're not supposed to be there, I will have to hurt you. You understand?"

Hayes: "Yes, thank you, I understand."

Raggedy: "Good, Hayes. I like you and I would feel bad about hurting you. The room is where the poker games used to be. I had to stop it, so you can now have the room."

Hayes: "When can I do that, Raggedy?"

Raggedy: "Tonight, Hayes. I am going to go and see a baseball game today. I also must go and do a few deliveries. I want to take you with me. Do you want to see a baseball game, Hayes?"

Hayes: "Yes, please take me. I haven't left this place since I came here. But I have no money to go."

Raggedy: "We haven't paid you anything, Hayes, and you never asked. That is another thing we like about you. It's trust, Hayes. We have a lot of people's money that come through here. None of it is ours. We just collect it and send it on its way. If anybody gets greedy or steels anything, they will just disappear one day. That's just the way it happens. So, don't get greedy or steal."

Hayes: "I will do anything, Raggedy, not to live on the streets or go back to the orphanage. I want to stay here. It's my home now."

Raggedy: "Hayes, I feel the same way. I have no other place to go. I have no other way to make a living. This is the only job I can do. Nobody would hire me. I am too big and ugly. With all the scars on my head, I scare people."

Raggedy talks to Hayes for a while longer. He tells him he wants him to learn how to cook. That one day he will get to be a cook for the restaurant. Or he could be a debt collector. Hayes tells Raggedy that he would rather be a cook.

Raggedy takes Hayes in his used green four-door 1928 Cadillac Model 341. Hayes is going through the city in the front seat of a Cadillac, looking out the window. He passes some street he remembers. Some of the streets seem familiar, but he doesn't know why.

Raggedy stops the car behind a bar. He tells Hayes not to leave the car. Raggedy reaches under his seat and pulls out a handgun. Raggedy puts it between his belt and his black pants. He looks at Hayes and says the word "trust." Raggedy gets out of the car and walks into the bar. Hayes watches him go inside. He is just waiting and looking around when Raggedy is seen dragging a man out from the bar. The man has a bloody face. Raggedy throws the man to the ground.

Raggedy then reaches down and takes the man's wallet. He takes the money out of the wallet and drops it on the man's head. Raggedy then kicks the man in the leg. Raggedy gets back in the car and gives Hayes two dollars from some of the money he took from the man. Raggedy looks at him and says "trust." Then he drives away.

Raggedys next stop is a truck repair shop. He tells Hayes there is a man here who is behind in his debt payment. It's too bad because the man has a couple of kids. Raggedy gets out of the car and asks Hayes to follow him. Hayes gets out of the car and follows Raggedy inside.

There are men working on trucks and some men are working on changing tires. Hayes goes into the office with Raggedy. Raggedy tells a woman behind a desk that he is here to see Al Peterson.

The woman tells Raggedy where he is. Raggedy and Hayes leave the office and walk over to the man working on a truck tire. Al Peterson. Raggedy asks the man to go outside with him. The man looks around for some help, but no one looks back at him. Raggedy grabs the man by the collar and brings him outside. The man is pleading with Raggedy to give him more time. He tells Raggedy that he has some money coming to him at the end of the month.

Raggedy has the man outside. Raggedy takes out brass knuckles and puts it on his fingers. Raggedy hits the man so hard the man falls to the ground. Raggedy then gets on his knees just over the man's right hand. He takes off his brass knuckles and puts it on the fingers of the man on the ground. Once Raggedy has the brass knuckles over the man fingers, he stands up.

Then Raggedy lifts his big right foot over the brass knuckle. Raggedy slams his foot down on the brass knuckles. The man on the ground screams in pain from having his four fingers broken. Then Raggedy takes another set of brass knuckles out of his pocket and does the same thing to the man's other hand. Raggedy looks down at the man who is crying with eight broken fingers and says, "I want my knuckles back after they manage to get them over those broken fingers, please."

Raggedy and Hayes get back into the car. Raggedy then takes Hayes to the baseball stadium.

Raggedy pulls into a lot outside the stadium. He walks Hayes into the building. Raggedy pays for Hayes and gives him a five-dollar bill. He tells Hayes that he'll buy him lunch, but he wanted Hayes to be able to get whatever he wanted without asking. Raggedy and Hayes watch the game and have a good time. Raggedy asks Hayes if he would like to know how he got the scars on his head. Hayes tells him he was told the scars are from the war.

Raggedy: "It was the end of The Great War 1918. A dozen fellow soldiers and I were in the frontline trench. We'd been in that trench what seemed like forever. It was nine months--about the same time you lived in the basement. The same time you were in your mother's belly. We did everything it that trench. We eat, slept, shit, peed, lived, and died in that trench. After freezing in it all winter, spring came. When spring came, the general started to get real brave.

"The enemy had their last offensive chance. So one morning, they threw everything they had at us. We held them off for as long as we could. By the fourth day of their assault on us, we had it. We had run out of everything from bullets to people.

"One of their hand grenades landed in the trench. It blew my helmet off and knocked me out. I think I was out for two days. I remember waking up and feeling this tremendous weight on me. I was unable to move it. Out of the corner of my eyes, I could only see gray shadows moving around. I tried to call out for help, but I was too weak. I started to pick up people talking. But what they were saying, I couldn't understand.

"Then something in front of me moved. I could see the enemy was in the trench. The weight on me was the bodies of my fellow soldiers. Then one of the people on top of me started to moan. One of the enemies heard it. I was wishing that moaning would stop. It was too late. One of them came over and started to put bullets in all the bodies. He must have got the right body because the moaning stopped. I was never so afraid.

"By the end of that day, I started to pee on myself. The pee felt like I was on fire down there. I had caught some sharp metal in my groin. There was blood coming out of my head and going into my eyes. All I could see between the bodies that were on top of me were gray shadows.

"The sun had gone down and the people in the trench got quiet. Everything got quiet accept my breathing. I tried not to make any sound, but one of them heard me. So he came over with a bayonet and started to stab all the bodies. He would have used a gun, but at night you want to stay quiet. He got close to me just stabbing away. Then all hell broke loose. Machine guns started to fire, and bombs started to explode.

"When the sun came up, somebody was pulling bodies off me. I thought this was going to be it for me. Then I was picked up and dropped on the ground outside the trench. When I was dropped, I let out a gasp of air. Then I heard someone in English say, 'This one is still alive.' The Americans had retaken the trench and pushed the enemies back.

"The next thing I remember was being in a hospital in France. My head was in bandages and my groin was gone. Six months later, I was back in the city of Chicago. Someone said I looked like the doll Raggedy something, and the name stuck. My mother got the name Rag because of me. She was called Rag's mother.

"I survived the war, Hayes, but paid the price. I should be dead. From what the orphanage said about you, we have a lot in common. That's why I picked you, Hayes. Out of every kid in that hellhole, I sometimes look at you and wonder if I saved you or signed your death warrant."

Hayes: "Sometimes I wonder the same. Raggedy, on the way over here, some of the streets looked familiar. I hope someday I can remember what happen to me like you can."

Raggedy: "You may not want to remember, Hayes. I remember being very scared and afraid to die. As big and tough I may look, I was scared."

Hayes: "Raggedy, what did you do before the war?"

Raggedy: "I played minor league baseball. I could hit a ball, Hayes. No major league teams thought a big, strong, muscle-bound kid could play the game. So, I never went beyond the minors. Then the Great War. And now I am here with you."

The game ends and Raggedy and Hayes leave. On the way back, Raggedy stops by the local horse track. He drives into the entrance for the trucks that transport the horses. The guard at the gate waves him past and shouts out, "Hello, Raggedy."

Raggedy drives into the stables and parks the car. He tells Hayes to follow him. Raggedy goes into one of the stable and finds a jockey grooming a horse. Raggedy pats him on the back and calls him by his first name, Jose.

Raggedy and Jose talk like old friends for a while. Raggedy ask Hayes to check the door to see if anybody is around. Hayes does as he is asked then looks back to Raggedy. "I don't see anybody, Raggedy."

Raggedy says, "Okay."

Raggedy reaches in his pocket takes out a couple of hundred dollars and hands it to Jose. Then Raggedy and Jose shake hands. Raggedy tells Jose to say hello to the wife and kids. Then Raggedy and Hayes walk out. On the way out, Raggedy stops by the gate guard and gives him a five-dollar bill.

Raggedy then starts the drive back to the restaurant. Along the way he stops by a butcher. Raggedy and Hayes go into the butcher shop.

Butcher: "Hello, Raggedy, how are you doing today?"

Raggedy: "I am doing good, Mario, doing good. How's the wife and kids?"

Mario: "They're doing good. My kids are always growing. If I didn't own this place, I couldn't feed them."

Raggedy: "Good, that's nice to hear. Mario, please give me two of the usual. One for my friend here. His name is Hayes."

Mario goes in the back for a minute, then comes back with two bowls of antipasto and two glasses of wine. Raggedy and Hayes take a seat at a table. After Raggedy and Hayes finish their antipasto, Raggedy approaches Mario.

Raggedy: "Mario that was as good as always, thank you. Mario, I have to ask you why you're buying your supplies from out of town."

Mario: "I am just trying to survive, Raggedy. The new supplier is about half the price. It is not meant to be permanent. It's just till I can get out of debt."

Raggedy: "We all have bills, Mario. Your old friends who helped you start this place a long time ago heard about the deal you got. So, every other business that promised to help each other feels hurt. You know what I mean?"

Mario: "I have kids, Raggedy. Please, I have kids. I like your kids, Mario. I like your wife. I promise to send her flowers, I like her so much. Mario, you make the best antipasto. I hope I don't miss it."

Raggedy says goodbye to Mario and walks out of the butcher shop. He and Hayes get in to the car and drive away. In the ride back, Hayes turns to Raggedy and ask the question.

Hayes: "Raggedy can I ask you what is going to happen to that butcher?"

Raggedy: "What happens to him is going to happen to him. He used some people and some people's money to open that store. He made some simple promise to help some other people with their stores and business. A couple of months ago, he made the decision to break that promise. He did it over and over. Some of the people who helped him were hurt in a small way. But they were insulted in a bad way."

Hayes: "I understand, Raggedy."

Raggedy: "That's good you understand it. You don't have to like it."

Raggedys next stop is a barbershop. Raggedy tells Hayes to use some of the money he was given to get a haircut. Raggedy stops in front of a barbershop and tells Hayes he'll be back in an hour to get him. Hayes gets out of the car then watches Raggedy drive off.

Hayes thinks to himself. He hopes Raggedy comes back for him. That this isn't a trick to lose him. Hayes turns and walks into the barbershop.

Inside the shop, Hayes sees a barber cutting somebody's hair. There are four other men on chairs around the shop. The man in the barber chair is reading the paper. All the men in the shop look at Hayes when he walks in. The barber smiles at Hayes and tells him to have a seat and he'll be with him next.

Hayes takes the last seat between some men. The men in the shop go back to talking about what horses are running and who they might be picking in the races. One of the men is cutting some cheese with a barber's straight razor, then eating the cheese. He is an old man with a bottle of wine under his chair.

Hayes sits in the chair and looks at the floor with hair lying on it. Then he sees pictures on the wall of old newspapers. The pictures are front pages of dead people who were killed in shootouts. Some pictures are of a lavish funeral procession. Then Hayes sees a picture of the barber and a heavy woman, and one boy with four girls. Behind the family in the picture is a grandfather clock. One of the girls in the picture is wearing a dress like Nitti wore last New year's. It must be the barber's family, Hayes thinks to himself.

Hayes sits and just listens to the men talk about the horses for a couple of minutes. Then he watches the barber remove the white apron from the man in the chair. The barber brushes the hair of the man and tells him it's, "Twenty dollars." The man in the barber seats pulls out a twenty-dollar bill and hands it to the barber. Hayes knows he doesn't have that much money. The barber takes the money from the man and puts it in his pocket. The barber brushes off the chair and calls out to Hayes.

Barber: "You're next, young man."

Hayes gets up and looks to the other men sitting in the chairs.

Barber: "Don't worry about those guys. They're just here to entertain me. You're next."

Hayes: "Thanks, sir, but I only have a couple of dollars for a haircut. I don't have twenty dollars. If you cut my hair, I'll give you what I have. Then I'll sweep your floor, sir."

The men in the shop laugh when they hear Hayes then go back to the paper.

Barber: "Don't worry about it, sport. Just get yourself up on this chair, and we will settle up when I'm done with you."

Hayes: "Okay, sir."

Barber: "Don't call me, sir, sport. Call me Nicholas."

Hayes: "Okay."

Nicholas: "And what name do the girls call you, sport? I'll bet the girls love those curly black locks."

Hayes: "My name is Hayes."

The barber starts cutting Hayes' hair. The men in the shop just kept on talking about the horses. Then Nicholas starts talking to Hayes.

Nicholas: "What brings you around here? I never seen you here before."

Hayes: "I just started living here."

Nicholas: "Just where about would that be?"

Hayes: "It's the restaurant by the tracks and the cemetery."

Nicholas: "What is the address of that place, Hayes?"

Hayes: "I don't know it."

Nicholas: "Hayes, what is the name of that place?"

Hayes: "I don't know that either."

Nicholas: "Hey, you're telling me you don't know where you live?"

Hayes: "I haven't lived there long. I work a lot and never needed to ask."

Nicholas: "Hayes, don't you think you should know where you live?"

Hayes: "Yes, sir. When I get back there, I'll find out. But I am so glad just to have a place to live. I lived on the street during the winter. Lived in an orphanage. The place I live in now is the best place I lived in."

Nicholas: "Hayes, whose green car is that I saw you get out of before?"

Hayes: "That car belongs to a man named Raggedy."

Nicholas: "That's the stupidest name I ever heard. Who would name their kid Raggedy?"

Hayes: "It's a nickname for him."

Nicholas: "Hayes, don't you think it's funny?"

Hayes: "Sir, I like him. I don't think it's funny."

The man with the straight razor turns to Hayes and says, "Boy, are you saying my son-in-law is a liar? If you are, I may have to go over to you and give you a haircut with my razor, boy. So, tell that nice man cutting your hair that you think that's a stupid name and you're sorry for calling him a liar."

Hayes: "Sir, I am sorry if I am causing a problem here. I should leave."

The old man gets up and walks over to Hayes. The other man watches as the old man walks over him. Nicolas steps back and doesn't try to help Hayes. The old man with the razer puts one hand on Hayes' chin and lifts his chin up. Then he takes the straight razor and puts it on Hayes' throat.

The old man then asks Hayes again and says, "That's the stupidest name I ever heard. Who would name their kid Raggedy?" With the razor at his throat being held by a man with hands that shakes.

Hayes tells the old man, "Sir, I been hurt really bad before. So bad I can't remember who I am. I have parts that were broken and sometimes they hurt. So, if you want to hurt me, there's not much I am able to do about it. But I can't tell you what you want to hear."

The old man pushes the straight razor against Hayes' throat just enough to draw some blood. Hayes doesn't move or say anything. The old man pulls his razor back, turns, and goes back to his seat.

Nicolas goes back up to Hayes and dusts the hair off him. Nicholas puts something on the cut on his neck to stop the little bleeding. Then he takes the apron off Hayes, pats him on the back, and tells him he's done. "You done good."

Hayes gets out of the chair turns to Nicholas and asked how much.

Nicolas: "It's on me, son. You earned it."

Hayes: "I can sweep your floor for you, sir, as a payment for the haircut?"

Nicholas: "Sure, why not. That's how I started. The broom and dust pan are over there in the closet."

Hayes gets the broom and dust pan and sweeps the floor. When he gets to the old man with the razor Hayes says, "Excuse me, sir," then sweeps up some cheese on the floor around him. Once Hayes has the floor swept, he takes the hair and what he swept up and puts it in a trash can and takes the trash out front and throws it away. Hayes comes back inside and puts the broom back. Then Hayes thanks Nicholas for the haircut. He turns to the old man and smiles at him. Then Hayes says he is going to wait outside for his ride back home.

Hayes is waiting outside by the curb. Raggedy pulls alongside the curb to let Hayes get in. Once Hayes gets in the car, Raggedy starts the drive back to the restaurant. Raggedy asks Hayes how he got the cut on his throat. Hayes tells him everything that went on in the barbershop. Raggedy listens to Hayes telling him what happened. Raggedy was in the backroom listening to Hayes and Nicholas.

Raggedy tell Hayes that he has a lot of enemies in Chicago and that he shouldn't try to be so brave next time.

Raggedy: "The first rule of any confrontation is to survive it. You can choose the time and place that gives you the best chance in any confrontation. Hayes, just try to survive."

Hayes: "Okay, Raggedy."

Raggedy and Hayes get back to the restaurant as the sun sets. Raggedy tells Hayes to move his stuff to the center room on the second floor. Hayes goes down to the basement, collects all his stuff, and puts it in a small laundry bag.

Hayes then goes up to the second floor and opens the door to his new room.

When he opens the door, he sees a window straight ahead of him at the other end of the room. Outside the window is a fire escape. Then past the fire escape he can see the lights of a Chicago night. It looks like every light in the world to him is on in the city. He walks to the window.

At the window he reaches down and pulls the bottom sash up. The smell of the fresh air fills his head. Then it's the sound of the city in front of him. The cars on the road at the other end of the dead-end street can be heard at his window. Then a steam engine train rolls by as it leaves the train yard.

Hayes looks around his new room and sees a dumbwaiter. Hayes takes a piece of wood and jams it into the door, so it can't be open.

Hayes goes back to the window and sits on the sill. He looks out the window, enjoying the lights and sounds, till he falls asleep sitting in the window on this 1937 Fourth of July.

CHAPTER SEVEN

Talking

The July of ' 37 passes quickly. Hayes spends the summer working every day at the restaurant. He has his same daily routine that he has done since his first day at the restaurant.

Hayes is now the most important person in the restaurant's daily operation. Hayes now makes up the work schedule for the cooks and waitresses. Now everybody knows who is to show up and when. Hayes has redone the menu, making the breakfast menu much smaller. He has downsized the restaurant's daily menu from three pages to one page.

The cooks, Randy and Joe, now have a limited amount of meals to prepare. The cooks have thanked Hayes for the change. They can now work on making those fewer meals. With less meals to offer, the food in the restaurant starts to improve.

Hayes had to go to Raggedy and have two waitresses fired. The two that Hayes had fired were stealing bottles of champagne. Hayes asked the two to leave. Raggedy gave Hayes the job of hiring two new waitresses.

One day in the summer, Hayes is covering for two waitresses. Hayes is working hard to take orders and buss tables.

A man comes into the restaurant and stops at the door. He looks around. He has a motorcycle helmet in one hand and a backpack in the other. He walks up to the bar and takes a seat. He drops his backpack to the side of the seat, then puts his helmet on the next one. He looks back over his shoulder to Rag, who is dressed as a telephone repairman and is counting money at a table.

Then he looks at the few other people in the diner. Hayes goes over to him and puts the menu in front of him. The man just asks for some apple pie, vanilla ice cream, and black coffee. Hayes calls back to Randy, "Hot apple pie," then he puts some vanilla ice cream on a dish .

The man reaches down into his backpack and pulls out a large notebook. He puts the notebook down on the bar. He opens the book and starts to write something inside. Hayes comes over to him and places the ice cream and pie in front of him. He pours the man some coffee then asks him if he would like anything else. The man just shakes his head no, then smiles at Hayes. He starts to eat his ice cream and pie.

Hayes looks at him for a moment then leaves the man to ring out a customer, who has finished their meal.

Hayes has just finished with a customer. Rag asks Hayes if he can get her some hot water for her tea. The man with the notebook watches Hayes get Rag the hot water, then turns back to his notebook. Soon, he finishes his pie and ice cream. He puts the notebook back in this bag. Then the man takes out a book and leaves it at the counter.

As the man walks toward the door to leave. Rag sees the man has left a book. She calls out to him and tells him he left something at the bar. The man tells Rag, "It's yours now." After the man leaves, Rag calls out to Hayes to bring her the book. Hayes picks the book up and brings it over to her. Rags reads the cover. Hayes just goes back to his always very busy, never-ending workday.

At the end of the summer, the restaurant has started to turn a profit. The owner, Nicholas Litti, and his father-in-law have seen a change in the money the restaurant was taking in.

Nicholas and his father-in-law had a talk with Raggedy. Nicholas has told Raggedy to let Hayes run the restaurant. "Let Hayes make all the decisions on just the daily operation of the business. If he wants to do anything bigger, to let us know."

Raggedy agrees with the decision.

At the end of summer, just two days before school would start for Nitti, she comes home from camp. Raggedy has driven to New York to pick her up.

The first-person Nitti goes looking for is Hayes. She finds him in the kitchen cleaning some pots and pans. Nitti goes up to him and puts her arms around him. That catches Hayes off guard. He drops a pot on the floor. The cook and the waitress both have a laugh at him. Hayes blushes a bit. After some "hellos" and "it's good to see you," Nitti tells Hayes that she will tell him all about her summer later. Nitti Leaves the kitchen and goes to her room to unpack.

Later that day, Nitti and Hayes meet at the bar. Nitti is eating her dinner when Hayes takes a seat next to her.

Hayes: "Hello, Nitti."

Nitti: "It's so nice to see you still here, Hayes."

Hayes: "I am happy still to be here."

Nitti: "I was afraid that you would be gone. Hayes, I was afraid that you would run away."

Hayes: "Nitti, I like being here. I think of this place like my home now."

Nitti: "This isn't much of a home. It's a dump, Hayes. It is where you work. A home has two parents and kids. This place is a dump. It has a bodyguard that's a killer. It has two old people who run numbers and take bets.

" It has an old woman who makes threatening phone calls for fun. They're left over from what this place used to be. They just haven't left this place yet. Someone needs to tell them to leave. The restaurant food is so bad, people have stopped coming here. Hayes, it's a dump."

Hayes: "I know, Nitti, but I have changed a couple of things. I may be helping."

Nitti: "Raggedy has told me about it. He thinks you're doing a good job. He thinks you're what this place needed."

Hayes: "I like Raggedy. He has taken me to a couple of baseball games this summer."

Nitti: "Hayes, when I first saw you, everybody didn't think you would last a day. Then I was hoping you would be nice to me. Now I would be sad if you were to leave. I would miss you, Hayes. I would miss you a lot.

Hayes: "I would miss you, too."

Nitti: "Really, Hayes, how much would you miss me?"

Hayes: "What do you mean how much?"

Nitti: "Hayes, I finished my dinner and I am going to my room. Bye for now."

Nitti goes back to her room. Hayes has finished his night work and goes back to his room. When he enters his room, he hears footsteps from the room above his. Then it occurs to him the room above his is Nitti's room. Hayes walks to his window and pulls the sash up. He puts his head out the window and looks up to Nitti's room.

There is a shade pulled down. He can see that there is a light on in her room. Then he looks at the fire escape outside his window that leads up to Nitti's room.

Hayes turns his one light out and lays down on his bed. He falls asleep looking up at his ceiling and wondering about Nitti's question about missing her.

In two days, September 1937, Nitti is fourteen years old and back in school. Hayes' days are just a repeat of the day before. As the days passed, Nitti would eat her meals at the bar. Sometimes, she and Hayes would sit together and talk about her day.

On the weekends, Hayes' days have become the same as the weekdays. Nitti would spend some time with her father at a store, dining out, or watching a movie. A couple of times, Nitti would get to spend a short time with her mother.

One weekend in October of '37, Nitti's mother being between boyfriends and bottles showed up at the restaurant. Sadie looked ten years older than she was.

Sadie had become a bad-mannered, foul-talking pain to all the restaurant employees on her last visit at the restaurant.

Sadie caught Hayes talking to Nitti about what she wanted for dinner with her mother. Sadie went right over to Hayes and grabbed him by his hair, pulling it so hard Hayes fell backward to the floor. Sadie started swearing at Hayes.

Sadie: "Don't you ever talk to my daughter, you gutter garbage. I will kill you, you son of a bitch. I know what boys at your age have on their mind. You just want to take advantage of an innocent young girl. You are all the same. You're just garbage. I don't want my daughter having anything to do with your kind of garbage. Do you know who her father is? All I must do is call him, and you're dead. So take your dirty little boy mind out of here or I'll take a knife and castrate your little boyhood myself!" Sadie yells at him.

Hayes gets up and says he's sorry, and then walks into the kitchen. Nitti, with tears in her eyes, watches as Hayes walks into the kitchen. Nitti waits for Hayes to leave. Once Hayes is gone from the room, Nitti turns to her mother and tells her, "Mom these are the last words you will ever hear me say. I don't want to see you again. I want you out of here. If you ever come back, I will tell my father to stop paying the money he gives you.

"If you come back here, I will take Raggedys gun and kill my own mother who is a drunk whore." Nitti in tears then leaves her mother and goes up to her room.

Sadie stands still for a couple of minutes then walks out of the room and out of the building for the last time. She never returns.

The next day, Nitti apologizes to Hayes for her mother. Nitti doesn't tell him the threat she made against her mother. Hayes tells her he understands and will go away when she comes back. That he doesn't want to be a problem between a mother and daughter. Nitti gives him a hug. They both go on with the rest of their day. No other words were spoken about what happened between them that day.

September has turned into October. October has become November. Nitti and Hayes have talked very little. Hayes has used his work as a reason to avoid Nitti. Nitti has given him space, hoping that he wants to be with her no matter what or who threatens him.

It is Thanksgiving 1937, and all the usual people are there. There are some new waitresses with a boyfriend or somebody's husband. Hayes has been there over a year now. All the people who are at the diner now like Hayes and think he is something special.

Raggedy has changed where people sit from other years. He has Nitti and Hayes sitting side-by-side. Randy has his wife and kids there. Rag is dressed up as a judge with a black robe. The cooks and some of the betters who have no place to go show up.

Nitti and Hayes have a good time together at dinner. They spend most of it serving all the other people. The two talk a lot with each other and work the day making the other people's day something special. At the end of this Thanksgiving Day, everybody is stuffed with smiles and laughter.

Raggedy thanks everybody for coming at the end of the day. He pulls Nitti and Hayes to the side and tells them it was the best thanksgiving he ever had and how grateful he was to them.

Then Raggedy takes Randy's family home. The waitresses and their dates leave. At night, Nitti and Hayes are in the kitchen cleaning up the mess from dinner.

Rag and Conversation have turned in for the night. After Nitti and Hayes finish cleaning, the two take a seat by the backdoor.

It's a Chicago November night. A very bright harvest moon has come out. Nitti asks Hayes to go for a walk with her. Hayes grabs a jacket for Nitti, and the two start a walk into the cemetery.

Nitti: "Thank you for thinking of the jacket. It's a little colder than I thought."

Hayes: "We could go back if you want."

Nitti: "No, Hayes, I want to spend some time alone with you. This cemetery has a lot of secrets. I know some of them. Let me show you some of them."

Nitti and Hayes walk down one of the rows of head stones. Nitti stops Hayes at a new-looking headstone.

Nitti: "Hayes, you see this grave that has the name Carl on it. There are two other people under him. Raggedy put them in there. There is another grave on the other side of the cemetery that is marked with the name Val. That grave has two people in it also.

"I know of another with four people under it. Could you imagine being the reason for a dead person? I think about that a lot."

Hayes: "How do you know that?"

Nitti: "Raggedy told me, or I saw him putting the people in them. The old man who they had before you is one of those people under Carl. I didn't like him at all, Hayes. He should have been nice to me. I didn't know I could be like my father."

Hayes: "Nitti, I don't understand. Did you do something to him?"

Nitti: "I just wanted him gone. Hayes, don't ask me anything more about him."

Hayes: "Nitti you shouldn't know about this. Or be thinking about this."

Nitti: "Okay, Hayes, what should I be thinking of? Please tell me. What are teenage girls supposed to think of?"

Hayes: "You should be thinking of school and your parents, Nitti."

Nitti: "I do think of school, and the work for it I have to do. I think of my parents and why they had me. How drunk my father must have been to like my mother. Why I must endure their mistake. Why I must be the one who has no parent I can call my own. I must be able to understand their decisions.

"I have a hard-enough time just being a teenage girl. Rag gave me the facts-of-life talk. Rag the old woman was dressed in a surgical suit and smelled of moth balls and alcohol. I must think about the rules that the church say that God wants me to follow. I must think about so much. I need a break from thinking about what other people think. Or what people tell me to think of.

"I must think about my mother and what I am going to do when she dies. I think about what I will be thinking. Will I be thinking that I will miss her? Or am I going to be glad she is gone? Someday, someone is going to kill my gangster father. It's going to happen. It's not if; it's when, Hayes. When it happens, I'll be all alone. Raggedy will leave me because no one is going to pay him to be my bodyguard. Rag and Conversation will have to find another place for their numbers and betting operation. Hayes, I have another problem. I can't tell you, but I think about him a lot. Someday, I'll tell you about it.

"Now can you please tell this girl, what is on your mind?"

Hayes: "I am sorry if I upset you. We should get back now."

Nitti: "No! I don't want to go back now. I told you something about me. Now you tell me something about you."

Hayes: "Okay, Nitti, but we need to go somewhere else. So, follow me."

Hayes takes Nitti over to the other side of the restaurant. He brings her to a place where they can see the train yard.

Hayes: "Nitti, see all those people who live around the train tracks?"

Nitti: "Yes, I see them. They're hobos and tramps. Those are dangerous people down there. We should leave."

Hayes: "That's where I am from. One day I woke up on a train track with a train over me. I was just a ten-year-old. I was beat up and left on the track. Those people down there took care of me. I lost who I was before they found me. Those people are no different than you or me. They just want a family, a safe place to live, and the ability to feed themselves.

"A few of those people are dangerous opportunist but the majority are just trying to survive the day. Nitti, that's who I am. That's what I am. I am a surviving young man, that's all."

Nitti: "That is what Raggedy told me. What will you do if you remember where you came from?"

Hayes: "Nitti, I don't want to change who I am now. I like being here and doing what I am doing."

Nitti: "Hayes, you may not have a choice. This is going to end. It's going to happen here where we live. I don't know when. When my father dies, our little world dies. You should leave our little piece of hell. Unless you have a reason to stay?"

Hayes: "I stay because it's the only place I have to go."

Nitti: "That's what I thought you would say. Hayes it's not what I want to hear. Please, Hayes, I don't like it here. Can we go somewhere else?"

Hayes and Nitti walk around for a while longer. The cold has Nitti wanting to go back inside. They say good night to each other then go to their rooms. Over the next days, the two go back to their hellos and goodbyes.

CHAPTER EIGHT

Bonding

The next Saturday, Raggedy takes Hayes to a college football game. He tells Hayes who Nicholas and his father-in-law are. He also tells him what a good job he is doing with the restaurant. He tells Hayes that Nicholas wants to let him run the restaurant and make the daily decisions. Nicholas and his father-in-law were very happy with him. Raggedy all so tells Hayes that the restaurant is just one of a couple of business that he has. Nicholas uses the place to launder money. So long as any changes to that end business isn't affected, he could do almost anything. Any major changes must be approved by Nicholas.

Raggedy tells Hayes that Nicholas is very concerned about him and Nitti. Then Hayes tells Raggedy that he likes Nitti as a friend, but he will keep away from her.

Raggedy tells Hayes that both of their lives will depend on it. It's just not who Nickolas Litti is. He is a father and that's his daughter.

Hayes thanks Raggedy for the job. He asks him to give him a couple of days to write down what changes he would like to do. Raggedy doesn't understand why Hayes must write it down. Hayes and Raggedy talk awhile about Nitti.

Then Raggedy asks Hayes why he never asks to get paid for the work he does. Hayes tells Raggedy he is just so great full for a safe place to live.

Hayes then tells Raggedy his memory has come back to him. He tells Raggedy who he is and where he came from. Hayes tells raggedy he is afraid to tell Nitti. Raggedy tells Hayes not to tell anyone or he could be in danger again. So long as nobody knows who he is or where he came from, he is safe.

Hayes asks Raggedy if he can spend a Sunday at Randy the cook's house. Raggedy tells Hayes he can but not to let anybody else know. After the game, Raggedy and Hayes go back to the restaurant.

That night, Randy takes Hayes home with him. The bus ride to Randy's house is about forty minutes. Then Randy and Hayes walk the two blocks to Randy's house.

The house Randy lives in is a multifamily rental. The house is a brown mortar building. Randy and Hayes walk up a flight of stone stairs.

Hayes sees the first floor is a ground-level apartment. The second floor is where Randy's family lives. The third floor above Randy's apartment is another rental apartment. The old mortar house was once a single-family home.

Randy brings Hayes into his apartment. It's a hall that Hayes walks into. One side of the hall has coat hooks that have a couple of old coats on them. Below the coats are series of different size shoes. Randy and Hayes hang up their coats and place their shoes under them.

Randy brings Hayes into the living room just off the hall. Randy's four kids are in the room. A boy and girl his age, and a boy and girl about ten years old are in the room. Randy reintroduces Hayes to his kids. Then Randy bring Hayes into the kitchen and reintroduces him to his wife.

Randy's wife is making rice. She has a large bottle of ketchup on the small counter to the side of the stove. Hayes is glad to see that the ketchup and the food is not from the restaurant.

Hayes eats dinner with Randy's family. It's Hayes' first family meal in years. It's been a long time since he sat down at a table with a set of parents for a meal. The talk of school and the problems that kids have are the subject at the table.

The youngest two are talking about who did what stupid thing to which stupid kid in school. The older two are talking about their schoolwork.

Hayes is asked where he goes to school. He tells them that he hasn't been to any school in years. The kids are surprised to hear that. Then Hayes tells the story of how he lost his memory. He tells the lie he still doesn't remember who he is. Randy tells his kids not to ask Hayes any more about himself.

The talk at dinner goes back to the kids and school. After dinner, the young girls get up and start to clean up the table and dinner. Randy takes Hayes back into the living room. Randy and his wife are sitting on the couch. Hayes sits in the other chair by a table with a radio on it.

Hayes looks around the room and sees a lot of nothing. The small room is filled with a couch a chair and two small tables. A small radio is on one of the tables. Hayes notices that the volume knob is broken. He asks to use the bathroom.

Randy tells him it's at the end of the hall where he put his coat.

Hayes gets up and walks out of the living room. He finds the bathroom. It has an old rusty toilet, a sink, and a small tub. Hayes goes back into the living room.

The oldest boy asks Hayes if he would like to go outside for a while and meet some of his friends. Hayes agrees and goes outside with the boy.

Hayes and Randy's oldest son are sitting on a set of stairs to somebody's house. It's an all-boy crowd on the steps.

The talk starts to become about girls. The boys were talking about what girl they would like to have. Some of the boys were telling tales, or tales that were promised never to be told.

One of the boys looks at Hayes, then asks him what girls he has had. Hayes, feeling the pressure of trying to fit in, tells them that he kissed a few but that was all. A couple of boys laugh at him. Randy's son take the pressure off Hayes by making fun of the boy who asked the question.

Some of the boys start to smoke and drink. They offer Hayes some cigarettes and some homemade liquor. Hayes passes on the drink but smokes a cigarette.

The boys sit there smoking and drinking till the drinks are gone. As it gets late, some of the boys go home. Hayes and Randy's son and two other boys are on the steps till midnight. Randy's son tells Hayes it is time for them to get back. The two start to walk back to Randy's apartment.

When the two enter the apartment, Hayes sees that Randy and his wife are on a makeshift bed in the living room. Randy's son tells Randy he is home. Hayes and Randy's son say good night. The two go into a small bedroom.

There is a bunk bed in the room. Hayes sees the two girls on the top bunk. The oldest son gets in bed with the younger boy. Hayes takes a pillow and blanket on the floor. Hayes lies down on the floor.

The younger girl and boy are now asleep. The older boy and the girl start to talk. The girl is asking the older boy about one of the boys outside.

Randy's son tells the girl to forget about him. "That boy is crazy and is always in trouble. One day somebody is going to hurt him bad. All he wants to do is make trouble.

So stay away from him. I told him to stay away from you. You better do what I say, or I'll tell Dad about your liking him."

The girl and he exchange threats for a while about who is going to tell their father what. Hayes listens to the two siblings go back and forth with insults and who is dumber. Hayes is amused by the banterer between them. He never heard a brother and sister talk to each other like what was going on between them.

Hayes starts to think about Nitti and him. Were Nitti and him like the brother and sister who were going at it? Or was Nitti and him like a boyfriend and girl-friend, the way the boys were talking about girls when he was on the steps with the other boys?

The rules and the threats that were given to him kept him away from Nitti. At first it was easy to stay away from her. Now, as the two were getting older, he would think more of her.

Hayes falls asleep on the floor listening two the siblings going at each like a pair of comics

The next day, Sunday, Hayes gets himself up. He looks back as the two girls and the two boys are still sleeping in the bed, checking to see that he didn't wake them up.

Hayes open the bedroom door and walks out to the living room. Randy and his wife are asleep on the small makeshift bed.

Hayes walks down the hall into the bathroom. He washes his face, combs his hair, and uses his finger to brush his teeth. After he finishes, Hayes goes back to the bedroom till everybody wakes up.

Randy is up in the kitchen making breakfast for his family. Randy's wife is put-ting the bed back in the couch. The four kids are in and out of the kitchen going back and forth to the bathroom. Hayes goes into the kitchen, takes a seat at the table, and looks at Randy making breakfast. Hayes has seen Randy do this a hundred times. But this was different. He couldn't see anything different, but there was something different about watching him cook for his own family.

Randy's wife and his four kids take their seats at the table. Hayes gets up from his chair that belongs to one of the four children. Then Randy tells the young-est to let Hayes share the seat.

Then Randy tells the oldest to say the prayer. The family goes silent. After the prayer, the family eats.

When breakfast is over, the two younger girls clean the table and do the dishes. The family leaves for the local church. Hayes goes with them on the four-block walk to the church.

The church is a one-story faded-blue painted building. The paint is peeling off the weather-worn siding. The windows are single-pane glass, six feet tall and three feet wide. There are six windows on each side of the building. The front door is wooden and has old, dirty, white-wash paint on it.

As Hayes walks into the small church, he sees plain wood benches to both sides of the aisle that lead to the alter. The benches have no backs to the them. They are just plain pine benches that are support by a set of two-by-fours in a frame.

The alter is on a platform two steps high that runs the width of the church. Behind the platform is a single door that leads to the back of the church. On that alter is a large black book.

Randy's family is greeted by some of the people in the church as they take their place on one of the pine benches. Hayes gets the end seat on the bench by the center row. The church fills up with people.

Hayes looks around to all the people in the church. There are no men in suits. The women are in dresses that are just plain everyday dresses. The children are dressed up no different than a school day.

As Hayes looks around, he notices that he is the lightest skinned person in the church. Some of the people he sees looking at him just smile at him and nod their head.

The church is filled with people on this bright Sunday morning. There is the sound of people talking that fills the room. The backdoor behind the alter opens. Four men in black suits walk out. They have a small black book in their hand, as they take their places on the wall by the door. Two men to the right side of the door, and two men on the left.

As the four men stand in their places, the inside of the church goes quiet. Finally, a short, heavy man walks out from the backroom. One of the men by the door reaches back and closes the door. The short, heavy man is in a white suit. He walks up to the alter, looks down, and opens the big black book in front of him.

The man turns a couple of pages until he finds the one, he was looking for. He clears his throat, then he thanks the people for coming out on this day to give a moment of their life back to the creator of it. Then, head down, he starts reading a couple of sentences from the big book in front of him.

When he's done, he takes his big book and closes it and takes a step backward. He brings the book above his head and then drops it on the floor. Then he says, as he makes his first eye contact with the people in the church:

The sermon

"Excuse me. You just heard his book talk, didn't you? The book said *bang*, didn't it? I know it did because I heard it. I know you all heard it because everybody looked to this short, good-looking, heavy man, who dropped the good book that spoke with a bang. Didn't you all just do that? You heard a bang and had a human response to the sound you heard. We do that in everything we do.

"We hear something and start the process of trying to analyze the sound because of our curiosity.

"I know that when I am up here at this place, where the words that sometime sound greater than what mortal man created them for. Words are just sound that give us information.

"Sometimes, the words we use are just a word that have already been said. Those words could get lost in the all-too-familiar sound of a person's voice.

"The book hit the floor and made a sound. No words were said in that sound. But you had to analyze the sound.

"So today, this morning, I am going to make some sounds. All of you will analyze the sound as if they had a greater meaning, then just some simple words from a familiar voice from this short, good-looking mortal man.

"I was sitting out back of this building the other day, trying to come up with the message for today's sermon. When a young boy, who is known for stopping by here from time to time to play that old game of checkers showed up.

"When I saw this young boy come by, my first thought was trying to avoid him. The pressure of coming up with the words to today's sermon had my attention. The business of my business was what had my attention.

"The young boy came up to me and asked me to play a game of checkers like he always does.

"'Can we play a game of checkers today, preacher please?' As always, I said okay to him. I then got up and went inside and got that simple game of checkers. I came back out and opened the board up, and then the both of us started to set up the checker pieces on the board.

"I asked the young boy if he was going to be red or black. The young boy asked me the question, 'Why does there have to be a red and black?'

"I had to think about that for a moment. Then I told him it's just a way to keep your side separated from mine. Then he asked me that simplest of all questions, 'Are people different colors so they can be separated?'

"I was at a loss on how to answer it. I had to think about it. The way the world is and the way we separate us and them, like the red and black of a simple game of checkers.

"The game of chess is black on one side and white on the other side. The Civil War was a blue against gray war. Sports team are done the same way. A team has a color. You are programed to like your team and color. You are programed to hate the other team and color.

"How simple does that sound? The simplest things in our world and the most complicated are separated by color.

"How do you tell a young person that in this land of the free, in this land that has no barbed wire fences on its borders, the simplest method of separation is color?

"For a man who can talk, for a man that people look to for answers on life's most complicated human emotion, for a man who went to school to learn how to talk, teach, and answer life's hardest question, this man was unable to answer that question. That question of 'Are people different colors so they can be separated?'

"I tried to tell the young boy he'll understand it better when he gets older. That was just the answer from a man who had no answer. But I did try to answer the question for myself of why we separate so much by color.

"Well, I had my work of writing this week's message and the question that young boy gave me of color and separation. I spent a lot of time trying to work the problem. I spent time working the what if and the what is the simplest explanation possible. But it took me nowhere.

"I even set up a checker board and looked at it with hope to solve the question. Then it occurred to me that the foundation of the game was broken down by the color of the board itself. Square blocks with two different colors. Hours I spent on this new quest in my life.

"I got tired of looking at the checker board with no answers. Then it occurred to me a chess game has the same separation of sides by color. A far more complicated game but the same simple separation by color.

"So, I set up a chess game on my desk. The board with different colors. The two opposing sides with different colors. Then I looked at the pieces and the board.

"After some more time trying to reason why the separation by color, it occurred to me we also separated people by who they are. A chess game, unlike a checker game, has even more layers of complication and separation.

"A chess game has different pieces with different statuses, from the pawns to the king and the queen. So now I was trying to comprehend this problem of different colors and different statuses.

"Then I looked at the calendar, and it said Saturday, and I still had no message to deliver for the Sunday sermon.

"I was feeling the pressure on this late Saturday. Then it struck me. Why don't I use the question of the young boy, 'Are people different colors so they can be separated?' for today's sermon?

"Why do we use color in our lives to separate sides? I was so happy with myself for about five minutes. I had an idea for a sermon for Sunday. So, I took out my notebook and pencil and started to write. The short happiness I had for having an idea for a sermon faded fast. I had nothing.

"I tried to think of some way to relate color and separation into a sermon, but I got nowhere. I spent a lot of time trying to figure a way to relate what I was thinking into something I could say today. After a couple of hours, I gave up. I started to think of using an old sermon.

"So, I looked back on some old ones that I have written. Then I found one that was written ten years ago by me. The name of this piece of writing genius by this good-looking, heavy man is:

Board Game of Life

"We all look for the feeling of being liked. To be a favorite of someone. Not to have to work on trying to get someone to like you. There is a benefit to having someone like you. It is a reward to your human emotions.

"As humans, we worry about being accepted. The hurt of not being accepted.

"Every day, when you enter the world away from your home, you're different. No matter how hard you try, something about you is different. You are as different to the people you meet as they are to you.

"There are places we would like to go, but we can't because it's only for somebody who is different than you. The reason may only be as simple as that game of checkers. The reason of a different color. But that difference is what may keep you out of the place.

"It hurts not being able to enjoy a place that you want to go to. If you show any part of that hurt, you may feel a sense of humiliation.

"We all are hurt when the rules of separation are made into borders, like the blocks on a board game. We may think to change what we are or try to become one of those who are allowed the freedom to enjoy the place we may wish to enter.

"Man's laws that allow separation or any borders by color are just current laws. Those current laws will change.

"You may never see those laws change. You may feel the unjust laws that are given to us should have been changed years ago.

"We have all heard the stories or seen the hurt your parents and grandparents had to deal with because of some unjust laws.

"We all are on the board game of life. We all are put on a side in this board game of life that we live in by the color of what we are judged to be. We were not asked to be on this unfair board game of life.

"This game with different sides, the game with square, colored places that separate and hold you to a given place on this board game of life, the game that will tell you how and where to move.

"The sides that were chosen for us by the so-called founders of the board. The founders of this game who draw the squares on the land we live on. The founders who handed down the rules for us to follow. We are who we are. We are people like the ones who made the rules.

"We can decide on what board we want to be on and what rules or laws we consider fair.

"Some people created the number of squares. Some people created which squares are which color. Some people created where the board ends and where the board starts.

"Why did they do this you may ask? They did it, so they wouldn't lose their self-given place on the board game of life. They came to the board game first.

"They were at the churches before we were. They were at the schools before we were. They were in the court house and the meeting house before we were. They were at the seats of the board of major corporations before we were. They made the rules before we got there. That's just the way it is.

"This board game of life that we must play every day, the side we must be on every day, the rules that are the laws that we must follow every day were put here before any of us were put on this corrupt board game of life.

"The board game of life that we play? Everybody plays in this game. Everyone wants to be a winner at this board game of life. Some people will cheat to win at this game. Some people will commit horrible crimes to other people who are on the board just looking to survive. They do this, so they can be called a winner. They do this, so they can call others the loser.

"The pieces on a chess board are like most people on this board game of life. Most people on this board are placed on the frontlines like pawns. What color you are, how much money you have, who you know and what power that person has could determine if you're a pawn.

"Rooks are the next step up from a pawn. They get to be in a better line than the pawn. They are place the farthest from the power. There are only two of them, unlike the many pawns.

"They are given greater latitude than a pawn, but they do have the bragging right of being in a different class than a pawn.

"The knights are next in line of power. They are given the privilege of being different than any other piece on the board. They are not bound by any given laws of moving in a straight line. They are not on the outside line looking in. The knights look down to the Rooks and the pawns.

"The knights have bragging rights of being in a different class than a rook and the pawns will never have.

"Then the bishops are next. They flank the royalty that is on the board game. They have that over all the other pieces on the board. They are given a place to be. They are given the law of not being able to leave the color space that they maintain.

"That is the price they must pay to be the closest to the royalty. The bishops have bragging rights that the knights, rook, and pawns don't have: the right of being in a different class. The right the rooks and pawns will never have.

"The mighty queen is next in the line of power. The powerful lady can go anywhere she chooses. She sits on the side of the king when she wants. She is his most powerful piece on the board. The queen has bragging rights that the bishop, knights, rook, and pawns don't have. She has the right of being in a different class that a bishop, knight, rooks, and pawns will never have.

"Then comes the king. He is given little movement ability. Every piece of the board has one mission: to protect the king. All the pieces will have to give up their place on the board to save the king. These are all the pieces on the board game of life, or a chess board. Every piece is given a status and color to give them an identity and a purpose.

"The pieces on the chess board are just a reflection of the status by who we are. The status we have is measured by how much power or money we have.

"The bragging rights of a place we hold that may be a higher class than someone deemed lower. Is it just a bragging right? The few at the top who have a prestigious place on our board of life will always look down on us as we struggle to maintain our current place.

"When we ask for change, we are told of the promise of following some golden, handed-down law that is the so-called right way to achieve the change we seek.

"The revolutionary thought we have of not being categorized into a square, with the hand-me-down given laws of what movement we are allowed. Or what race that you are. from the beginning to the end of your life will be a man-made law of which side you are on or what square somebody wants you to be on.

"On your way home today, before you forget the message of this Sunday sermon, I want you to think of a new piece for this board game of life.

"I came up with what name I would give my newfound piece on this game of life. I would call the new piece Elegant Father.

"There would only be one piece for both sides. I would place this new piece high above the center of the board, on a rainbow made up with the colors of all our children.

"My new Elegant Father will see no borders. My new Elegant Father will see no squares. My new Elegant Father will see no separation.

"When you look at your kids and have the want that they will live their lives with the freedom of no borders or separation, not being given laws or rules that are corrupt with prejudice of separation, border, and status.

"Given those laws and rules by people. When it is my Elegant Father that is my king.

"To the young boy who came around and asked to play checkers the other day.

"Don't look at yourself as a piece on a board game. Look at yourself like my Elegant Father. Put yourself above it. Put yourself above the separation by color. Put yourself above any borders that are given to you by some man-made law. Put yourself above any given status.

"Please don't tell my Elegant Father I dropped his book

"Amen."

CHAPTER NINE

Changes

A couple of days later, Hayes has come up with what he calls a Plan of Business for the restaurant. Hayes suggests that they turn the restaurant into a diner. He wants to have the first floor rebuilt. To cut the restaurant in half. The diner would be in the first half of the building. The kitchen and the staircase in the back half. The bar would be made into a counter for people to eat at. Rag and Conversation can do their businesses in the backroom. The rooms upstairs will stay the same.

Hayes will change the menu again. He wants to get one new cook but keep Randy as the morning cook. Hayes wants to be one of the night cooks and close the diner. Hayes would still work in the day with the same duties.

All the waitresses should wear the same uniform. Every cook would cook the same way. Every table would be placed the same way every day. The waitresses would write and take the orders the same way for every table.

Some of the other changes would be to sell cigarettes and alcohol to go. Free coffee to uniformed police officers after 6:00 PM. Another change would be to change the name of the place to Nitti's Diner.

Raggedy takes the changes to his boss Nicholas Litti and Nicholas' father-in-law. The owner and his father-in-law give their okay to almost everything. No free coffee to police any time. The name of the place would stay the same. In a couple of days, the restaurant closes for good. A week later, a new diner opens at the same place.

It is an early Friday Chicago morning. The sun is breaking over the horizon. The front door of this three-story, just-painted-white diner sits on the side of a worn-out old road facing the early morning Chicago sun.

A closed sign hangs in the front door of the unopened diner. Above the front door sits a black-and-white sign with the diner's same name on it. There is a big square window on each side of the front door. The windows have a couple of wooden tables behind each of them inside. The top two floors the windows shades are pulled down. In front of the diner is now a parking lot.

This small diner is at the corner of Railroad Road and Cemetery Road. To one side of the building is a cemetery. On the other side is a train yard. Behind the diner, the two roads meet at the dead end.

The changes Hayes did start to take effect immediately. A new group of people call commuters who ride the rails, and the buses start to use the new diner for breakfast and dinner.

Over the winter and in to the spring the diner has become very busy. The diner is turning a nice legal profit for Nicolas Litti. Nicolas starts to give Hayes a share of the profit. Hayes gives the money to Raggedy to hold.

Nicholas Litti is so happy with what Hayes is doing he has Raggedy set up a business meeting with Hayes. Nicholas Litti his father in law, Raggedy and Hayes have a meeting at the barbershop. Nicholas tells Hayes how happy he is with him and the new diner.

He tells Hayes the diner is a business. His daughter is his daughter. Nicholas makes it clear to Hayes that he is not to be anywhere with her alone. He doesn't want to see the two together away from the diner in public. Hayes is never to have her as a girlfriend or he would kill Hayes himself. Then he tells Hayes not to tell Nitti he met him. Hayes agrees with Nitti's father on everything.

In the month of April 1938, Rag dies. Raggedy buries his mother dressed in a white wedding gown in the cemetery under someone else's grave. Conversation is told to leave and never come back, or he'll be killed. He leaves without saying a word.

Nitti has the whole third floor to herself now. Hayes is so busy with the diner, she hardly gets time to talk to him. In the summer of '48, Nitti goes off to her summer camp.

In September, Nitti comes back, and Hayes is always busy. Hayes doesn't close the diner for Thanksgiving, and there is no thanksgiving dinner for the employees. The day after Thanksgiving Nitti spends with her father.

As the year passes, Nitti is in school one day when she is call to the principal's office. Raggedy and Hayes are there waiting. It's the first time Hayes has been to her school. Nitti walks into the principal's office and see the two. Nitti looks at them for a moment and asks, "Who is it, my father or mother?" Raggedy tells her it's her mother, and she has died. Nitti starts to cry then goes over to Hayes and puts her arms around him. Nitti holds him tight, then starts to whisper in his ear.

Nitti: "Thank you for coming for me, Hayes. I always knew this moment would come. I always wondered how I would react to the words 'your mother has died.'

"I wanted to be unfazed by it. I wanted to be unhurt by it. I had it all planned out like a script in a play. I would know what I would say. I had plans if I got the news in school I would go right back to my class. I wouldn't let her change anything in my day. I would go on as if I wasn't affected.

"Hayes, I am hurting. I can't do anything right now but cry. I can't think of anything but crying. It's not like I planned. Now I'm sorry I will never see her again.

"Hayes I am sorry I couldn't help her. What hurts the most is that I couldn't help her. I wish I could have helped her. Now my mother is gone. My mother."

Hayes: "She is looking at you now, Nitti. I think you're showing her how much you do love your mother. It's okay to cry, Nitti. Please cry."

Raggedy and the principal walk out of the room and leave the two alone. Hayes puts his arms around a crying Nitti.

Nitti's mother was found outside a hotel window. She was thrown out of by her latest drug-addicted boyfriend.

Two days later, Raggedy, Hayes, and Nitti are by a grave burying her mother. Raggedy paid to have her buried with a casket and a normal funeral.

1938 passes into 1939. The only thing that changes with Raggedy, Hayes, and Nitti are their ages. Hayes is a workaholic and has total control over a booming diner. The diner now has takeout food. Nitti just comes home from school, eats, and goes to her room most of the time.

Spring of 1939 comes and goes. It's now the summer of 1939. Nitti is now fifteen years old. Having just graduated from high school. This is her first summer where she will not be going to summer camp. Hayes is a nineteen-year-old young man and his life is the diner. The cooks and waitress are now doing everything the way Hayes wants it done.

Raggedy is no longer a collector. He is now just a Nitti sometime bodyguard. Nitti has asked Raggedy to let her go out alone. Raggedy did what Nitti asked her to do. Nitti is now able to leave the diner and go out into the city by herself. Sometimes, she is with some friend from high school. Sometimes, it's to meet her father for a meal or a movie.

On July 4, 1939, Nitti goes out on her first date. She and a girl from school and two other boys go see a movie. Raggedy doesn't go with her and spends the day at a ball game. Hayes works the day. At 6:00 PM, Nitti comes home from her date and movie.

Nitti walks through the front doors of the diner and sees the place full of people again. All the tables are filled, and the waitresses are running between the tables and the backroom. The busboys are cleaning the tables just in time for the next group of people. Nitti makes her way past the workers and the people to the backroom and into the kitchen.

Nitti finds Hayes behind the diner talking to a new very pretty waitress. Nitti stands by the backdoor waiting for Hayes to come back in. Nitti is at the door for ten Minutes before Hayes sees her standing there. Hayes and the girl finish talking. The waitress walks in to the diner first. She smiles and grins at Nitti and brushes her shoulder against Nitti.

Hayes follows the waitress up to Nitti where he stops. "How was the movie, Nitti?" he asks her.

Nitti answers him with, "I'll tell you later, Hayes. Can you please stop working early today? I would like to talk with you later."

"Okay, Nitti, I'll see what I can do."

Nitti turns, then walks upstairs to the bedrooms.

At 8:30 PM, Nitti comes down from her room and into the diner. She walks up to Hayes and tells him she has a problem in her room and needs a hand. Hayes ask her to give him five minutes and he'll be up. Ten minutes later, Hayes is knocking on Nitti's door. Nitti opens the door and asks Hayes to come in.

Hayes has never been on the other side of her bedroom door.

He investigates the room and sees everything is painted white—the walls, the ceiling, and the furniture. The room has several lamps with different colored glass shades on some small tables.

A large rug is on the center of the floor. Her room is bigger than Hayes' room below hers. To one side, Hayes sees an open door that leads to another room. Hayes walks into her room.

Hayes: "Nitti, what can I help you with?"

Nitti: "Hayes, you never been in my room before. Do you like it?"

Hayes: "It's a lot bigger than mine. You have furniture."

Nitti: "Don't be shy. Come in and look around."

Hayes goes on into the room and looks at all the nice things she has. He looks at the pictures on the walls. One of the pictures is of her mother and her father. They are much younger and happier in it. Another picture is her mother holding a baby and smiling. Nitti tells Hayes that's her, the baby. Rag's old six-by-nine pictures of a young Raggedy in a baseball uniform is there.

Hayes walks over to a bookcase and sees some books. Hayes picks up a child's book called *The Wizard of Oz*. Hayes sees the book *Romeo and Juliet*. It was the book Nitti was holding when he first saw her. Hayes tells Nitti he read the *Wizard of Oz* when he was a kid.

After looking around and seeing that she has her own bathroom in the next room, Hayes asks her what she needed help with.

Nitti: "I don't need help with anything, Hayes. You and I are going to watch the fireworks tonight." Hayes: "Nitti, I can't. I have to go back to work."

Nitti: "No, you don't. I talked to Raggedy. He is going to lock up tonight. You can do whatever you want or must do tomorrow. Hayes, look out my window. There is a blanket, some sandwiches, and soda pop for us to have."

Hayes: "Nitti I am not supposed to be up here in your room."

Nitti: "When was the last time somebody told you that, Hayes? How many years ago was it? I don't think you ever wanted to hurt me, Hayes. There is no reason I can't have you in here. Can you think of a reason I shouldn't have you in here?"

Hayes: "No, Nitti."

Nitti: "Then, Hayes, you can leave if you want to or you can come out on the fire escape and enjoy some fireworks."

Hayes: "Okay, Nitti, please give me a couple of minutes and I'll be back here. I have a few things to do."

Nitti: "Okay, Hayes."

Hayes leaves her room and goes on down to the diner. Nitti goes out onto the fire escape. She sits down on the blankets and puts the picnic basket with sandwiches to her side. Below her is the diner's front door.

She can see people coming and going from the diner. Out in the distance is the city of Chicago. The fireworks are set to start in about a half hour.

Nitti looks out at the skyline and thinks about how much it has changed from her first memories in the room. She was very young when her mother left this place. Nitti's mother told Rag to watch her for a while. Nitti remembers the nights she went to the window and cried for her mother.

Nitti's thoughts are broken when she hears Hayes' voice below her. Nitti looks down and sees the pretty waitress kissing Hayes. Nitti hears Hayes tell the waitress, "I will see you tomorrow." The waitress walks away, and Hayes keeps looking at her till she is at the end of the block and turns the corner. Then Hayes goes back into the diner.

Hayes goes up to his floor, washes himself, then goes back to his room and changes. Nitti is still on the fire escape when she hears Hayes knocking on her door. Nitti gets up and goes to her door and opens it and Hayes is there with two plates of apple pie and ice cream. Nitti is surprised and happy with the treat. Hayes and Nitti go out onto the fire escape. They start eating the pie and ice-cream before it melts.

Nitti: "Thank you for the treat, Hayes. That is very nice of you to think about doing it."

Hayes: "I love this stuff. If I could, I would eat it all day."

Nitti: "I thought you bought this up here for me, Hayes?"

Hayes: "It is nice to have you here, Nitti. You make it more special."

Nitti: "It would be nice if we had more time together like this."

Hayes: "Nitti, can I ask you something?"

Nitti: "Sure, Hayes. I would like it if you talked to me more."

Hayes: "I was thinking of making the diner bigger. Would you like to know what I want to do?"

Nitti: "No, Hayes, I don't care about the diner right now. I want to enjoy this nice day and some fireworks with you. Can't you forget about this place? There are other things we can talk about. You haven't asked me how my date was today. Don't you think I would like to talk to someone about it? Do you want to know what movie we saw? If I liked the movie? If I had a good time? Or if I even like the boy I went with."

Hayes: "I am sorry not to think of that, Nitti. Why don't you tell me about it?"

Nitti "You just don't understand. I don't want to tell you. I want you to ask me about it. I want you to think of me and what I may be doing. Hayes, I think of you and what you are doing. I see you kissing that waitress. I am curious about why you two were kissing."

Hayes: "I tell—"

Nitti cuts him off. Nitti: "Hayes, don't tell me. I don't want to know. Let's talk about something else for now. Hayes look down there to the street. A father is taking a picture of his daughter. Someday, Hayes, you may get to do that."

Hayes: "What would you like to talk about, Nitti?"

Nitti: "You know I am going off to college this fall. I can stay there all year 'round if I want. I may never come back here. A lot of girls meet their future husbands at college."

Hayes: "Is that what you're hoping for, Nitti, to meet your future husband?"

Nitti: "I was hoping that I already met him. How about you, Hayes. Don't you want to meet some girl and fall in love with her?"

Hayes: "It won't be at college. I never finished elementary school."

Nitti: "Hayes, when you were in my room before, you saw the book *The Wizard of Oz*. You said you read it a long time ago. How long ago was that? From the first day I saw you, I never saw you with a book. The story you told me is that you can't remember anything before you were ten. Hayes, did that change?"

Hayes: "I was at the orphanage for a while. I must have read it there."

Nitti: "Hayes, how much money do you have?"

Hayes: "I don't know. Raggedy has it. He is holding it for me. Why, Nitti?"

Nitti: "Where do you want to be in ten years?"

Hayes: "I want to be right here at the diner with you and Raggedy."

Nitti: "Hayes, I won't be here. When I go off to college, I may never come back. If my father wants to come and see me, I'll be okay with that. I like Raggedy, but it wouldn't bother me if I never saw him again."

Hayes: "I understand, Nitti."

Nitti: "Hayes, Raggedy said he has to go away this weekend. I have no one to take me to church. Can I ask you to take me this Sunday morning, please?

Hayes: "Sure, if Raggedy lets me. I will ask him, Nitti."

The fireworks start and the two watch the show from the fire escape. When the show ends, Nitti and Hayes say good night. Hayes goes down to the diner to check it for the night. Nitti turns her lights out and goes to bed.

CHAPTER TEN

We're Off

The next day, Hayes asks Raggedy if he can take Nitti to church. Raggedy gives him permission to. Hayes then finds and tells Nitti that he will be able to take her.

Sunday morning comes on a bright, warm day. Hayes is in the diner wearing new pants and a new shirt with shiny shoes, waiting for Nitti.

Nitti comes down the stairs in a soft pink sundress. She has a white handbag with a long strap that goes around her neck. She gets to the bottom of the stairs and stands feet from a quiet Hayes. Nitti smiles at him and turns around a couple of times. Her sundress spins in a circle as it follows her turns. Nitti stops and looks at Hayes.

Hayes: "I wish your mother could see you."

Hayes walks with Nitti the two blocks to the church. Hayes looks at the church.

It's a two-story new stone building with a shiny, gold-plated, large cross on the top of it with a large bell. There six stone stairs as wide as the church that lead up to the front doors that have big heavy, black hinges.

The large windows are cut crystal glass from Metz in France. There are twelve of them on each side of the building.

Inside the church are two rows of new oak benches with high backs. At the front end of the church is the alter. The back wall has several lit candles burning in gold candle holders. To the side of the alter are gold-covered pipes from an organ. Everything in the church is new and beautiful.

The walls inside the church are Chestnut oak that reach up to the wood-plank ceiling of quarter-sawn red-and-white oak. Four octagonal

wood columns on the side of the room hold up the ceiling.

At the front doors of the church stand four well-dressed men against the wall holding long-handled wicker baskets.

Hayes and Nitti take a seat on one of the benches by the doors.

Nitti is greeted by some of the people. Some ask where Raggedy is. They also comment that this is the first time he has not shown up for Sunday mass.

Nitti tells them that he couldn't make it and introduces Hayes as her friend. The church fills up with people.

Hayes looks around. All of the men are in suits. All of the women are in bright summer dresses. The children are dressed up for the day.

As Hayes looks around, he feels that he is out of place in this church. He is one of the darkest skinned people. Some of the people he sees looking at him and Nitti just smile and nod.

The church is filled with people on his bright Sunday morning, filling the room with the sound of their voices. The backdoor behind the alter opens. Two men in white robes walk out, followed by a man in a black robe. The three men are carrying a small black book in their hands. The man in black walks up to a front alter and starts to talk.

The sermon

"I would like to welcome all the people who showed up to your church this beautiful summer day. Remember, the more prayers we make, the more of your prayers are answered.

"As I look out onto the faces this morning, I see a lot of smiles. I see some of the same faces I see every week. And as always, I see some new faces. So, to the new faces, I say welcome and I hope to be calling you the same face next week.

"Today's sermon is about fences. Yes, that's it. Yes, it's that simple—just fences. It's so simple we can just close our books that are in front of us and go back home.

"No, I'm sorry, please don't do that quite yet. We haven't passed around the basket. The bookkeepers of this church would not be very happy with me.

"Sometimes, I would like to put a fence around the bookkeepers of the world. They are always making the numbers work so another bookkeeper can make the numbers not work. Both bookkeepers may be in next week to give the sermon, will see.

"Anyway, back to fences. When we hear the word fence, the picture we first put in our mind is the simple six-foot spruce stockade fence. But we know there are more than one type of fence. They all have different names and they look different. Some fences have different uses and purposes.

"This church has some fences. We have some around the parking area. Our baseball field out back having a home-run fence. They are probably the most noticeable fence. We see them and don't think twice about it.

"This church also has some fences that we know are fences but we don't think about it. We just react to them. Like the three little steps up to this platform. It just a simple three steps. But you know it's to keep us up here and not let us three down to you.

"No, I'm sorry, I have it backward don't I. It is to keep you down there and us up here away from you, isn't it?"

The man looks back at the other two men by the back wall and they have a silent laugh. Then he looks back at the people in the church.

"The three steps and this platform that I now stand on is just, so I could see you. Or you could see me. It's that simple. But in our mind, we make the three steps and the platform a fence to separate us.

"Our big wood front doors are a fence. We do open them and let people in. We open them to let people out. Our large stone walls on the exterior of our church are a fence. The benches you sit in with their large backrest are a fence. They give the person who sits in them a place to lean against and a separation from the person behind them and in front of them.

"We live in a world of fences. Fences are all around us. Some fences we make to separate. Some fences we make. Some things just happen to become a fence.

"What I am going to talk to you, the audience, about is the fences in our lives.

"What fence are you making in your life? Why are you making those fences? Are those fences needed? Are those fences you are making out of hatred? Are those fences you're making designed to keep something fenced in when you should let it go?

"Are you a person that has a fence around you? Are you somebody? Are you somebody that is only known to you? Are you hiding who you are behind a fence? Do you want to tell that person who is close to you who you really are? Do you want to take that fence down and let that person see the real you? Are you using a fence to shield yourself from the reality of who you are?

"How many fences do you have around yourself? Do you put up those fences out of hate? Do you put up those fences for protection? Do you think what would happen if you took down those fences? Would your life change? Would it change for the better or maybe for the worse?

"Do we know people who put up fences around themselves to keep others out? Maybe they are looking to keep you out. We as humans don't like that feeling when we are kept out. Even if we really don't want in. Just the thought of being kept out by a fence makes us unhappy.

"I've felt it. We've all felt it at some point in our life. We didn't need to see the fence that was keeping us out, but we knew it was there. It was there, and we didn't like it.

"Depending on who put that fence up will affect how you react. If it's somebody who is close to you, your reaction may be withdrawn.

"You may step away from that person. You may do this, so you can analyze why that fence was put up. Then you're going to analyze what you're going to do about it.

"Your goal will be to confront your own feeling about that fence, which gives you that feeling. Your goal may be to put up your own fence, so you are not affected by the other person's fence.

"Have you ever trusted a love one? Then that loved one purposely did something that hurt you. They did it not by any mistake on their part. They planned what they were going to do against you.

"Then, after you see the act and all the parts of what they did, you put up a fence that may last a lifetime. That fence may never come down.

"So that may be some of the fences that you encounter every day of your life. Some of those fences are just temporary and soon forgotten. Some of those fences are ones you will never get over or get around. Some of those fences may lead you to tear them down with anger. Some of those fences will make you put up your own fence with anger.

"Today we are going to take those fences down and put up something called a gate of acceptance. To replace a fence with a new structure called a gate. Today when we walk out the doors of this church, we are going to open some gates. Are we going to put up out newest, latest and greatest gate?

"Are we going to walk over to someone we never talked to and say a simple hello? Are we going to shake somebody's hand? Are we going to offer somebody a ride home if they need it?

"Are we going to invite somebody we know but never had over to your home for Sunday dinner? Can you put that fence down for a day to open a gate and let someone break bread with you? Can you just imagine some of the conversations you may have?

"Imagine just going for a walk in our city with someone you never even talked to. You may have gone to the same church for years and never said hello. You may have sat next to each other many times and never thought twice about it. How many times did you walk into this church together then walked out together but never went farther than that?

"Is it that fence I spoke of that keeps you going further than doing nothing about getting to know that person? Is it a fence in your head that says you can't be seen with that person? Is it a fence in your head that keeps the hate for who that person is?

"Can it be the fence of the color of a person that is a fence which prevents you from opening a gate? Opening a gate could just be you being friendly to that person. Maybe it's that person's race that keeps you on the other side of the fence. Because your perception of that person's race is unacceptable to you. Open a gate.

"Maybe it's a fence of someone that will harm your status in the community that keeps you from totally accepting this person. This person may be so much like you and you never know it. You may find a joy in this person that we would all like to find in other people. Open a gate.

"Maybe it's the fence of economics. You may have a different bank account than someone. Have you gone to a ball game? You have your home crowd and the people who sit in hometown seats. You'll have a group of fans all cheering on their team together.

"There is no economics fence among them at that time. They're just sports fans. No one is checking bank accounts or if anybody has one. Any fence that may be use outside the stadium is left outside the stadium. People open gates to common interest.

"It's not so simple sometimes to get around, get over, or take down that fence in our minds. It's the words like acceptance that should take down a fence. If words like understanding that should get you around a fence. It's words like compassion that should get you past a fence. It is as simple as opening a gate that lets you get on the other side of any fence.

"It's words like acceptance, understanding, and compassion that you can use when you need help opening a gate.

"We need to start as a community taking down some of these fences we put up. We need to start as a community to start to open some gates. Our town is made up of many different nationalities and many different people.

"It's what makes our city one of the best in our nation. With all the different people we find ourselves creating fences between us. We have clubs for different ethnic groups. We have different clubs for different parts of our society. Some of these clubs belong on a different world. But that is another sermon. We have different schools for our kids.

"There are restaurants, stores, sports stadiums, swimming places, places for transportation, churches, housing, movie theaters, and maybe one of the simplest places: a barbershop. They all have fences around them. We walk into these places and do our business in them knowing that they have an unseen fence around them. Help open a gate.

"We need to think of those fences as if they were meant for us. Each one of us. We are all part of the same group that make up our city. Every person that is part of our city is part of the fence.

"When we choose to keep out a race of people, that is part of our human race. We have problems. We have the beginning of the end of a community.

Open a gate.

"A community needs to change. For it to change, it needs to take down the fence and let the new in. When the community puts up fence to keep the old in, the end for the community has started.

"On a building in another big city there are the words written, and I quote By Emma Lazarus:

'Give me your tired, your poor,

Your huddled masses yearning to breathe free, The wretched refuse of your teeming shore.

Send these, the homeless, tempest-tossed, to me: I lift my lamp beside the golden door'

"Those words ring so true today. Every place I walk in our city, I see those fences I talked about. I think of what our city will be in one hundred years. We need open our gates to let the new in. They need to come in and give new life to our city.

"The new will pull down the old and build a bigger and better city. They will walk the sidewalks. They will shop the stores. They will send their young children to our school and churches we have built. Those young children will be the future caretakers of the city. Open a gate for a child.

"Our parents and grandparents came to this city and other cities and built them. Our parents and grandparents came to this city after a cow made us famous and rebuilt the city. Can we open a gate to our future children and grandchildren?

"That's what a city needs to survive and become a great city is to open the gates. Have the new take down, go around, and go over the old fence we have put up.

"We need the young and the new. We need to make sure all children have no borders, no fence that will be an obstacle they cannot overcome. All our children will be the future us.

"All the children will have this as their new homeland. All the children will have their parents' nationality as their ancestral history. Just like we do. They will be no different than us. We are the melting pot of the nations of his planet.

"We will take any children another nation will give us. We should open any gate for a child. We have the diversity to let those children become a part of who we are.

"What great nation has ever done that? What group of people anywhere has let children come to them and embraced them? Those children we embrace will be the strength this nation needs to be what our four fathers imagined for a young colony.

"Our four fathers, having the greatest power at the time, wanting to keep our vast untapped natural resources for themselves, put a fence of a powerful naval fleet around us.

"They sent brave soldiers dressed in red. They stood shoulder to shoulder like a red picket fence.

"Sadly, a lot of the young men who stood like a red picket fence fell. We won our independence by men and women who wanted the freedom of living in a land of the free. A land that there was no fence imposed on us by a nation or by any one group of people who thought to quarantine the rights of people to be free by putting a fence around them.

"At that time, many of the other nations wanted to cut off parts of our land and put fences on the parts they wanted for themselves. It was a race among them to have the biggest slice of this land. The only reason that didn't happen was because of the people who came here from different lands just wanting a place to be free of fences.

"It was the sons and daughters of the children from those same nations that wanted to put a fence around us that fought and died for their new homeland.

"Our country owes a depth of gratitude to those children whose parents came from other lands. Those children became the builders, the teachers. Those children found the gate open to this nation.

"Any time a fence was put up in the path of our nation, it was the children of the parents of other nations who took it down or opened a gate.

"The wars our country has fought have never been about us wanting to put a fence around another country.

"We have sadly had to send our young and brave back to the land that some of our children's parents came from. We have sent them because we will pay the price of giving our young in the belief that freedom is something that is worth paying the price with our young.

"We have opened our gates to other nations for their children. They have watched their children, their own future, leave for the promise of this land.

"Soon our nation will send its own children to war again. Some of which had family that walked other nations' land years ago. They will save a nation, save a nationality, save a race of people who are being wiped out.

"As I looked at the paper this morning, I thought of fences. The land to the east where most of our parents came from is on the edge of human crises. I wish I could put up a giant gate and let all the good people just wanting to be free come here. But I can't.

"The people over there are in trouble. There's something called evil. It's the same evil that has us putting up fences here. It's the same evil that has us separating people by color here. It's the same evil that has our young and old on the streets with hunger here.

"At no time in the past has one evil person had the power to change the world. The world has now found that person. Our world is going to change.

"The children of the past eighteen and more years are going to go where Hell is now, walking on existence of humanity. The sacrifice that is going to be made by them will be the only way to stop the hell that is the deadliest horror man will face.

"The children who just survived what is known as the Great Depression will now find themselves in the battle to put a gate in a fence of evil. Just to find when they open that gate, Hell is on the other side. Help us help those who just want to live life with the freedom we have. Help us see that humanity can only be in a place that has no fence in our hearts or minds on our land.

"Amen.

"Now let's pass around the baskets."

The mass is over. The preacher is by the door greeting the people as they leave. Nitti and Hayes are walking out the door.

Nitti grabs Hayes' hand and brings him over to the preacher. The preacher sees Nitti and gives her a cheerful hello. Then he asks her where Raggedy is. Nitti tells him that Raggedy couldn't make it today. Then she introduces Hayes to the preacher as her friend while still holding his hand.

Hayes lets go of Nitti's hand then shakes the preacher's hand. The preacher shakes Hayes hand then turns and greet another man standing on the side of Hayes. Hayes and Nitti are quickly lost when the preacher finds other people to greet.

Nitti takes Hayes to the bottom of the stone stairs. She stands at the bottom of them looking up, waiting for someone. Hayes tells her he should take her home now. Nitti tells him to please wait a couple more minutes.

Hayes is just looking around waiting for Nitti to want to be taken home. Then he sees Nicholas Litti talking to the preacher.

He is there with his wife. He has a boy his age and two girls from the picture Hayes sees at the barbershop.

Hayes tells Nitti again that they should go. Nitti tells Hayes just a bit longer.

Nicholas and his family come down the steps and walk right into Nitti and Hayes.

Mr. Litti stops when he sees Nitti and Hayes holding hands right in front of him. Nitti is looking right at him.

Mr. Litti: "Hello, Nitti, it's nice to see you at church today. You're looking very nice today. I don't see Raggedy. Is he here?"

Nitti: "No, he said he had to be somewhere. This is my friend Hayes."

Mr. Litti: "I know Hayes. He's been coming into my barbershop for a couple of years now. Hasn't he told you? He is doing a very good job with my diner."

Nitti doesn't blink an eye, hearing what her father just said.

Nitti: "Hello, Mrs. Litti. Hello Junior, Marie, and

Lisa. It's nice to see you again. It's been a long time."

Mrs. Litti: "Nitti, you are growing up so fast. You should come by and see us more often. Oh, by the way, we are late for a brunch. We are breaking bread again with some old friends. So, goodbye Nitti and Nitti's friend whomever. Let's get in the cars Junior, girls and wait in our new car. Sorry we can't give you a ride were late. Say goodbye now."

Junior: "Bye, Pretty Nitti."

Girls: "Goodbye, Nitti."

Mrs. Litti: "I will be in the car with your and my son and your favorite nieces."

Mrs. Litti and the girls walk to the car when Maria says, "Lisa, wasn't that your dress last year?"

Nitti, Hayes, and Mr. Litti stand as they watch Mrs. Litti, Junior, and the girls walk off then get into a new car. Then Nitti and Hayes just look at Mr. Litti.

Mr. Litti just looks back at Nitti and Hayes.

After a minute or two, Mr. Litti says, "Well, Nitti, I have to go now. I'll stop by and take you out next week, okay?"

Nitti: "Thank you. I always like to spend time with my father. I understand you have to go, so bye."

Mr. Litti: "By, Nitti. By, Hayes. You and I are going to have a talk real soon."

Mr. Litti turns and starts to walk to the car. Nitti just looks at him walk away. Then she yells out "Dad!" She lets go of Hayes' hand and runs to Mr. Litti. He stops and turns around. Nitti says a couple of unheard words by anybody but Mr. Litti.

Mr. Litti bends down and gives Nitti a kiss on her cheek. Mr. Litti stands there, as he watches Nitti walk back to Hayes. Nitti takes Hayes' hand and walks away from the church. Mr. Litti's thoughts are broken up by the sound of his car horn being blown.

On the walk back to the diner, Hayes explains why he couldn't tell Nitti he knew her father. When Nitti and Hayes are back at the diner, Nitti lets go of Hayes' hand and tells him she is going to her room to cry.

Nitti: "I had to ask my own father for a kiss goodbye today. Then I had to hear you explain to me how unimportant you think I am and how important doing what Raggedy tells you to do is. If you smell something burning from my room, it's his hand-me-down dress I wore today that was two sizes too big.

"So, I had to take in this tent of a dress. I thought it was something special, this dress that my father who I love gave me for an early birthday present."

Hayes and Nitti go back to their hellos and goodbyes as they pass each other the following days. Nitti see Hayes and the pretty waitress talking more and more. Most of the time, it's when they are behind the diner. July passes and August comes. The local movie theater is showing the new movie called *The Wizard of Oz*.

Nitti see Hayes talking to the pretty waitress on a late-August day, just days before she must go off to college. Nitti goes up to Hayes in front of the waitress and asks him if she can see him behind the diner.

Once they are alone, Nitti says, "Hayes I will go away to college September first, this Friday, on my birthday. I will be sixteen then."

Hayes: "I know, Nitti. I will miss you."

Nitti: "The movie *The Wizard of Oz* is playing in the movie theater. I want to spend my last day here with you. I want you to take me to see that movie."

Hayes: "Okay, Nitti, I will be happy to go and see the movie with you. How about we go Thursday and catch the matinee."

Nitti: "Thanks, Hayes, that will make me very happy to spend the day with you."

On the way back in, Nitti walks into the diner first. She smiles and grins at the pretty waitress and brushes her shoulder against her.

It is Thursday, August 31, 1939. A nineteen-year-old Hayes and a fifteen-year-old Nitti are on their first date. It is 11:00 AM when the two leave the diner. It is a beautiful late-summer day. Hayes dresses in a new button-down shirt with new pants and clean shoes. Nitti has on a new dress.

Hayes takes Nitti out to lunch. He takes her to a café with tables on the sidewalk. They talk about all the people they remember who worked at the restaurant and diner. The day they heard about Randy the morning cook dying. Nitti's mother and the last day Nitti saw her. The bartender Gus and a cook named Joe who left one day.

Then a week later, Raggedy started to ask if anybody noticed they left.

They tried to figure out how many bodies were buried by Raggedy in the cemetery. They talked about the days of having a Thanksgiving dinner. They talked about the crossword puzzle of secret hellos.

Nitti tells Hayes if the old man who was there before him wasn't killed, they wouldn't have met.

Across the street, Nicholas Litti's father-in-law is watching Hayes and Nitti having lunch. He's seen enough. He turns and goes and tell Nicholas about the two.

At 3:00 PM, the two of them walk in to see *The Wizard of Oz*. After the movie, Hayes and Nitti walk out of the theater. Nitti is upset at Hayes and he can't figure out why. They start to walk back to the diner. Hayes is asking Nitti what he did wrong. Nitti isn't talking or answering him; she's just walking as fast as she can, trying to stay in front of him.

At a corner in the middle of Chicago, Hayes puts his hand on Nitti's shoulder and asks, "What's wrong?"

Nitti looks at his hand on her shoulder. Then she looks up at Hayes and says in front of all the people around them, "I love you, do you understand that, Hayes? I am a girl who loves you. I wanted you to take me to a movie and kiss me. Not talk about what happened to Dorothy when and if she came back. You're a boy. You're supposed to want to kiss me in a movie theater. That's what boys do—they kiss girls. Boys like pretty girls. I know I am a pretty girl because my father tells me it all the time. You never said that to me, Hayes, not once, and I wanted you to. I would pray one day you would look at me and want to kiss me.

"I would dream of you coming up the fire escape and tapping on my window, so I would come to the window. Then you would kiss me, Hayes. When I went to summer camp, I was thinking of you. Did you think of me?

"Hayes, I can't take it no more. I am hurting myself too much over you. I didn't need you to be in love with me. But I need you to like me the way boys like girls. Hayes, you must really hate me."

Hayes: "Nitti, I think it's time I tell you all about me."

Hayes and Nitti walk back to the diner. On the way back, Hayes tells her he does remembered everything that led up to him ending up at the diner.

As the two of them walk up to the diner, they see the diner's closed sign in the window. Hayes tries to open the front door, but it doesn't open. Then Hayes and Nitti go around to the back.

Hayes walks into an open backdoor and sees no one in the kitchen. The stoves are lit, and pots and pans are thrown about. He walks into the dining room.

In a lone seat at a table, leaning back in a chair, is Raggedy. He smiles at the two and says, "How was the movies?" Raggedy has a gun in his bloody hand. His other hand is over a patch of blood on his chest. In front of him are two machine guns.

Hayes: "Raggedy what happened?"

Raggedy spits blood. "It's over. This place has come to its end. I got all the people out. Nitti, your father is dead, everybody is dead. There is a suitcase under the next table with a lot of money in it. You two need to disappear. Nitti, I can't protect you anymore.

All you have is What's in that suitcase and Hayes. Hayes, I told you what to do when it happens, and it happened. Hayes, it's your job now to protect her. There will be people looking for revenge. Junior will not last a week. Hayes, you need to hide her.

"I have a box of dynamite under my seat. I may have a couple of more minutes before I pass out and become daisy food. Get the suitcase and grab what you can, Nitti. I am going to light the dynamite to have it go off, so run. There is nothing you can do now but run and hide."

Hayes grabs Nitti and runs up to her room. On her floor is her dead father and his old father-in-law. Nitti screams and cries. Hayes grabs some pictures then picks up two suitcases Nitti had packed for college. The two come downstairs and find Raggedy dead on the floor. Next to Raggedy is a burning wick and some dynamite. Nitti gets the suitcase of money that Raggedy told them to take. Hayes and Nitti make their way to the train station when they hear the dynamite go off.

The next day, September 1, 1939, Hitler invades Poland. The news in the following days is about the new war in Europe. The diner fire the dead body's get lost in the news. Hayes and Nitti escape Chicago together with a suitcase full of money. The war ended in 1945.

The forties end. The fifties turn in to the sixties. The sixties turn in to the seventies, Hollywood was always looking for the next great movie to be made. The gangsters and the stories made of their lives found their way into Hollywood legends.

So the life and the times of Nicholas Litti was made into books and movies. The one part of his life that remained a mystery was the myth of a long-lost daughter.

CHAPTER ELEVEN

Daisies

In the vast expanse of the state of Texas sits just an average city with average people. The city has all the average things that a city has: a large domestic airport on the north side, a hospital located on the east side. In the center of the city sits the police department. On the south side sits the main newspaper building. On the city's west side there is an old coal-fired power plant.

The old coal power plant is fed by a set of old train tracks that comes up from the south. This city grew after the war with two new major highways and a big new domestic airport.

Alongside the old train tracks that fed the old coal plant runs an old service road that goes in and out of some small towns.

About twenty miles south of this city is a small, dying town with old train tracks, and the service road that runs alongside of it. The town has the usual small local streets with small-town names, like Main Street, Bank Street, Park Street, and other familiar names.

The town has lost its post office and police department years ago. As the city to the north grew this small town lost most of its population. They either moved to the city for the jobs or moved on to another city.

On this old service road is a small diner. The diner was once a two-story service building for a water tower that supplied water for the old steam engine trains. Behind the diner and alongside the tracks is that old abandoned water tower. On the other side of the tracks is a small car junkyard.

In 1945, the railroad put the old service building up for sale as their train engines turned to diesel engines. The old service building was purchased by a young married couple in their early twenties.

The young couple turned the old service building's first floor into a diner. They turned the second floor into an apartment and lived in it.

The couple had a baby boy the first year at the diner. The boy was named Andy. They struggled to keep the diner open. The service road that ran in front of the diner carried less and less traffic as the years past.

In 1965, the couple's only, child was drafted into the Vietnam War. He became an airborne pathfinder for an elite ranger company. During his time overseas, the diner was broken into at night.

The diner was closed one evening when the couple who were asleep upstairs heard someone breaking into the diner. The husband went downstairs to scare off the intruder. When the man went downstairs, he saw two people running out his broken front door. The man ran outside the building and saw the two people in a car that was driving off.

The man ran out in front of the car trying to stop them. From the second floor, the wife saw the car drive into her husband.

He fell onto the hood of the car and broke it's antenna off. The woman then saw the car drive off north to the city. She then ran down the stairs to find her husband dead on the ground holding the car's antenna in his hand.

The next day, the diner was closed. A Texas Ranger and a newspaper reporter were there. The state Texas Ranger made out some reports. The newspaper-man and the Texas Ranger promised the now widowed woman help find the people who killed her husband.

A couple of days later, her son returned home from Vietnam. The woman and her son buried her husband and his father.

As the day after the incident passed into weeks, and then months, and then years, no arrest for the murder of the man was ever made. The woman died about ten years later of a broken heart. She was buried alongside her husband whose murder had gone unsolved. Their son is now the owner and running the diner.

It's now 1986. Andy the only son of the young couple who purchase an old railroad service building that was made into a diner is now the owner and cook for the converted diner.

The town that diner is in has only a couple of dozen people left in it. The service road has not been repaved in decades. There are no more street signs on any poles on any streets in the town. The last building that was built was over twenty years ago.

The service road that follows the train tracks was the only thing that kept the diner alive for the past four decades.

Tourists that are lost trying to find the big city to the north will end up on the service road by mistake. Truck drivers trying to avoid the state troopers or weight station will use the old rough service road.

The diner has some people from the city to the north who will stop by for a cheap, secluded meal. Those people are usually married, but not to each other on their way to a no-tell motel twenty miles farther south.

Those couples would stop by the diner at night, laughing and talking and looking for that cheap meal called time away. Or the meal called free-pass night. Talking about how they're not understood, the problem of a marriage they no longer want to be a part of, and how it's now about staying together for the kids.

Then early the next morning, on the way back to the city, those same couples would stop by for breakfast trying to get their stories straight. They are making plans to do it again. Some of them may come back with a different dish. People's taste do change.

Sometimes, the women will be trying to hide their face behind makeup and wigs. The women looking at the beer-belly man across from them. How the few minutes with him on top of her were a few minutes too long. How she and the young men she once knew would make the earth move. Now she must pretend as if it was just as good for her as him.

The man wishing he could have just paid the woman off and left her there when they were done.

The alternative lifestyle couples who must pretend like they're at a business meal, even in 1986. When they get to the hotel, it is side-by-side rooms they want. It's just for business, they must tell the clerks. It isn't pretty. It's just enough to keep the small diner in the black sometimes.

The diner opens its doors at 6:00 AM, Monday-Friday. The diner closes some of the time at 9:00 PM, Monday-Friday. Saturday the diner is open 7:00 AM to 3:00 PM.

Andy the owner closes the diner on Sunday because of lack of business. The other reason is the few waitresses work too many hours during the week. Andy closes the diner Thanksgiving, Christmas, and New Year's Day.

On weekdays, the first waitress comes in at 5:45 AM and leaves at 2:00 PM. The next waitress comes in at 11:00 Am and leaves at 7:00 PM. The last waitress of the day comes in at 4:00 PM and stays to closing.

Andy gets up at 5:00 AM and will be there from opening to closing every day. The first waitress comes in and unlocks the front door. Andy locks the front door every night. Sometimes, Andy must bring in a cook or waitress from the big city north of the diner.

Andy pays his waitress very well. The waitresses often wonder where he gets the money to pay them and keep the diner open. They have told Andy he works himself and the waitresses too hard and too many hours.

It is an early Friday Texas morning. The sun is breaking over the horizon. The front door of this two-story white diner sits on the side of a worn-out old service road facing the early morning Texas sun. A closed sign hangs in the front door of the unopened diner.

Above the front door sits a black-and-white sign with the diner's name on it. There is a big square window on each side of the front door. The windows have one wooden table behind each of them inside.

The top floor has three small windows with the shades always pulled down. In front of the diner is a small dirt parking lot. On the side of the parking lot is a glass phone booth.

The owner of the diner, Andy, comes down from his apartment above the diner at 5:30 AM, which he does Monday-Saturday. He has been doing the same routine for the past twenty-one years.

Andy starts the burners for the flat grill. He pulls a couple of dozen eggs from the refrigerator. He goes out the backdoor picks up two metal garbage cans and brings them around front.

He then walks over to a small box at the base of a flagpole. He pulls the flag out and puts in the box from the previous night. Andy attaches the flag to the pole then raises it. He sees a pile of cigarette ashes and beer cans on the ground. Somebody dumped their car's ashtray and cans on the ground. Andy gets a shovel and scoops up the mess and puts it in the trash can.

He then walks back around the diner and goes to a sink to wash his hands. He goes over to the grill and put some bacon he cooked last night on the center to reheat it. He then goes around to the front of the diner behind the counter.

Andy fills the coffee machine with water then turns them on. Then he collects yesterday's papers from around the room.

He pulls a crossword puzzle off the counter and looks at it. Throughout the day, the waitresses will do parts of the crossword puzzle when it gets slow. This was passed on by Andy's parents. Andy can tell how busy the day was by how much of the puzzle was done. The paper is from the city to the north of them and would sometimes have a reader make a crossword puzzle, and if it was good, the paper would publish it and print the name of the person who created it.

At or about a quarter to six, the first waitress comes in through the backdoor of the diner. At the age of twenty-five, she's a single mother of a boy. Sometimes, she is late and on occasion has failed to show. Andy would know if she would be out when his phone upstairs would ring early in the morning.

Andy had known the girl since she was a baby. Her father would bring her in and sit with her at the counter. Michelle the girl has grown into a very pretty woman with long blond hair. She found a boy she liked while working at the diner and they started dating.

The boy was older then Michelle. Andy had to fire him because he was caught stealing from the register.

Two years later, the boy left town with another pretty girl and left an unmarried pregnant Michelle to grow into a woman. Michelle and her son now live with her parents.

Michelle comes into the kitchen and yells out to Andy, "Good morning, Andy. I made it." Andy from where he is at the time would thank her for being here. Michelle would go to the front door and turn the closed sign to open and unlock the front door.

Michelle would take the dishes, cups, and utensils out of the dishwasher. Then she would start to set up the two wooden tables with dishes and cups the way Andy wants his table set. Then she would set some cups and dishes across the counter.

The morning coal train passes behind the diner. It is laboring, pulling its heavy load of coal to the power plant. The power of its engines and the heavy coal cars shake the diner. The glass and the dishes rattle as the vibrations from the train travel unobstructed up and into the diner. Andy comes out from the kitchen and greets Michelle.

Andy: "Hello, Michelle. How is your boy doing today?"

Michelle: "I think Paul is catching a cold. I was going stay home with him. But he missed too much time from school already, so I kicked his butt off to school."

Andy: "Yeah, I hear that there is something going around again."

Michelle: "Andy, he is so smart, the school teacher has him doing long math."

Andy: "Michelle, he gets his smarts from his mother."

Michelle: "Thanks, Andy. My father wants to know if you would like to come by the house on Sunday and have dinner?"

Andy: "Tell you mother and father I said thank you but not this time."

Michelle: "I will give him that answer again. When he asks me why, I'll give him the same answer you give me every time I ask you: 'I have to get ready for Monday.' And when he asks me what you do on Sundays, I give him the same answers: 'I have to cut my hair and do the laundry and separate my black shirts.'"

Andy: "Michelle that's what I do. I have my routine. I have my life. That's who I am."

Michelle: "I know, Andy, but if you change your mind, please just show up."

Andy: "Right. Michelle, has that deadbeat sent you any money lately?"

Michelle: "No. I got a letter from him asking for a picture of Paul. He is somewhere with that girl."

Andy: "Michelle, here comes a customer. Let's get to it."

A man called Tad and a woman called Betty come into the diner and take a seat at a window table. Betty is in her late-thirties and Tad is in his early twenties.

She is dressed in a woman's pants suit. The man is dressed in a pair of tight blue jeans and a lavender shirt with several buttons undone. Michelle brings over a coffee pot and two menus.

She hands them the menus and fills the cups with coffee. She asks them if she can get them anything as they take the menus. The woman looks at the menu and starts to read it. The man picks up the menu and starts to check Michelle out.

Betty: "Give me a moment, dear. I'll let you know."

Michelle walks back to the counter and puts the pot of coffee back on a burner.

Betty: "Tad, I don't think that waitress can afford to put gas in that car of yours. Unless you want to find another place to work, stop looking for the opportunity. There aren't many jobs that pay stock boys what I pay you. Just remember whose shelves you're supposed to be stocking."

Tad: "Just looking, Betty. It's just a look. I really don't like them that young, you know."

Betty: "I know what you like. But right now, I want to eat and get back home. So call her over here and order what you really like."

Tad calls Michelle over and orders his breakfast and Betty orders hers. Michelle fills their cups with coffee again then goes back to a kitchen window and hangs the breakfast order up.

A policeman who rides a motorcycle comes to the diner and takes a seat at the counter. The policeman, whose name is Dan, comes in a couple times a week. He is a marine from the Korean War. Dan is in a short-sleeve police shirt just long enough to cover a large marine emblem on his big right arm. Michelle goes over to Dan and fills his cup with coffee.

Michelle: "Hi, Dan. Will it be the regular heart attack on white bread, toasted?"

Dan: "Yes, Michelle, two bacon, lettuce, and tomato sandwiches on white bread, toasted, with extra mayo. You know I can't get it at home. Please, Michelle, I've been thinking of it all night."

Michelle: "Dan, you'll be thinking of it tonight when you are pulling the graveyard shift again."

Dan: "Please, Michelle. I promise OJ and wheat bread tomorrow."

Michelle yells back to Andy in the kitchen, "Two Dan heart attack it's-my-last-one-again special please."

Tad laughs at the table by the windows when he hears Michelle.

Betty: "Quiet, fool. I don't want to be recognized. I don't need any policeman remembering me being here, you understand."

Tad: "I hope that cop has a heart attack on that bike."

Betty: "I hope someday you become a man and not a talking vibrator."

Michelle brings Betty and Tad their breakfast and refills their cups with coffee. Then she goes and gets Dan more coffee.

Michelle: "I am sorry, Dan, if I embarrassed you with that sandwich, but I do care about you."

Dan: "Thanks, Michelle. My wife is always asking how you and the boy are doing."

Michelle: "Please tell Patty that were just fine."

Dan: "I often wish I killed that boyfriend of yours that night. Drinking and driving with you in the car. When I found him tossed from the flipped-over car that he drove off the road. And you stuck in the car upside down. I wanted to bash his head in with a rock and do society a favor."

Michelle: "Thanks, Dan. I know you mean good, but he wasn't worth you having to deal with that in your life. Or what it would have done to your family, but thanks again for getting me out of that car."

Dan looks back to the table with the man and woman eating breakfast. Then he looks back at Michelle.

Dan: "Another Mr. and Mrs. Smith?"

Michelle: "Yes, and that guy is a walking bottle of perfume. I wanted to puke at that smell of I-didn't-have-time-for-a-shower-so-I'll-just-wear-this-gallon-of-cheap-perfume."

Dan: "Someday something's going to happen, and they'll be caught together and can't get out of it."

Michelle: "That would be funny. Your BLT is up. I'll get it."

Michelle goes and get Dan's BLT and brings it back to him with some extra mayonnaise.

Michelle goes back and forth with Dan and the people at the table.

Betty and Tad have finished their breakfast.

Michelle puts the check by Tad. Betty takes the check, looks at it, and hands Michelle ten dollars for an eight-dollar tab.

Betty: "That meal was worth every dollar I spent on it, dear. It was a very good breakfast. I wish everything I paid for could deliver like that breakfast. Right, Tad, you know what I mean?"

Tad: "Sometimes the second dish is better than the first. You know what I mean."

Betty: "Speaking of promises that are just promises, we're late for a meeting I promised to be at."

The couple leave the diner. Michelle grabs the dishes and brings them back to the kitchen. Dan is now on his second BLT.

Michelle brings him over a new napkin. She can see an eighteen-wheeler pull up in front of the diner and parking parallel to the road.

Two men walk into the diner and look to the counter where Dan is sitting. The bigger of the two truckers see Michelle behind the counter and says out loud, "The chick in this place looks good. I wonder if she is on the menu."

Dan clears his throat loudly, then looks at and smiles at the two men. The two men nod their heads at Dan and take a seat at the counter. Michelle gets a pot of coffee and brings it over to the two men.

Michelle: "Here's the menu, guys. It's all the coffee you can drink with any of the diner's breakfast specials. I'll be the chick behind the counter. You two can be the nice customers in front of the counter. Please call me Michelle. I will stay behind the counter. Thanks for coming in."

"I'm Dave, Michelle, and this big, ugly guy next to me is Pete. Give me an egg, mushrooms, and a side of hash browns," the smaller trucker says.

"I'll have a bowl of grits with lots of butter. Bring me some shit on a shingle on toast, babe. Please call me Big Pete."

Dave: "Thank you, Bill. Please excuse my friend, Michelle."

Michelle: "No problem, guys."

Michelle writes up the ticket and puts it in the kitchen window. Then she goes back over to Dan who finished his second BLT and three cups of coffee. Dan leaves ten dollars for the meal and thanks her.

Then Dan tells her he will be back tomorrow to have the wheat bread breakfast. Then he calls out to Andy and tells him he'll talk to him tomorrow.

Dan passes the big truck driver and tells him, "I'll be up the road checking people's vocabulary." Then Dan walks out of the diner and around the eighteen-wheeler, then gets on his motorcycle and drives off.

The truck drivers have finished their meals. The diner has a couple of other people come into it. Some people are at the counter and some are at a table.

The big driver gets up and walks to the diner's single restroom. The driver called Dave pays the tab and goes out to his truck and waits for the other driver, Bill. Fifteen minutes later, Pete walks out of the bathroom and leaves the diner.

A bad bathroom odor starts to overcome the diner. Michelle walks over to the restroom. When she sees the mess in it that Bill left, she holds her nose and walks inside to open a vent.

Then she goes back into the kitchen and tells Andy the toilet is backed up again. Andy comes around with a plunger, mop, and bucket and cleans up the mess.

It's about 9:00 AM when the city newspaper is delivered to the diner. The diner is the last stop for the driver's route. Michelle goes up front and picks up the six copies of the paper. Michelle looks at the front page. It tells of another victim of a serial vigilante. A vigilante that has beaten suspected drug dealers.

CHAPTER TWELVE

Grind

Michelle puts a copy of the daily paper on each of the tables then takes one of the papers and opens it to the crossword puzzle. She takes it out and reads the name of the person who created it. The paper would let one of its reader write a crossword puzzle. This puzzle today was created by a reader named Path Man. Michelle pulls it out and clips it to the kitchen window for all the waitresses. The diner waitresses have been doing this since before Andy was born.

Several people have come into the diner, eaten, and left. Michelle and Andy have managed to feed the people and clean up after them like they always do. Michelle has three words figured out on the daily crossword puzzle: door, path, tower.

It is now 11:00 AM and the second waitress comes in. She puts on her apron, picks up her pad, and says hello to Andy and Michelle. The second waitress's name is Noreen.

Noreen is in her thirties. She has two boys in the local high school. Noreen is just the mother type to everybody. She will be the one to bring the food to any event. Noreen married her high school boyfriend and prom date. Noreen's husband works at the coal-fired power plant. The diner starts to fill for the lunchtime rush.

Noreen finds the crossword puzzle in the ordering window. She looks at it for a minute. Michelle has found three words. Michelle would write her words in black ink. Then Noreen goes back to serving the people in the diner. Michelle and Noreen push the lunches out to the customers. The people in the diner start to thin out after lunchtime.

It's 2:00 PM and Michelle hangs up her apron. Then Michelle goes to an old broken stove. She opens it up and takes out last night's deposit that Andy uses as a safe. It is Michelle's job to bring it to the bank.

Andy has known Michelle to forget to bring the deposit to the bank. Sometimes, Michelle would have her father bring it to the bank.

One day Michelle forgot about the deposit and left it in the car. That night after putting her son to bed she remembered the deposit. Michelle ran out to the car and found the deposit on the front seat. That night Michelle put the deposit in her freezer. Andy knows Michelle wouldn't steal a penny from him. She yells goodbye to Andy and Noreen.

Michelle gets into her car on the side of the diner. She is thinking of her son and what time she must pick him up from his daycare. As Michelle backs her car up, she sees an old wrecked pickup by the phone booth. Michelle turns her car to the back of the pickup. On the back of the pickup she sees a boy and girl no older than her child. The two children are dirty and wearing torn, dirty clothes.

Michelle looks at the other people in the back of the truck and sees a group of migrant workers. The ages of the people are from the too-young-to-be-working to the too-old-to-be working.

All the men and women are in dirty, worn, and torn clothes. A man is in the phone booth, looking at a newspaper, while trying to make a call.

Michelle puts her car in park and watches the people in the pickup and the man in the phone booth. He makes several attempts but fails to dial the correct number and is now out of money.

The man comes out of the phone booth with the paper and walks over to the people in the truck. He talks to a couple of them and points at the paper.

A woman gets out of the truck and goes over to the phone booth with the man. Michelle turns the car off and gets out of her car. She walks over to the two children who are sitting on the truck's tailgate on this hot Texas midday. Michelle says hello in Spanish to the two children and smiles at them.

The boy and girl smile at her and give her the peace sign. Michelle gives them the peace sign back and looks to the front end of the bed of the pickup. All around the truck bed are black garbage bags filled with clothes and garbage.

Michelle then looks over to the phone booth and sees the two people still having problems. Michelle walks over to the phone booth.

She knocks on the booth to get their attention. The woman inside the booth comes outside. Michelle asks the woman if she can help.

The woman shows Michelle the paper and the number on it. The woman points to the number and says in English, "We are just looking for work."

Michelle nods her head and says, "Please follow me." Then Michelle takes the woman's hand and has the woman follow her. Michelle motions for the man to follow them. The man is hesitant to follow but Michelle grabs his hand too. Michelle leads the two to the back of the diner. From the backdoor she calls out to Andy. She tells him that there is a pickup out front with some migrant workers and they are lost.

Michelle gets the paper from the woman and brings them to the diner phone. Michelle picks up the phone and dials the number for the woman. Andy is looking at the man and woman and shaking his head. He gets two glasses from the counter and fills them up with water then hands them to the man at the door and the woman. Michelle gets somebody on the phone and tells that person about the people lost and looking for work.

Michelle gets the address and writes it down on one of her order tickets. She takes the ticket and the man out front and explains the best way to get where he needs to go. Then Michelle goes back inside to the woman.

Michelle and Andy come out a couple of minutes later with the woman. Michelle and the woman are carrying plastic milk bottles filled with water and a bag. She walks to the back of the truck and puts the water on the bed. Then Michelle pulls out two bananas and hands them to the two children.

Andy looks at Michelle and tells her, "That's coming out of your Christmas bonus, young lady." Then he reminds her about her boy and picking him up. Michelle lets out an expletive and runs to her car. Michelle spins the tires and squeals them on the road, then drives away. The man and woman get back in the truck, thanking Andy. Then the migrants drive off. Andy goes back to work in the diner.

Andy and Noreen are now taking care of the customers. At 3:00 PM, one of the regular locals enters the diner. He is third generation from immigrants. His parent purchased an old wooden-structure hotel fifty years ago. In the past fifty years, the family has put little money into the building.

The building is now used as a rental property. Martin is now the owner and self-appointed manager for the building. He rents the building out to the transit population.

Most of them are seasonal workers and some are just locals who can't afford to own a home. The building is a permanent home for the bugs, mice, rats, and roaches. The day Martin left high school, he walked home and never left.

Martin, now thirty years old, walks into the diner with a baseball cap on sideways. A cheap gold chain hangs around his neck. He is dressed in his favorite green, red, and white running suit. Martin takes his usual seat. Noreen comes over to him and greets him with, "Sorry, Martin, no free food today."

In a fake Italian accent, Martin asks Noreen, "Please call me Martino, Noreen."

Noreen: "Your mother named you Martin. Your name is Martin."

Martin: "Noreen, did I miss the free giveaway?"

Noreen: "Always with the free with you. I have things to do. What can I get you today, Martin?"

Martin orders the cheeseburger special. After Martin places his order, he gets up, goes to the counter, and picks up a newspaper. He calls back to Andy, "Give me some extra fries today."

Andy replies, "Like you need them. Always wanting something for nothing. And that new phrase, give me! Not can I please have."

Martin goes back to his seat trying to sing some old Sinatra song.

Noreen starts to pull some glasses and dishes out of the dishwasher and sets them on the counter. She cleans the seats at the counter. Andy rings the bell for Martin's food. Noreen picks it up and brings it to Martin. Noreen puts the plate down with his drink and tells Martin, "Write the words to the song on the back of your hand and it will help you remember them." Then Noreen goes back to cleaning.

A man comes into the diner and stops at the door. He looks around the diner. He has a motorcycle helmet in one hand and a backpack in the other. He walks up to the counter and takes a seat. He drops his backpack to the side of the stool then puts his helmet on the next stool. He looks back over his shoulder to Martin eating at a table. Then he looks at the few other people in the diner. Noreen comes over and puts the menu in front of him. The man just asks for some apple pie, vanilla ice cream, and black coffee.

Noreen calls back to Andy, "Hot apple pie." Then she gets some vanilla ice cream in a bowl.

The man reaches down into his backpack and pulls out a large notebook. He puts the notebook down on the counter. He opens the book and starts to write something inside. Noreen comes over to him and puts the ice cream and pie in front of him. She pours him some coffee then asks him if he would like anything else. The man just shakes his head no then smiles at her. He starts to eat his ice cream and pie. Noreen looks at him for a moment then leaves him to ring out a customer who finished their meal.

Noreen has just finished with the last customer. Martin asks him if he could put the check for the meal on his account. Noreen tells him that he doesn't have an account and that this is a cash business. Martin pays the tab and walks out while trying to sing the words to an old Italian love song. The man with the notebook watches Martin walk out, then turns back to his notebook.

Noreen picks up a paper and walks over to the customer eating the pie and ice cream and writing in the book. She looks over the paper and tries to see what he is writing. Unable to make out anything, Noreen goes back into the kitchen where Andy is. Noreen talks to Andy about wanting to take some vacation time next month.

Andy puts it on a calendar he has on a wall. Noreen then goes back out to the front of the diner. The man was finished with the ice cream and pie, then he asked for more coffee, black. Noreen gets him more coffee then goes to an old couple who walked into the diner.

Noreen was working on some other customer when the man who ordered the pie and ice cream was at the register to pay his tab. Noreen looked back over to where he was sitting. The man left a paperback book on the counter. Noreen tells him that he left a book there. The man pays his bill and tells Noreen it is hers now. He leaves her a tip and puts his backpack on and walks out of the diner. Noreen sees him get on his bike and drive away. She goes over to see what book he left. Noreen picks it up and reads the cover.

Its 4:00 PM and the next waitress comes in. She is a fifty-year-old woman. She is the only employee left who knew Andy's parents. Harley raised three children and sent them off to college. Harley's husband died in the early parts of the Vietnam War. Her husband was a helicopter pilot who was shot down and listed as MIA for years. Andy's parents paid the young widow's mortgage off. Andy's parents asked for nothing in returned.

Harley comes into the diner and finds Noreen at the counter working on the daily crossword puzzle. Noreen has found a couple of words. Noreen would write her letters in blue ink. Noreen had found three words in the puzzle: coal, car, tracks.

Harley goes back into the kitchen and says hello to Andy. Then she grabs her pad, pencil, and, apron and goes around front. The dinner crowd slowly starts to fill the diner. Noreen and Harley work the counter and tables.

Noreen calls back to Andy and tells him it is 4:30 PM and the game's about to start. She then goes over to a black-and-white TV. She puts the TV on and turns the sound down. On top of the TV is a small transistor radio. Noreen turns the sound up. On the radio you can hear a man doing a beer commercial. After the commercial, the man starts describing the weather for today's baseball game.

An older couple walks into the diner and takes one of the front tables. That side of the room is Noreen's tables. The couple sits down and starts to call for a waitress. Noreen, who is writing an order for another customer, answers the couple. "Be right with you two."

Noreen finishes writing the order and takes the ticket to Andy. She picks up a meal for a customer at the counter and places it down for the customer then goes over to the older couple at the window.

Noreen gives them her name and thanks them for having patience. Then she takes out her ordering pad. The old man asks Noreen what the score of the game on the TV was. Noreen turns to the TV and back to the old man. "It just started," she tells him.

The woman looks at Noreen, then calls her Nora and tells her that they were seated before other people. They were hoping to get some help quicker. Noreen looks at both and explains it's the busy time of day and they can place their order now. Then Noreen tells them her name again.

The old woman then looks back at her menu and sighs deeply. The old woman starts to read the menu out loud to herself. She lowers the menu and looks over it and asks the old man across from her if he was listening. His reply is a low with the words, "Always, dear, always."

The woman then raises the menu back in front of her face and starts to read it out loud to herself again.

Noreen looks at the old woman then asks, "Would you like me to come back when you know what you would like to order?"

The old woman lowers the menu and looks up at Noreen and tells her, "We may have a question for you. Just be patient with us." The old woman looks up at Noreen name tag and says, "My mother's name was Noreen and she had the patience of a saint, so please just give this old lady a minute."

Noreen looks at the man across from her. She see the old man has fallen asleep. She looks away from this table as she looks to find Harley. Harley is starting to pick up some of Noreen's customers and tables as she works her tables and the counter.

Noreen then hears the old woman ask her if the food has any salt in it.

"Yes, it does," Noreen answers with a smile.

The old woman then tells the sleeping old man, "The food has salt, Harold. You know that with your heart condition salt is not good for you. But I guess they don't care here."

"If you like, ma'am, I will ask the cook to hold any salt," Noreen says.

"Oh, I don't want to be the problem. If your cook must cook with salt, then who am I to make such a request. It's just Harold's heart."

"It's not a problem. Let me give you another minute with the menu. I must get to some other customers. Please excuse me for just a moment. I will be right back, promise."

"Well, don't let me and my husband be the reason for your lack of customer service."

Noreen runs back and forth between some tables and the ordering window. She and Harley are pushing out the meals and taking the orders as fast as they can. Noreen goes back to the table with the old couple.

"Sorry for the wait, folks. Do you know what you would like to order now?"

The old woman looks out the window and points to a green Coupe DeVille parked sideways next to the road. "Do you know we had to park way over there. That's such along walk for us. We are not young like some of the other people in here. You would think that they would be more considerate of us older people. Did I tell you my husband has a heart problem? He shouldn't walk so far."

"I am sorry he had such a long walk. Most of the time there's plenty of parking. This is just one of the busy parts of the day," Noreen explains.

"Well you need not worry about us. It's not like we are one of your more frequent customers. I am sure a place like this and your great service just brings in all the important people. When you get to our age, you learn to just settle. You settle for any service. You just get into a line and wait till all the young and important people are taken care of. When you are this age, it's about knowing the young people rule the world.

"When I was young, it was about respect for your older or else. Now it's all about how many toys a person has. It's like that material girl. When I was young, there were wars and depression to teach us life lessons. Now it's 'I want it all now.'"

"Ma'am, I don't want to be rude to you or rush you, but I have other customers waiting for me. If you know what you would like to order, please let me take it, so you can eat," Noreen says with her teeth showing in a smile.

"Harold do you want to order so she can leave us and help the more important people? Harold please tell this lovely lady what you would like to have."

The man being asleep doesn't hear his wife ask him the question. Noreen suggests the salad special for him.

The old woman tells Noreen, "A bowl of pea soup and a sleeve of crackers for him. I'll have a butter sandwich on white bread please."

Noreen, frustrated, doesn't even write it down. She turns and walks to the order window and yells the order to Andy.

Then Noreen goes and catches up on the other customers. Harley sees the frustration on Noreen's face. She catches Noreen between customers and tells her, "Your lipstick is showing." It was a phrase the waitresses used to tell each other their frustration was showing. Noreen thanked Harley then took a deep breath and went back to work.

Andy has the old couple's meal at the window. Noreen picks up the order and brings it to them. She places the dishes in front of the two and asks them if there will be anything else.

"Don't let us keep you," the woman says. The woman picks up the salted crackers and opens the bag. She then takes the crackers out and empties the whole bag of crackers into her husband's pea soup. She wakes her husband up and tells him to eat the soup before it gets cold.

Noreen is now all caught up on her customers. She goes back to the table with the old couple and asks them again if she can get them anything else. The woman has half of the sandwich eaten. The man had maybe a spoon or two of soup. His bowl of crackers and soup is still filled. The man has fallen back to sleep. The old woman asks Noreen for the dessert menu.

Noreen looks at the next table that has a menu on it. The people who have eaten there have left and the table hasn't been cleaned yet.

Noreen takes the dessert menu off that table and gives it to the woman. She asks Noreen if the cheesecake is good. Noreen replies with "It is from the city and is very good."

The woman says, "Of course it would be good. Anything from the city would be good. I can't expect to find something good like cheesecake down here with the cows.

"Harold the lady wants you to have the cheesecake. She must have forgotten about your heart. I bet they push that day-old cheesecake on all the out-of-towners, Harold." Then the old woman orders a cup of tea and says to Noreen, "Please use a new tea bag for me."

Noreen grinds her teeth again, says sure, and goes for the tea. Noreen brings the old lady her tea, some milk, and sugar. She puts the tea on the table and looks at the old man who's asleep. Noreen picks up the man's uneaten soup, empty plastic sleeve, of crackers, and napkin.

The old lady then says, "I know you want us to leave so you can give the table to somebody who can eat more than us. But can you please leave my husband a napkin to wipe his face."

"Sure," Noreen tells her. She reaches across the other table and finds an unused napkin. Then she places it in front of the sleeping man.

Sometime later, Noreen brings the check over to the old woman. The man is still asleep and snoring loudly. "If there is nothing else, I can help you with, I'll leave you the check. It looks like your husband is asleep. If it's cash, you can leave it on the table. Credit cards have to go up to the counter," Noreen tells them.

"I always pay by check. I have my checking book right here, so it will just take me a minute. Do you have a pen?" the old woman asks.

"Ma'am, no checks. Diner policy. Cash or credit cards. It is on the front door," Noreen tells her.

The woman answers back with the line, "I never heard of such a thing."

Noreen leaves the check.

The woman fishes out the money in the bag. She calls Noreen over to take the cash to the register. Noreen goes over to them, picks the money up, and brings the check and the cash to the register.

Noreen takes the paid ticket and the change to the old woman. The woman counts her thirty-five-cent change. She leaves the twenty-five cents on the table. The old woman wakes her husband up. He stands up and tells his wife, "I'm still hungry. They don't give you much food here." Then he looks at Noreen asks her what's the score of the game.

Noreen turns around and sees the TV is off because the game has ended. Noreen turns back to the old man and says, "The game ended. I lost."

"The baseball games are getting shorter and shorter. In a couple years, they will play a nine-inning game in under an hour, you wait and see, Nora."

Noreen watches the old people walk out to the green Coupe DeVille. The old woman gets into the driver's side. Once her husband is in the car, the woman puts on her left turn signal. She then drives over the concrete curb in front of her car. Noreen shakes her head and looks at the twenty-five-cent tip.

Noreen and Harley work through the dinner rush. Some of the regulars come in and a few new people. It now 7:00 PM. Noreen has finished her shift and her day is over. She hangs up her apron and says goodbye to Andy and Harley.

CHAPTER THIRTEEN

Closing Time

The dinnertime rush is over. The hot Texas sun is low in the sky on this Friday night. Andy and Harley are the only two left in the diner for the day. Andy is in the back cleaning up from the day. Harley is behind the counter by the ordering window working on the crossword puzzle.

Harley has added three more words to the puzzle: bridge, victim, and antenna.

Harley looks up, then out the front window. She sees a large Chrysler state trooper car pull into the diner's parking lot. The car belongs to a Texas state detective. Haden has been with the Texas State Police for thirty years. Haden was the second law officer to show up the night Andy's father was killed. Dan the motorcycle policeman was first.

Haden wanted to be the detective who broke the case and found Andy's father's killer. Haden never got to break that case. He spent too many years dreaming of being a private eye.

Haden wanted to retire and be a private investigator. Haden just couldn't find that something he needed to investigate. It looked so easy in the movies to him. But Haden just couldn't get it started.

Haden gets out of his car and takes off his blacked-out sunglasses. Haden is a tall man, six foot three, from an Irish line of police. Haden walks into the diner and says, "Hello, Harley. How is my favorite female?" Then Haden walks down to the last stool at the far end of the diner's counter.

Harley answers back, "You'll be my fav if you would sit at this end closer to the order window. It may not look like a long walk but do it a couple dozen times a day for a couple of decades."

"I understand, Harley, but it's just a habit of wanting to see everybody in the room. I also like to see who is coming and going."

"You can take the detective off the job, but you can't take the job out of the detective," Harley tells Haden.

Haden calls out loudly, "Andy, good evening. They let me out for good behavior. I'll have some of that chili today, boss!"

"Why do I even have to be here if you are just going to yell out what you want to eat? I have a pad and a pencil here Mr. Detective. Please let me be the waitress and you can be the customer."

"Right, Harley, it's your laws in here. I know my place."

Harley and Haden talk about the hot day. Haden asks how her grandkids are doing. Harley shows Haden some pictures. Andy puts the chili on the order window and calls out to Harley who, at the far end of the counter, is talking to Haden. Harley walks back, picks up the chili, grabs some crackers and some napkins, and then walks down to Haden and gives him his meal.

A couple of minutes later, a blue Ford Pinto pulls into the lot and parks alongside the trooper's car. A short man gets out and puts on a Trilby rabbit hair hat. The man reaches back inside his car and pulls out a briefcase and a newspaper.

The man's name is Harper. Harper is a writer for the big city paper. Harper was the third person to show up at the diner when Andy's father was killed. He wrote the headlines for the story that next day. It was his first headline as a young reporter.

Harper had tried to find the killer, but Harper found no leads and no more news that would help.

Now Harper just wants to write a book a publisher would publish. All his work gets the return letter of, 'It's not something we could use at this time' or the standard-form rejection letter.

Harper walks into the diner and sees Andy in the back of the kitchen and walks up to the kitchen door. He pokes his head in and says hello.

Andy says hello back and says, "The gossip hour has already begun and you're late. Your friend has already started his dinner and didn't wait for you."

"Thanks," Harper says." Then he walks down to join Harley and Haden.

Harley: "Glad you can make it tonight, Harper. We were starting to wonder if maybe you lost your hat and couldn't find it."

Harper: "How are my two friends doing today?"

Haden: "Harper, what would you do if you lost that hat?"

Harper: "Haden, you will lose your Belgian Texas Ranger 38-six shooter before I lose my hat."

Haden: "That's not going to happen. I am going to be buried with this gun. There is no way I could lose this big bad-ass gun."

Harper: "My hat is bigger than that so-called little pea shooter you have."

Harley: "It always happens when two men start to talk. One man will start to compare size. It doesn't make a difference on what object they are talking about. But it always comes down to who is bigger."

Harper: "Yes, we do that, but it was a woman who first said size doesn't matter."

Haden: "It was probably Eve. And we've been paying for that sin ever since."

Harley: "That will never change. Let's blame the female. Two men talking size. Then they find a way to blame a female for man and their shortcomings. You know what I mean, guys."

Harper: "As always, you win, Harley. You always get the last sentence in the on-going war of words."

Harley: "What will it be tonight, Harper? Mac and cheese or the meatloaf?"

Harper: "I'll have the meatloaf and a beer, Harley. I wish the wife could cook a meatloaf like Andy. I even gave her Andy's recipe, but it's like dog poop."

Haden: "Harper you better be careful with that wife of yours. I don't think she likes you anymore."

Harper: "She stopped liking me after we had that delinquent kid. I think she would have killed me if we had another."

Harley: "There you two go again. Excuse me, I'll have Andy heat the meatloaf up for you."

Harley goes around back to the kitchen. Andy is working on tomorrow's meals. Harley asks Andy to heat up some meatloaf for Harper. Andy puts the meatloaf in the oven. Andy asks Harley if they said what they were going to be doing tonight.

"No, they didn't get to it yet. I wish they came in here one night and just didn't try to hide it," Harley answers. Then she goes back out to the counter.

A young couple has walked into the diner and taken a seat at the table by the front window. It's a boy and girl about high school age. Harley grabs her pad and walks over to the young couple.

Harley gives them the menu and then gets a couple of cokes that they ordered. Harley then takes their order of cheeseburger well done for him and grilled cheese for the girl. Harley takes the ticket to the window and tells Andy the order. Andy takes the ticket from the window and tells Harley five minutes.

Harley asks Andy to look at the young couple. Andy looks through the order window and smiles at them. Andy asks Harley to give them some chips for free.

"Maybe they will come back with some friends," he tells her.

Harley takes a bag of chips to the young couple and tells them, "These chips are on the house while you wait." Then she goes back over to Haden and Harper and looks to the young couple.

Harley: "Do you see that young couple over there? What I wouldn't give to be a young girl again on a date. What I wouldn't give to just be young again. What do you say, guys?"

Haden: "If I was young again, I'd join the FBI or CIA. I hear those pensions is the golden parachute of all pensions."

Harper: "I wouldn't get married and I wouldn't be working for a daily paper. I would be an investigative reporter for a national paper. I would have spent more time working on my books, instead of trying to make that wife of mine happy. Not that she isn't happy with my Howard Hughes-size paycheck."

Harley: "You two just don't get what I am thinking of. It's the feeling of wanting to be alone with another person. I am sure those two were thinking of each other all day. That young girl was thinking about what she would wear. What jewelry to wear. How much makeup to put on. The talk with her girlfriends on what they think of the boy. What she should eat when they go out. How the night should end. Would I let him kiss me on the lips or would I just give him a kiss on the cheek first. If we go to a movie would I let him put his arm around me. If I wanted him to put his arm around me, I would tell him if was cold in the theater. To have a boy spend his money on you because he likes you, what could be better?"

Haden: "Harley your mind is stuck in a date that may have happened back in the thirties. The boys now are looking for more than a kiss from a girl on a date.

"The reports we get from the colleges are something the US Supreme court would want to sensor. When I was that age, we had to worry about the girl's father and a shotgun or a good ass-kicking."

Harper: "Harley if I could write a book the way you describe a date, if I had your rose-colored glasses to look at the simplest things in life… How you could draw those thoughts from just those two having a dinner date. They may be on a date with someone else next week. A lot of young people just are dating to get out of the house.

"When we were young, dating was a process to find someone to marry. My grandfather told me the story of how his future father-in-law, went on the first couple of dates with him and his future wife. It was a different world back then."

Harley: "You two guys would ruin a Shakespeare play, given a chance. It's just boy meets girl. Boy likes girl. Girl likes boy."

Haden: "It's now boy meets girl. Boy really wants the girl. The girl needs to know self-defense."

Harley: "Excuse me, guys, their food is up. Let me get them their meal before you two have them in a divorce court."

Harley serves the young couple their meal then goes back over to Haden and Harper. The three of them talk about the same things they always talk about. Haden and Harper finish their meal. Harley is working on the crossword puzzle.

Harley: "What is an eleven-letter word that starts with, in? To self…?"

"Incriminate," the girl with the boy says.

Harley writes the word down on the crossword puzzle then hangs it up in the order window. The words on the puzzle are door, car ,track, coal, car, track, bridge, victim, antenna, and incriminate.

Haden and Harper finish their meal. Haden leaves first. He calls out to Andy, then walks out the door. He gets in his car and heads south. The boy on the date with the girl asks Harley for the check. Harley gives the boy the check. He pays it and leaves with the girl. As they walk out the door, Harley yells out to them, "If you two ever get married, please come back here and invite me."

The girl blushes and the boy shakes his head. They get back in the car and head back to the city.

Harper gets up and leaves some money on the counter. Then he tells Harley he has to go out of town for a while. He will not be back till next month.

Harper says good night to Harley and Andy and walks out the door. He gets in his car and heads south.

Harley goes to the back where Andy is working and tells him that harper went south too. Andy nods his head. Then he tells her to close it up for the night. Harley says okay.

Harley goes to the front door and turns the sign around and locks the door. She goes to the register and gets a printout of the day's numbers. Then she finishes adding all the receipts for the day.

It takes her just a few minutes to count the drawer. When she is finished, she calls back to Andy and tells him the numbers match. Harley takes the cash and puts into a bag then brings it into the kitchen. Harley puts the bag into an old stove then hangs up her apron. She puts her pad in the apron and tells Andy, "That's it, we're done."

Andy walks Harley out of the back of the diner and to her car. They say good night then Harley drives off to go home. Andy then takes down the flag and puts it in the box.

Andy walks around to the back of the diner. He locks the door behind him. He walks in the diner, looks around, turns the lights off, and goes back in the kitchen. He checks the stoves to make sure they are off, turns the loaded dishwasher on, turns the kitchen lights off, and goes upstairs.

CHAPTER FOURTEEN

I Did It

Andy walks into a dark room. He reaches over and flips a light switch on. The floor has an old blue rug on it. Straight ahead is a small all-white kitchen. On his right side is an old wooden color TV that sits on short wooden legs. To each side of the TV are two doors. One door is to the room that was his parents' bedroom. The other door is to his bedroom. That is the same room Andy had as a kid.

Between the bedroom doors and over the TV is an old picture of Andy's parents in front of the diner the day they opened it. There is an old, small picture on the television of a young baseball player named Andy Johnson. It is who Andy is named after. There no other pictures of his parents.

To his left side is one large, single-pane glass window that looks out over the back of the diner. Andy walks over to it. In the distance, you could see the railroad tracks. Across the tracks you could see piles of old junk cars. The junkyard security lights reflect off all the broken car glass, resembling the stars at night.

Andy takes a seat on a wooden stool and looks at the lights. He does this almost every night. Then Andy starts to let his mind wander to thoughts of the two people he has become.

What should I do tonight? Should I take a shower and turn in? Should I stay here and watch the light show? The show from the stars above and the broken glass across the way. Wait for the coal cars to come by and take me on that trip?

The trip I learned how to take years ago. My father who learned to ride the rail. Then he taught his son the same. He gave his son the talent to jump a freight train and ride it like a seasoned well-weathered hobo. Or should I stay here and be the proprietor of this establishment?

To be the cook. To be the waiter. The busboy. The dish washer. The floor sweeper. The man with a plunger to clean up another people's shit.

The days I spent in the back of this never-ending burden of a long-time past dream, of a long-dead parent. The days I spent of just waiting to have a catch with a father. Then I found the back wall of this rectangular pine box. The rectangular pine box of two parents. The back wall that would throw a baseball back to me. Anytime that I wanted to have a catch, the wall of the pine box would be there for me.

Then I found the water tower. The empty water tower down by the tracks. The very private water tower. The water tower that was in plain sight of anybody. Anybody and everybody never even gave it a second look or thought. Anybody but me, a young teenager who was at the awakening of puberty.

The one round wall inside the water tower. The one round wall where no one could see a young teenage boy. The round wall with a couple of gaps between the old clapboard. The gaps just big enough for me to see out. Just small enough for nobody to see in. The collection of magazines and pictures that help pass the time. Pass the time till it was time for a new picture or magazine.

Then the time came when it was time to find something new. The talent, the skill I had to ride a coal car. The thought of taking the train ride to the city. The thought of something new. It was what I put on today's special menu.

As night fell on that any clear, bright, starlit night, this young, curious teen went for a ride to the city on a coal car.

Out the backdoor of the rectangular pine box. Down the dirt trail. Past the water tower. Down in the gully of weeds and loose railroad track stone. Then the wait for soon-to-be heard sound of a group of big diesel freight train engines lumbering up the steel rail. The long groan that starts low and slow. Then the sound changes to a louder, steady, constant rumbling over the gaps in the rails. The end on one rail and the start of the next rail.

Then the burst of wind, as the deafening exploding sound of a massive steel force pushes by you. The alternating sounds of wheels and flexing steel.

You watch the coal cars go by. Then you pick the one that awaits you. You get up two cars ahead of it. Then you start your run at the pace just fast enough to time a jump. It's a strong right hand and arm to catch a bar.

Then the timing to plant a foot on a cross bar. The left-hand swings over and catches another bar. You're on a moving coal car. The car is part of a long line of coal cars being pulled by those massive steel diesels.

You climb up the back of the coal car. Over the top and onto the black chunks of the dirty coal. You lie with your back on the coal as you look up at the stars. The train and the car movements are like being rocked in a rocking chair.

After a few miles, your mind wants to put you to sleep. Stay awake, you call out to yourself. The end of your ride is just ahead. You see the same familiar landmarks that tell you you're close.

Then the mark of the end of a bridge. You set yourself up for the jump. Up on your feet. Bend your legs at the knees. Down low to the coal. Your feet between the top rail and the coal.

Then the next mark. The side of a grassy hill that is as high as the coal car. You jump straight ahead and land on your feet. You then take a roll in the tall, soft grass. The roll ends as you see the coal cars pass you by. You turn, then get up and walk to the top of the grassy hill.

At the top of the hill you see the lights of the big city. The lights all along the streets. The lights up and down the tall buildings. The different smells of a big city. All the different sounds.

Then the walk from the grassy hill into the city. You walk till you find the all-night stationary store. You enter the store and look around with the hope to find no familiar faces. Your walk around, satisfied that you will stay unknown. Then into pictures and magazines of possibility.

Then the look at the faces and the shapes. The hope you find the right face and shape quickly. Then she is looking at you. She is the one. You picked her out and she is waiting for you to take her home.

But one more wouldn't hurt, so leave her and tell her in your mind you'll be back. Then quickly you get another. You take it off the rack then walk back to the first one. The one with the face. The one with the shape.

Then to the register. You hope for a quick check out. You will come up with a dozen reasons why you buy such things if asked. As the face and shape get put into the brown paper bag. You pay for your future entertainment of a dream. Then it's out the door. Up the street. You make sure your shirt is tucked into your pants.

You take the brown bag and put it down the front of your shirt. No one can see it. It's safe and your hands are now free.

You walk the same street back to the grassy hill. You look for the next slow-moving train leaving the power plant. You check your shirt and your bag to make sure it's set.

You time it good. A train is leaving the plant. You walk over to the southbound tracks. Then watch as the train creeps past you. You pick a car and just take an easy step onto the coal car. You use both hands for a grip. Then you plant both feet onto the car. You can't climb up the car this trip. You must be low next to the ground when you get off. There are no soft grassy hills.

The train is almost up to speed when it nears your jump-off point. Then you use one hand to steady yourself. You jump and hit the ground hard with two feet. Your feet slide a bit on the railroad track stone. You fall forward, landing on your knees.

Your arms and shoulders will take your rolling till you stop. On the ground, you check yourself. You're fine. Just scraped up a little. Then you check your package inside your shirt. Everything is okay. The train goes on its way.

Across the track and to the water tower. Up the tower stand. Then you get into the tower. You have a car battery and a headlight you took from a junk car. You hook up the battery to the headlight. You take out what will occupy your time alone. Then…

The night is getting late as you make your way up the dirt path. You look up to the single living room window. Someone may still be up. When the TV light is seen in the window, somebody is up.

The diner is closed. You take the hidden key to the backdoor and open it, then lock it. Upstairs you go. They could be in their room asleep and left the TV on. They could be waiting for you with questions.

Andy wakes himself up from that same dream. It always end with him coming up the stairs, never past the door.

He knows what he must do. Out the diner and into the city. The same way he has learned to do and has always done. But it's different now, back from the war. He learned so much. He learned the ability to end a life. It wasn't long after he returned home Andy was on the coal cars again. But it wasn't for the enjoyment he once found in a water tower.

Now Andy found car antennas from the junkyard. He just found a person in the city. Andy has beat somebodies face in with the antenna. Then Andy finds himself back at the diner with a bloody right arm. Was it a dream. No, the blood is real.

Andy walks up the dirt path from the railroad track this early morning. He goes behind the diner to wash his bloody right arm. He looks up and notices the backdoor open. Something's wrong. He never left the door open before.

Andy then hears a loud voice yelling. Then he hears two gunshots from the front of the diner. Andy runs around the front of the diner to see Dan the cop's motorcycle running. The headlight is on and pointing to the front door. Then he sees Dan with his helmet in his left hand and a handgun in his right hand.

Andy walks up to Dan. Dan looks at Andy without saying a word. Dan then points the gun at a young man lying on the ground with a bloody neck. The bullet took out half of this young man's neck. Both men are looking down at the motionless figure.

Dan: "He's dead. I checked him for a pulse. He's dead. He shot himself."

Andy: "What happened?"

Dan: "Saw a car up the road. Got here to turn around to check the car, I saw somebody coming out your front door. I yelled for him to stop. Then he pointed that gun at me. I had no time to think. I yelled drop the gun. Then I fired a shot in the air. He tripped over those untied shoes. His gun went off and he shot himself in his neck."

Andy: "You'll be okay, Dan. Anybody can see what happened."

Dan: "You may want to take a look at who that is on the ground first."

Andy bends down and takes a closer look at the face.

Andy: "Oh shit, Dan, it's Paul. Michelle's old boyfriend. He looks like he aged twenty years."

Dan: "Crack and meth, I guess. He was robbing you. There is a bank bag under him. Andy, I threatened to kill him a couple of times in public."

Andy: "Dan you will be okay. I know what happened. Go inside and wash your face and I'll join you. I know what happened. You will be okay."

Dan: "Okay, Andy. Maybe I should clear my head and go over what happened. Good thing you were up and around back. Andy, what were you doing up? What were you doing around back? Andy, why is your right arm all bloody?"

Andy looks down at his bloody right arm. Then at Dan.

Andy: "Dan, go inside and wash your face. Give me a minute and I will tell you."

Dan puts his gun back in its holster then goes inside to wash his face and clear his head. Dan finds the light switch and turns it on. Then he goes over to the sink behind the counter and turns the cold water on.

He rubs some water on his face. He looks at the crossword puzzle hanging in the order window and reads the words. Then Dan puts them together. Door, car, track, coal, car, track, bridge, victim, antenna, incriminate.

Then it is the bloody right arm of Andy and why he was out late. Then the last call over his radio before he saw the car by the diner. The call of a another beating in the city. Dan unhooks his gun and walks out the front of the diner.

Paul's body is gone. The car he saw on the side of the road is pulling into the lot with no lights on. Dan recognizes it as Paul's old car. The one he flipped with Michelle in it. Andy pulls it around back. Dan follows the car. Andy gets out and Dan meets him on the side of the car.

Dan: "Andy, what are you doing? This is all evidence. You're not supposed to touch anything."

Andy: "I don't know what you're talking about, Dan. Evidence for what?"

Dan: "We have a dead body here. People are going to think I killed him."

Andy: "What body? I don't see no body or anybody, Dan. And you don't see anybody. And nobody will ever find any such body. This car is going to be in the junkyard. I am going to drive it there as soon as you leave, Dan. I didn't see you, and you didn't see me and my bloody arm. So, Dan, you need to leave now. When you get home to your wife, tell her it was just another boring night.

"Now go or we're both going to be eating bad prison food. What you may be thinking that I am responsible for. Should just stay that just think it. I promise it won't happen again, Dan. It's over. Please leave."

Andy gets in the car and drives it down the path and across a section of track the horses used to pull the wagons across. Andy drives the beat-up car into the lot and parks it by a car crusher. He takes the plates off then puts them into another old car.

Andy then walks across the tracks up the dirt path. He walks around the front of the diner, and Dan and his bike are gone. Andy picks up the bloody bank bag that Paul dropped and walks into the kitchen. He tosses it on to the old stove then goes back into the diner. He looks around to see if the diner looks the way it should. Andy locks the front and back door, turns out the light, and goes upstairs.

It is an early Texas morning. The sun is breaking over the horizon. The front door of this two-story white diner sits on the side of a worn-out old service road facing the early morning Texas sun. A closed sign hangs in the front door of the unopen diner. Above the front door sits a black-and-white sign with the diner's name on it.

There is a big square window on each side of the front door. The windows have one wooden table behind each of them inside. The top floor has three small windows with the shades always pulled down.

In front of the diner is a small dirt parking lot. On the side of the parking lot is a glass phone booth.

The owner of the diner, Andy, comes down from his apartment above the diner at 5:30 AM. He has been doing the same routine for the past twenty-one years.

Andy starts the burners for the flat grill. He pulls a couple of dozen eggs from the refrigerator. He goes out the backdoor and picks up two metal garbage cans and brings them around front.

He then walks over to a small box at the base of a flag pole. He pulls the flag out of the box he put it in the previous night. Andy attaches the flag to the pole then raises it. Andy sees a bloodstain on the ground. Andy kicks some dirt on it.

Andy walks back around the diner and goes to a sink to wash his hands. He goes over to the grill and puts some bacon he cooked last night on the center to reheat it. He then goes around to the front of the diner behind the counter. Andy fills the coffee machines with water then turns them on. Then he collects yesterday's papers from around the room.

At or about a quarter to six, the first waitress comes in through the backdoor of the diner.

At the age of twenty-five, she's a single mother of a boy. Sometimes, she is late and on occasion has failed to show. Andy would know if she would be out when his phone upstairs would ring early in the morning. Andy has known the girl since she was a baby.

Her father would bring her in and sit with her at the counter. Michelle the girl has grown into a very pretty woman with long blond hair. Then she found a boy she liked while working at the diner and they dated.

The boy was older than Michelle . Andy had to fire him because he was caught stealing from the register. Two years later, the boy has left town with another pretty girl and left an unmarried, pregnant Michelle to grow into a woman. Michelle and her boy now live with her parents.

Michelle comes into the kitchen and yells out to Andy, "Good morning, Andy. I made it."

Andy from where he is at the time would thank her for being here. Michelle would go to the front door and turn the closed sign to the open sign and unlock the front door. Michelle would take the dishes, cups, and utensils out of the dishwasher.

Then Michelle would start to set up the two wood tables with dishes and cups the way Andy wants his table set. Then she would set some cups and dishes across the counter. The morning coal train passes behind the diner. It is laboring, pulling its heavy load of coal to the city.

The power of its engines and the heavy coal cars shake the diner. The glass and the dishes rattle as the vibrations from the train travel unobstructed up to then past the diner. Andy comes out from the kitchen and greets Michelle.

Andy: "Hello, Michelle, how is your boy doing today?"

Michelle: "I think Paul has allergies."

Andy: "Yeah, I hear that is common at that age."

Michelle: "I saw Paul last night. Little Paul's father. He looks like an old man, Andy. The girl he left with left him like I did because of the drugs and drinking. Most of his hair was gone. He lost a lot of weight and all his muscles."

Andy: "Did you let him see his son?"

Michelle: "No. Andy you wouldn't recognize him. I don't want my son to see his father like that. One day I am going to tell him what really happened to me and his father. And hope he can understand his father is just sick.

"I want my son to remember his father as a strong young man who was at one time such a good person who loved his mother.

"I have a picture of his father on a wall when he had all his curly blond hair and beautiful smile. For now, that's where I want his father—a picture on a wall nowhere near his son. If he never sees his father again, I wouldn't care. Andy, he was also trying to borrow money from me.

"Then he was asking about the diner and if we still do everything the same way. I was going to call you and tell you he may want to borrow money from you."

Andy: "Well, Michelle, let's get the day started."

Michelle: "Okay, Andy, but we have a problem. Some things are not right. The bank bag is on the stove, not in the stove, and there is blood on it. The crossword puzzle is missing."

CHAPTER FIFTEEN

Guest

It is a late Wednesday night. Later that year in 1986, the night before Thanksgiving, Andy is up in his apartment above the diner. He has put a sign in the front door that the diner will be closed on Thursday for Thanksgiving.

Andy is looking out his back window, sitting on his wooden stool, thinking about his lonesome life. The wife he once had. The pine box he lives in. The children he never had. The one parent who loved the diner. The one parent who loved the father and his son. A happy nest he never found. How in ten years of a marriage he found himself just waiting to be alone.

Talks with the wife had just become words like maybe tomorrow, maybe tomorrow, maybe next week. Maybe next time. The effort on his part just to avoid any conversation was his biggest effort in a failed marriage. The excuse not going home at night just to work in his pine box. Telling his wife the diner needed work and he will be there all night when he was just up in the apartment wanting to be alone.

The days of working at the diner was the hiding place he needed to cope with a life he now found himself in. He should never have left the life he found in the military. It was the place where he found peace with who he was.

The independence from any emotional attachment, that was the expected price to be paid for a wife.

A couple of dollars was the only emotional price that was expected to be paid to rent a wife.

His parents' relationship. The days of just hellos and goodbyes. The only two things his parents had in common was their address and they both had a son. His parents who never had an argument. His mother who let her husband work any time and all the time. She never asked for his time. She just loved the man who loved his life in the diner.

His father who worked harder on his relationship with the diner than the relationship with his wife.

His parents never being able to leave the town. The secret he was told. The void of not having any other relatives.

Coming out of the military after his father is murdered to help his mother cope with her loss. To keep the diner going. His father's dream, his father raising and doing what he could to nurture the other sibling, the diner.

So often he would find himself down by the tracks or at the junkyard. The water tower. Just to get away from the same smell of a diner. The same routine he saw his parents do every day.

Then the odd jobs his parents found for him to do as he got older. Those odd jobs like taking the garbage out. Sweeping the floor. Cleaning the windows. Then washing the dishes. Bussing and waiting on tables. Then food prep and cooking.

The time he got to do what he wanted became less and less. After high school he was working from 5:00 AM till 10:00 PM at the diner. This was how the next part of his life was going to be till he was drafted.

He went away and found the place he wanted as a boy—away from the back of the diner. Away from the same smell every day. The same routine every day.

He was in a world that gave him the escape he needed from his other sibling, the diner, that always needed more attention than him. The twenty years or more could be spent here.

Then the short visits home to see his parents. Then I must leave, sorry, good-bye-for-now excuse.

Female relationships were no more than the short time they needed to be. There were no long-term plans. No long-time commitments were needed to be promised.

At last, his time wasn't the never-ending burden he lived as a prisoner. Then the officer who came to him one morning with a letter from home. It started with "My dear son." Somewhere in it, his father died, and he had to go home. The letter ended somehow. He never saw the whole thing.

His thoughts, to his loss of a father who never talked much of his early childhood. The man who worked all the time. The man who was such a good man. The man who showed his wife respect.

His mother now alone and no one there for her. No other relative she can reach out for. Her only friend was her now dead husband. The woman who gave him my life was out there alone. His mother who loved somebody from the moment she first saw him. He would never have a love like that.

Andy's thoughts are broken up by blue-and-white flashing lights reflecting off the junk cars out his window. They are police lights coming from the front of the diner. Andy gets up and goes down into the diner and turns the lights on. He then goes to the front door and opens it.

Outside on his motorcycle is Dan the policeman. He is talking to the migrant workers Andy saw months ago. Dan saw the pickup was parked by the phone booth. So, Dan pulled into the diner's lot. He has his headlight pointed to the back of the bed of the truck. Andy sees the same little boy and girl he remembers from before.

The young woman who he let use the phone and the same man who was driving the truck are talking to Dan. Andy walks up to the three of them.

Andy: "What's going on, Dan?"

Dan: "Hi, Andy. I hope I didn't wake you. I was driving by and saw this truck in your lot. I turned in here to see what they were doing. The man had a plastic milk jug and he was filling it with water. I don't think they were doing anything else. I talked to the woman and she said the kids didn't have any water all day. She also said that they stopped here before."

Andy: "Yeah, they were here before, I remember them. They look a little more worn than last time. Last time they had a couple of men with them."

Dan: "I asked if there was anybody else with them and she said there was no one else."

Andy: "Did she say where they were going?"

Dan: "She said that they have no place to find work and the truck is low on gas. They were hoping to get some water and stay here till morning. If you look at those tires, they would be lucky to make it out of your of lot."

Andy asked the woman where the other men were from last time. She tells him in English they all left and went different ways. Then she begs him for some water for the kids.

Andy and Dan look at each other than Andy says, "Dan they're not looking to steal anything. Just let them go. I have no problem with them trying to get some water. They can stay in the lot. It is no problem."

Dan: "Okay, Andy. If you don't mind, there's nothing I need to do then. I must get back on the road. I will stop by in the morning after I get off my shift. Then I must get home for some turkey and football."

Andy: " Yeah, tomorrow's Thanksgiving. Okay, Dan, I'll be fine seeing you tomorrow."

Dan puts his helmet back on and drives away on his bike. Andy looks at the woman, the two little kids, and the old man. Then he looks at the open front door of his diner. Then he looks at the name of the diner then back at the two young children.

Andy turns to the woman and tells her to bring the man and the children inside and he'll get the children some clean water. The woman tells him that she has no money to pay for it. Andy tells her not to worry about it because water in Texas is free.

After some explaining that he didn't want any money she agrees and takes the children and the old man into the diner.

Andy takes the chairs off one of the tables by the window and motions for them to sit. The woman, the children, and the man take seats at the table. Andy goes back behind the counter and fills a pitcher up with water. He takes four glasses down from the rack. Then Andy brings the pitcher of water and the glasses over to the table.

Andy puts a glass in front of each of them and pours water into each of the glasses. Then he tells them to drink. The woman smiles at Andy then tells the children to drink in Spanish. The kids start to hastily drink the water.

Andy looks at the kids drinking. Then he tells the woman he'll be right back. Andy goes out the front door and walks up to the truck. He looks inside and sees the seats torn down to metal. Half the dash missing. He then goes to the back and investigates the bed of the truck. Just some black bags with dirty clothes in them. Then Andy goes back to the cab of the truck and takes the key out of the dashboard. Then he goes back into the diner. Inside, he locks the front door. The four of them have finished the pitcher of water.

Andy picks up the pitcher and goes behind the counter and fills it up again. Then he brings it back to the table. Andy leaves the pitcher at the table then walks back and takes a seat at the counter and watches the four of them drink more water.

Andy asks the young woman to come over and have a seat at the counter, so he can talk to her. She comes over to Andy and sits in the seat next to him.

Andy: "I am sorry, but I don't remember your name."

Woman: "Maria."

Andy: "It's nice to meet you, Maria. My name is Andy."

Maria: "Thank you for the water. It is very kind of you."

Andy: "Where were you going tonight?"

Maria: "My father was hoping to find a job somewhere. We are down on money and gas. The children were thirsty, and we didn't mean to be a problem."

Andy: "It's okay, we have plenty of water. Can I ask you where the kids' father is?"

"I don't know. He got sick and couldn't work. One day he just went off and didn't come back. I don't know what happened to him. The children ask where he is. I must tell them he'll be back when he is better."

Andy: "When was the last time the kids ate?"

Maria: "A couple of days ago. My father got paid from his last job. We ate, put gas in the truck, and went looking for work. It's harder for him to find work now. People want to have strong men to work, not an old man and a woman with kids."

Andy: "Yeah, I understand. That may never change, young lady. You know winter is coming and even a Texas night can get very cold. What are you going to do a when winter comes?"

Maria: "I don't know."

Andy: "I have some food in the back that hasn't been eaten. If it's okay with you, I would like to give it to you and the kids."

Maria looks at her kids.

Maria: "Please, that would be very nice of you."

Andy: "Okay, just give me a couple of minutes. If they need to use the bathroom after all that water, it is over there."

Andy goes back into the kitchen. Maria goes back to the table and talks to the old man and the kids. Andy comes out from the kitchen with some cold cuts and bread and some milk and cookies. He Leaves it on the table and goes back into the kitchen.

After a while, Andy comes back out to the table.

All the cookies are gone and most of the food. Maria stands up and then tells Andy how kind he was and thanks him for the food. That her father would work all day tomorrow for free just to pay him back for the food. Andy laughs and tells her "This is a diner. We have more food than anybody can eat." Maria doesn't get the joke.

Andy asks her to wait here for him to come back. Andy goes into the kitchen then upstairs. Andy comes downstairs with some blankets and pillows, then puts them on the counter.

Andy tells Maria that they can spend the night in the diner, but they can't take anything out of the refrigerator and display cases. It will ruin the food if they open it and leave it open. Maria talks to her father, she then thanks Andy.

Andy shows her the light switches and gives her some hand soap. Andy then leaves and goes upstairs wondering if he is going to have a diner the next day.

The next day is Thanksgiving Day. The diner is closed. Andy is awakened by a horn blowing in his parking lot. Andy puts on his pants and shirt then walks down to the kitchen then the diner. He sees the people he forgot about. The two kids in blankets on the floor. Maria and her father looking out the window. Andy walks to the window and sees Dan standing outside his car.

Andy unlocks the front door and walks up to Dan. The two talk for a while then Dan drives off. Andy goes back in the diner and tells Maria everything is okay. Andy tells her he will be back. Andy goes upstairs and takes a shower. He gets dressed and comes downstairs.

He finds the kids sitting at a table, all the blankets and pillows folded up. Andy asks Maria where her father is. She tells him he lost the truck key and is trying to find it. Andy doesn't tell her he has it. Then he tells her he is going to make himself some breakfast. That if the old man can't find the key by then, she and the kids can join him.

Andy goes back into the kitchen and picks up the phone and calls Michelle. He tells her that he has a problem at the diner and needs her help. Michelle reminds him it's Thanksgiving and it's her day off. Andy says he knows, and he wouldn't ask if it wasn't important. Michelle tells him okay. Give her about a half hour and she'll be there.

Andy makes himself, Maria, and the kids breakfast. Then he brings an egg sandwich out to the old man who is still looking for the truck key.

Michelle then shows up driving very fast and slides into the parking lot. Michelle gets out of the car. Then she goes into the back of the car and gets her little boy.

Michelle walks over to Andy and the old man.

Andy: "Hello, Michelle, and her getting-to-be-very-big boy. How are you both doing today?"

Michelle: "I am here, Andy. What is the problem?"

Andy: "Michelle you remember this gentleman and his truck, don't you? Well he lost his key and he can't find it. Would you like to help him?"

Michelle: "Andy I owe you a lot, but if this is a joke, I am not going to like it."

Andy: "Michelle may be a little. I have that woman and her two kids inside the diner. They showed up here last night. Dan found them in the parking lot just trying it get some water. To make a long story short, I think they're in more trouble than last time we saw them. Can you please go in there and talk to her? She speaks some English, but you are a woman and able to speak Spanish. Well find out what you can please. I have the key to the truck. I didn't want to give them to this old man till I did what I could."

Michelle: "I understand her name is Maria, isn't?"

Andy: "Yes. I'll be out here."

Michelle and her son go inside the diner. Michelle talks to Maria for a while till Michelle convinces Maria to tell her everything, because they may be able to help her and the kids. Michelle comes out of the diner without her son and marches up to Andy.

Michelle: "Those people in their smell because they haven't had a bath in months. The kids are wearing the same dirty underwear from the last time they were here. They haven't had any real food in a month. They went two days with no water. The little boy has a fever and the girl has a bad case of diarrhea. Andy, how does this shit happen to these kids? I called my father and I am taking Maria and her two children home with me today. You take your new friend and let him clean himself out back. When you get him clean, you can bring him over to the house. I know you don't own a car. You can use his since you have the key. That's where his daughter and his grandkids will be. Don't ask me anything about tomorrow, Andy.

"What did those kids in there do? This isn't supposed to happen!"

Michelle goes back into the diner and gets her son. Maria comes out with Michelle and her two children. Maria stops by her father and tells him not to worry, they will be back later. Michelle has Maria and the three children in the car. Michelle does a donut in the parking lot as she speeds away.

Andy and the old man just look at each other. Then Andy motions for the man to follow him. Andy takes him around back of the diner and in simple hand gestures asks him to stay put.

Andy goes upstairs. Then he comes down with some soap, towels, and some of Andy's old clothes from the seventies. He then directs the old man to a garden hose for a shower. The old man gets the idea. Andy goes back inside and cleans up the breakfast.

The old man has cleaned himself and changed to some of Andy's old clothes. He walks in the backdoor in a pair of plaid bell-bottom pants and a tie die tee shirt. Andy just looks at him and smiles.

Back at Michelle's parents' house the kids have been given a bath. The little boy was given some of Michelle's boys' clothes. The little girl was given some clothes by Michelle's neighbor who has a girl her age. Maria has taken a shower and put on some of Michelle's clothes.

The two boys are playing with a race car game. The little girl is by her mother's side. Michelle's grandfather is there. He has come over from the same nation sixty years earlier the same way. He spends a lot of time with Maria talking about their country and some of the same hardships they both encountered.

The family sits down to a Thanksgiving dinner with Maria and her children. After dinner, Maria asks if she can call her father.

Michelle calls Andy's home number. Andy picks up the phone and talks to Michelle. Andy puts the old man on the phone with Maria. You can see a smile come over the man's face after he talks to his daughter.

The Thanksgiving Day ends. The football games get played. People around the country eat and drink. Some people go home, and some just lived another day.

Maria and her kids spend the night at Michelle's family's house. Andy and the old man have pushed the truck of to the side because the old man still can't find his keys. Andy knows he must get ready for tomorrow.

Andy starts to wonder if Michelle would show up late or at all. Then what is he going to do with Maria the kids and the old man? The reality of his real work world starts to set in. The real world of real living people and real problems start to hit him. Somehow, he must send them on their way and get back to be a diner owner.

The sun has set. Andy hands the old man a blanket and a pillow for the night, so the old man can sleep on the floor. Andy makes sure the front door is locked then turns in for the night.

Andy comes down from his apartment above the diner at 5:30 AM. He has been doing the same routine for the past twenty-one years. Andy starts the burners for the flat grill. He pulls a couple of dozen eggs from the refrigerator.

He goes out a backdoor, picks up two metal garbage cans, and brings them around front. He then walks over to a small box at the base of a flag pole. He pulls the flag out and puts in the box the previous two nights before. Andy attaches the flag to the pole then raises the flag. Andy sees an old truck in his lot. He finds the old man up looking for his key. Andy walks up to him, pulls the truck key out of his pocket, and hands it to the man. The man's face breaks out in joy. The old man kisses Andy.

Andy walks back around the diner and goes to a sink to wash his hands and his face. He goes over to the grill and puts some bacon he cooked last night on the center to reheat it. He then goes around to the front of the diner behind the counter. Andy fills the coffee machines with water then turns them on.

At or about a quarter to 6:00 AM, the first waitress comes in through the backdoor of the diner. At the age of twenty-five, she's a single mother of a boy. Sometimes, she is late and on occasion has failed to show. Andy would know if she would be out when his phone upstairs would ring early in the morning.

There was no ring of the phone this morning. Andy hears Michelle's car race across the parking lot. He is glad that he doesn't have to call another waitress to cover her.

Michelle finds the old man out front trying to start is truck. Then she tells him in Spanish that Maria and the kids will be back in the afternoon so please don't worry. Michelle comes in and says hello to Andy and tells him that her parents are going to take Maria and her kids to see a doctor today.

Michelle gives Andy a hug and a kiss on the cheek and thanks him. Andy asks for what? Michelle tells him for saving another young woman.

Andy asks her to get the place ready. Then Michelle tells him that the man's truck won't start. Andy tells her he took the points out of the truck.

Andy and Michelle open the diner. The old man has worn the battery out in the truck. He spends most of the morning sleeping in it.

Dan comes by in his own car to see what happened with the family. He pulls into the parking lot and sees the old man sleeping in the truck.

Dan goes inside and takes a seat at the counter. Michelle goes on over to him and asks him what brings him in on his day off.

Dan tells her about the family he found out front the night before. Michelle fills him in on the rest. She tells him that they need a place to live and a way to work. The help her family is doing could just be temporary. Dan tells her he understands. That maybe he could do one thing that may help.

Dan leaves Michelle and goes on back to Andy who is working the grill. The two talk for a bit then Dan leaves. Noreen comes in later that day and Michelle tells her what Andy did.

Noreen and Michelle talk about the family and their own ancestors and how they came over. In the afternoon, Michelle leaves for the day and tells Andy she will call to let him know what happened to Maria and the kids. Then Michelle goes out and talks to the old man. Then she leaves. When Harley comes in, she is told about what Andy and Michelle did.

Later that day, Michelle returns with Maria and her two children. They are clean with clean clothes and have eaten a couple times during the day. The kids were checked out by a doctor and given some medicine. Then Maria was told they would be just fine in a couple of days. That night Maria, the old man, and the kids sleep on the diner floor again.

Saturday morning comes. Andy comes down to see the four people sitting at a table. The blankets and pillows are folded and placed on the counter. Andy looks at them and smiles. He knows they can't live on this diner floor. By Monday, they must be somewhere else.

He asks Maria to get them some breakfast. Maria goes in the back and makes some cold cereal for the others. Then Andy explains that he needs to have the kids away from where he must put the customers.

Maria says she understands and will have the kids in back today. That when the truck runs, they will leave. Andy, not knowing what to say, nods his head and walks away.

Maria and her father and kids go out back behind the diner. Noreen shows up to do her Saturday shift. The diner opens, and the few customers come in then eat and leave. Noreen and Andy finish the day. They close the diner and Noreen leaves. Andy goes outside and asks the four to come back in.

Andy tells Maria he called a friend to come and look at the truck. They don't have to worry about the money. But Monday they will have to leave. Maria tells him she will leave Monday.

Maria and the old man and her children spend another night on the diner's floor. Sunday morning comes. Andy comes down to find the blanket and pillows folded on the counter. The kids are eating breakfast.

About 8:00, a tow truck pulls into the parking lot. Andy goes out and talks to the driver. Andy gives the man the points to the truck and tells him about the family. The man then puts the points back in the truck, hooks battery cables up to it, and cranks the engine.

After a lot of cranks, the engine starts. The old man comes from the diner smiling ear-to-ear.

The tow truck driver checks the truck over. Then he tells Andy this truck couldn't make it to the junkyard on the other side of the tracks. It's not worth the tires Andy offered to put on the truck. Andy thanks the tow truck driver and watches him drive off without the old man's truck.

Andy's now stuck with this old truck. Stuck with an old man who speaks no English. A young woman with two kids. Andy drops his head and starts to walk back to the diner. He leaves the old man in his running truck that is going to run out of gas.

He walks into the diner and sees the two kids playing on the floor. He goes around the counter and gets two cookies then hands them to the kids. Andy then asks if he could talk to Maria outside.

Andy and Maria are outside. They hear the truck run out of gas. Then the old man try starting it again, but the battery is still dead.

Andy looks at Maria and tells her that she needs to leave Monday. That he helped her as much as he could. He will give her some money to get a bus ride for her and her family.

Andy turns his attention to a car that pulls into his lot. It's Dan's car. The car stops, Dan gets out of the driver side, and Michelle gets out of the passenger side. The two walks up to Andy and Maria.

Dan and Michelle say hello to Andy and Maria. Dan looks at Michelle and says, "You tell him."

Michelle: "Maria, could we please talk to Andy alone?"

Maria says okay and walks to the diner where her kids are.

Michelle: "Andy thank you for what you did for them. It means so much to me. I will never be able to thank you. You and Dan have helped me through some hard times. I thought this was my chance to pass that help along. With some help from Dan's ability to twist an arm, he found a place for them to live for now.

"Dan got Martin to rent them a two-bed room in his dump. It's not the best place, but it's a safe place for them short-term. My dad who owns a landscaping company is going to give the old man a job. Then he says it's up to him. But it's a start. I talked to Noreen and Harley and we need another waitress. Andy, we love you, but you work us too much and too many hours.

"The night Maria was at my house, I talked to her a lot. She used to be a manager and bartender in her country. That is how she learned English. We need another waitress bad. We really need two more. But we will talk about that later. Her kids can stay with me. My kid can stay with her. She can work weekends. Andy please just give it a try. I can't talk to Maria about it till you say yes. If I say anything, it could be just another letdown her and her kids. Please, Andy."

Andy: "Michelle I was just telling her that she had to go Monday. I didn't want to do it, but I had to. I don't know if your plan will work, Michelle. They may not want to do it. The old man may not have enough in him. Maria may not work out. You're really trying to help them."

"Michelle If you think you could make her into a waitress who can work for me then you go in there and ask her."

Michelle reaches up and kisses Andy then Dan. Michelle runs off to the diner to tell Maria of her plan.

Andy looks at Dan.

Andy: "That young lady better not forget I am her boss. And that kissing up to the boss or kissing the boss may not be permitted. "

Dan: "You need to wipe the lipstick off your face and stop blushing, boss."

CHAPTER SIXTEEN

Talk

In the vast expanse of the state of Texas sits just an average city with average people and filled with average things. The city has a large domestic airport on the north side of the city. On the east side of the city, a hospital is located. In the center of the city sits the police department. On the south side of the city sits a main newspaper building. On the city's west side sits an old coal-fired power plant. The old coal plant is fed by a set of old train tracks that comes up from the south. This city grew after the war with two new major highways and a big new domestic airport.

Alongside the old train tracks that feeds the old coal plant runs an old service road that goes in and out of some small towns.

In 1945 the railroad put the old service building up for sale as their train engines turn to diesel engines. The old service building was purchase by a young married couple in their early twenties.

The young couple turned the old service building's first floor into a diner. They turned the second floor into an apartment and lived in it.

About twenty miles south of this city is a booming town. This small town has a set of old train tracks and that service road that runs alongside of it. The town has the usual small local roads. The roads in this town have the same names other roads in small towns have, like Main Street, Bank Street, Park Street, and other familiar names.

The town has a new post office and police department. As the city to the north stagnated, this small town grew with people and jobs

On this service road that runs along the old train tracks is a small diner. The diner was once a two-story service building for a water tower that suppled water for the old steam train engines. Behind the diner and alongside the tracks is that old abandoned water tower.

In 1987, a national chicken processor purchased the old car junkyard across from the diner. The new owner purchased it, so he could use the railroad and the highway to ship his processed chicken around the country. The plant would process chicken twenty-four hours a day.

The plant opened its doors in 1988. It had to hire migrant workers at first because of the lack of a labor pool in the nearby town.

Andy, the son of the young couple who purchase an old railroad service building. The old building was made into a diner. Andy is the owner and cook for the converted diner.

The town that diner is in has a housing shortage. The town has all new street signs and twenty new buildings in the last year. The chicken processing plant and the service road that follows the train tracks has made the diner into a money-making machine. The workers from the plant would cross the tracks to eat at the diner.

The diner didn't have to rely on tourist that are lost trying to find the big city to the north that end up on the service road by mistake. Truck drivers trying to avoid the state troopers or weight station.

It is now 1988. The small diner is always full of people. Most of the customers are Spanish speaking people that work at the chicken processing plant. Maria is now working at the diner full time, all the time. Maria's father watches her kids while she is at work.

The diner has been so busy, Andy has had Maria working every hour that it is open. Maria, needing the money, has worked the hours and asked for more. She even asked Andy if her father could come in and clean the diner on Sundays. Andy, who has always done it himself, tried the old man out one Sunday. The old man impressed Andy so much, he now has him come in every Sunday and clean.

At the diner, Harley and Noreen have been working for more hours and much harder than they wanted to be. Maria has worked much harder and longer than the other two. Maria has started to give directions and guidance to Harley and Noreen.

Harley and Noreen, who have been nothing short of kind and helpful to Maria, have started to have problems with her. Maria is always trying to handle the next customer that walks through the door, jumping ahead of Harley and Noreen.

When Maria hears Harley and Noreen having communication problems because of the language barrier, she will come over to either waitress and take the order and then dictate it to the other waitress in English. Some of the new Hispanic customers want to only talk to Maria. This has embarrassed Harley and Noreen.

Maria has now started to ask Harley and Noreen to be more patient with the Hispanic speaking customers. One day Maria told both Harley and Noreen to stop talking to customers about things outside of the diner. Maria told the two to keep the conversations about what the customer wants to eat. That talking about movies or what was on TV with the customer was a waste of time and cost the diner money.

Maria also took her receipts, Harley's receipts, and Noreen's receipts. Maria added them up and took the average money of each of them. Maria showed Harley and Noreen that her receipts were thirty-three percent more than the other two.

Harley and Noreen had come to the end of their patience with Maria. Harley and Noreen had Andy outside the diner one day. The two women gave Andy a whole new set of problems that he never had to deal with.

For the first time that Andy could remember, the diner was making a lot of money. For the first time since Michelle and her boyfriend worked at the diner, he had an employee problem. Andy thought about it for a couple of days.

He was making a lot of money now. The two waitresses that he had depended on for years wanted Maria dealt with or fired. Maria was now his most valuable employee. Maria helped more customers per hour and had fewer wrong orders with her bilingual skills.

Andy asked Maria to stay late after he closed the diner. The two closed the diner down the same way since Maria worked the hours that Andy worked. Andy and Maria take a seat at a table by the window. Andy gets himself a beer. Maria gets herself a tea and some Milano cookies.

Andy: "Maria I know you want to go home and see your children. I'll try to make this quick and easy. Is there anything you would like to tell me before we have a talk? Any problems you're having. Any problem with the people you are working with that you would like to talk to me about?

Maria: "Andy I don't have problems here. You're not going to fire me, are you? I promise you I will work even harder. I need this job, Andy."

Andy: "Please, Maria, trust me, I am not here to fire you. You're the hardest working person here since my father. Only you could work as hard as him. I want to thank you for your hard work. Thanks to you and that twenty-four-hour plant, this place is making some money. More thanks to you and your always happy demeanor. I am starting to enjoy this diner. So please trust me, you're not getting fired."

Maria: "Thank you, Andy. But I must be doing something wrong or else why would you have me here?"

Andy: "Maria let me tell you something about me and the diner first."

Maria: "Okay, Andy."

Andy: "Maria, like I said, I want to thank you for all the hard work you do. My father loved this place. This was all he wanted to do. He wanted me to have the same love for this diner that he had. Maria, I didn't. I joined the army when I was young and loved it.

"I was away from here, which is what I always wanted as a kid. I could come back and see my parents who I loved. But I needed to get away from my parents' life, like any child who grows up does. The army life let me come back time to time and see them. Maria, I found what and where I wanted to be. Then one day I was told my father died. I had to go home and bury him.

"After my mother and I buried him, the diner came back into my life. My mother couldn't run it. She was only capable of being a waitress for a couple hours of the day. Then she had to get out of here. She just loved my father too much. She let him have this pine box, so long as she could have him. After he was gone, my mother couldn't cope.

"I made a promise to her that I would run the diner and keep it going. I regretted that promise the next day. But here we both are. You a young woman with an old man and two kids to support. Me with a diner and four employees.

"Maria the reason I must talk to you is Harley and Noreen are having problems with you. I asked Michelle about you. She confirmed that Harley and Noreen have told her that you are just too eager to help. To put it nicely."

Maria: "I am sorry, Andy. I don't want to be a problem to them. I am just trying to do the right thing. It's just about working hard to do a good job."

Andy: "Harley and Noreen have been with me a long time and I owe them a lot. They help me through hard times with the diner and personal things with my ex-wife. When they came to me and said what they said, it was just to help me, Maria, with what was wrong. As an employer, you must know the problem before your business has the problem. So, Maria, the problem is you."

Maria: "Me? Andy I am sorry. I don't want to be the problem. I will change and tell them I am sorry."

Andy: "Maria, you are going to have to go and work it out with them. Maria, I don't want you to change. The way you do things it is just you. You need to learn how to work with people. You need to understand your coworkers want to help this diner and me, and I want to help my workers.

"Michelle needs this job. I knew her father from school; he is a good man. I knew Michelle from a baby to a girl. Then to a young girl in trouble who found herself with a baby. She works so hard for that boy.

"Her father has enough money so Michelle doesn't have to work. But she does as much as she can.

"Harley has her kids and grandkids she is helping. Noreen is working for money for her kid's college.

Maria, I know they waste time talking about things that have nothing to do with the diner. I know Harley will talk to some customers way too long. Maria, I can't change them. Maria you need to change.

"You must go to them and tell them what you must. You need to find a way to work as hard as you do and still do what you think is right.

"If you think they need help with a customer, help them. If you think they need space, give them the space. Maria you may be the best waitress this diner ever had. But this diner doesn't need that.

"What it needs is a good waitress. A great employee who can work with others. If you must stop running at your pace to a walk so that you can walk with a coworker and help them.

Then, Maria, that's what I need you to do. Not everybody works or thinks the same.

"Harley and Noreen will leave someday. I am not going to have them change in any way. Maria, I don't need to change them. I am not going to fire them for a cheaper worker that will be a problem in a different way.

"Michelle is a very smart person. When her son is older and goes to school all day, she will probably get a different job. Then, Maria, it maybe you I will be depending on to keep the employees in line.

"If you work with Harley, Noreen, and Michelle, I will know that I can trust you with any other employees, Maria. For the first time, I want to come down these steps in the morning and make this place work."

Andy and Maria end the talk about Maria and her future work with employees.

Andy walks Maria home. After Andy says good night, he turns and starts to walk home.

It is a late Saturday night when Andy starts to walk home. He is wondering if he just made a mess of the whole situation at the diner. He is asking everybody to work harder.

He is asking a new employee to change herself to make it easier for the two older employees. No one in their right mind would do that.

Andy notices some lights at the end of a street. He makes a turn and starts to walk down the street. Then he starts to hear some music. It's not rock and roll and it's not country. The music is Hispanic.

At the end of the street, Andy finds the old town park. In the park are dozens of people. Some are barbequing. Some families have little kids on blankets. On the hood of a car is a teenage boy and girl hugging and kind of dancing to the music.

It's been a long time since Andy saw this park with people in it at night. When he was a boy, he would walk up here and watch all the teenagers from the fifties. The birth of rock and roll.

The boys would be by their hot rods. The cars were mostly built from parts from the junkyard across the tracks. The cars would have a pair of dice hanging from the review mirrors. Now he sees those cars with different flags with different colors of different nations hanging from the rear-view mirror. The boys would have on T-shirts on the warm Texas nights. A pack of cigarettes rolled up in their T-shirt sleeve. All the teenage boys with the greased back hair.

All the pretty girls in their Saturday date-night dress. Poodle skirts with sneakers and the chewing of bubble gum. The girls with no dates would walk to the park with other girls. The girls hoping that a cute guy would try and make some time with them.

Andy takes a seat on some rocks and watches the mostly Hispanic group having a good time. It's been years since Andy had a good time like he sees happening in the park. It's been a long time since the park had so many people.

The music changes to some old Sinatra music. Andy kicks back and listens to the music as he looks up at the stars.

How long have people been coming here on a Saturday, he wonders. Then he hears a voice from across the field that's all too familiar. It's Michelle and she is walking with a man a little older than her. Andy puts his arm over his face as they walk past him; she doesn't recognize him.

Andy hears him talking about the work he does at the chicken plant. He is head of human resources. As they walked past, Andy could tell it was the first date by the way they were talking. The two walks out of the park and out into the night.

She is young and very beautiful, so of course she is going to have a life away from work. It shouldn't feel so awkward. But it does.

Everybody but me has a life away from work. I am the diner. I am the clock on the wall. That clock is always set at work time.

I have four people now at the diner. I wonder if they look at the diner like I did when I was young. I hope they don't.

How about Maria? She is a young and attractive woman. She says she's single, but she was married. What if her husband comes back and takes her away? Is that story of her husband true? Or what if she finds a man that can support her, and the kids and I lose her? I think I may be in trouble.

I just started to like the diner and what it is. I never realized how fragile it is. For years, I didn't care if it went bankrupt. Now that it is making money and I like it, I could lose what has kept it going for all those years: the people who work it.

I must find a way of ensuring some stability with the workers. I must find some stability with me. I only found that stability when I was away from it in the army.

I must work on that. I may have to get some help for myself but where or who can help me? I can't go back to those train trips to the city. It was just a matter of time before they caught me. If I don't get on those train cars, I can't do what I did.

You and I need to talk a little bit about the way things are going around here. This diner has never seen so many customers. The waitresses that have worked here are having trouble coping.

The next day is Sunday. Andy gets up and calls Maria. Andy tells her he will be away from the diner most of the day. He wants Maria to tell her father who cleans and works on the diner to call Maria if he has any problems.

Andy has put on new locks for the front door.

More people are coming around after the diner closes looking for a place to eat.

When the old man shows up at the diner Sunday morning, Andy goes over what he wants him to do for the day. Andy shows the man the new locks on the front door and tells him to keep it locked. In broken Spanish and broken English, Andy tells him no people inside.

Then Andy points to the phone booth and the water faucet. It is what somebody may ask for, like he did. Andy tells the old man it's all his today and please take care of it.

Andy shakes the old man's hand, pats him on the back, and walks out the backdoor. This is the first time Andy has left the diner open with someone else.

Andy walks out of the back of the diner. He gets to the service road and looks back at his diner. Andy turns back to the road and starts his walk. At the other end of town, Andy walks into a cemetery. He finds a path he has walked before. Along the path he sees some new stones with recent dates on them.

Andy finds the two stones that he has seen before. Two stones that he has not seen in just over ten years. The day he put his mother in the ground. Andy stands in front of the two stones and looks down at them.

His father's stone is on his right side and his mother's stone is on his left side. He sits down on early-morning wet grass between the stones.

Andy starts to talk to the two stones. All you can see is the back of the stones and Andy sitting between them.

"Hello, Mom and Pop. It's been a long time since I have seen you. I can't remember a longer stretch of time. Even when I went into the army it wasn't this long. I wish back then it was longer. I didn't ever want to come back to the diner and live there ever again.

"Pop you would be happy with the diner now. We just had the biggest week ever. I made more money last month than all last year. We are so busy. There is a chicken processing plant across the tracks. You would have to work forever to kill all the chickens they do in a day, Pop.

"A lot of people work there, and we are the closest place to eat. We have people coming to our front door all hours of the day. Harley is the last person you know who still works at the diner. Everybody else you know is gone.

"I have two waitress named Noreen and Michelle. You would like them, Pop. Ask Mom, she knew them. I hired a Hispanic woman with two kids and no husband. She also has an old man to take care of. I know it sounds crazy, Pop, but I think a found the next you. Yeah, Pop, she as tuned to the diner as you.

"I look out the order window and watch her work. And that girl knows how to work. I think she has radar or eyes in the back of her head.

She can tell when a customer is coming through the front door. She knows how long people will take to eat. She can take orders for three tables and not have to right down the order. Yeah, Pop, I had to add a couple of tables we are so busy.

"Like I was saying, this girl is something else. She's so good at it, I have a problem. She is making the other waitresses crazy. I talked to her, Maria, last night and I hope it helps.

"Pop, for the first time, I like working at the diner. It feels like a business now. It's not the other sibling that I always felt the diner was. The sibling that got all the attention. The problem child that got all the grease. The child that took all your time away from me.

"Mom, Pop, I did something to some people I shouldn't of. I had a lot of anger in me. The diner and my life and the promise I made to Mom to keep it running for you. The drug dealers who sell that death to people. The young girl Michelle's boyfriend had his life ruined by it. The boy had so much promise. What a nice young couple they made till he found that death.

"One day at the diner a man came in and was bragging about how good his drug dealer was. How his drug dealer was the one other drug dealers went to for the good stuff. I couldn't take it. That night I found him in the city and I crippled him for life. I wanted to kill him.

"The papers made me into a vigilante, so I did it again and again. One night I was caught by a cop who figured it out. He kept silent about it because he knows me.

"Well, Mom and Pop, I don't have that anger anymore. I think when I saw Maria and how her life was, it changed me. Pop I could never understand how hard your life was. But I think I am starting to understand the privilege it is just to live a life.

"Pop like I said, the diner is so busy and doing so well, I have to change some things. I want to take the diner to twenty-four hours a day seven days a week. You could only dream of that. I bet you would try to work it all, wouldn't you? I am not going to even try it. The diner has enough money and business to change. Pop I am going to change your business to mine.

"Mom I am still going to keep the same name. Who you are is just between us and the daisies around us. Mom before I leave you two today, I will collect some of the daisies for you.

"I wish my two parents the best. You both got what you wanted in life. Pop you got a home and a place to work and call your own. Mom you got Dad forever. Just four feet from you.

"It's not a fairy tale like in that book you had me bury you with. You really have your Romeo that took you away from your early life and your real name."

Andy kisses his mother's stone then he collects some daisies. Andy leaves the graveyard. The sun is now at the high point of the day when he returns to his diner.

Andy sees the gravel parking lot has been raked and the grounds have been cleaned and detailed like the cover of *Home and Garden*. Andy goes inside and sees the old man scrubbing the floor. Andy and the old man spend the Sunday cleaning and working the diner. At dinnertime, the old man makes Andy a Spanish chicken dish on the grill.

The Sunday ends, the old man walks home, and Andy goes upstairs and separates his black T-shirts by sizes to get ready for his next week.

Andy has a talk with Harley and Noreen asking them for patience with Maria. As the week passed, Maria finds what she does best. She is a multitasker. Maria finds her niche with Harley, Noreen, and Michelle.

In a month, Harley leaves the diner. It was a sad day. Harley found the new customer difficult to understand. Her age and the old-time customer not coming around as much.

Andy also expanded the hours of the diner. Monday-Saturday the diner is open 5:00 AM to 10:00. Closed on Sundays.

Andy found himself in a bind looking for new help. He had so many Hispanic customers, he wanted to hire people who spoke English and Spanish. Andy had Michelle and Maria interview new people, and Andy hired who they would suggest.

A new cook was also needed to help Andy with the volume of people. Andy hired two new full-time cooks with an eye on keeping the diner open twenty-four hours a day.

Maria and the two cooks had a sit-down talk with Andy one day about changing the menus to a more Hispanic flavor. It took Andy, the new cooks, and Maria to change the forty-year-old never-updated menu.

Maria was working more hours at the diner than any other employee. She was supervising the new waitresses and the busboys. Maria had the tables set, the counter worked how she wanted it done. Andy was spending so much time in the kitchen, he wanted to hire a manager for the cooks, waitress, and busboys.

Andy offered it to Michelle. Michelle thanked him then told him that Maria should run it. Noreen told Andy the same. Noreen also told him that day she was planning on leaving soon too.

Andy gave Maria the title of Diner Manager and ability to do whatever she wanted to do. Maria was able to let her father stay at home and not work as a laborer anymore. Maria's father was able to watch Maria's kids and that saved Maria some money on babysitters. Maria still had to live in Martin's roach, mice, and bedbug rental apartment.

The first thing Maria did the first morning when she opened the diner as a manager was take down the crossword puzzle in the ordering window. Noreen, who was feeling the pressure of all the changes and the difficulties of communicating with all the Spanish speaking customers, left that day.

Noreen went to Andy that day and told him it was her time to leave. Andy and Noreen only had a minute to say their goodbyes because the diner was so busy.

Six months later, Michelle got a job at a daycare with her ability to speak Spanish and English. The chicken processing plant built a child care school because of all the workers who had kids.

Michelle became engaged to the new manager for the chicken plant who helped Michelle get the job. Andy was so upset with her loss and her good news, he had to take the day off.

Andy bought Michelle a brand-new 1987 Buick Grand National GNX as a present. Michelle, who helped save Maria who helped save the diner and Andy. Maria had just taken on a great deal more responsibility with the loss of Michelle.

CHAPTER SEVENTEEN

Change

It is 4:00 AM. Maria is up. She takes a shower and dresses for work. Before she walks out the door, Maria kisses her sleeping kids goodbye. She will see them again at 11:00 PM later that night after work when she kisses them good night.

Maria saw her father and mother work for years just trying to survive. Her mother died five years ago. Her father worked as a laborer doing any job he could find. The last twenty years, he worked on a horse farm. When he started, the people called him the bull because he was so strong. Then time and the back-breaking labor that was asked of him took its payment. The payment of his youth and his strength

The bull was an old man when the horse farm was sold off. The old owners gave the old bull the old pickup truck that the farm let him use. Then the bull left the horse farm with his daughter, her two kids, and a couple of farmhands.

Six months later, they were at Andy's diner using a phone looking for work. Then six months later, Maria, her two kids, and the old man just looking for water found the diner again.

Maria walks out of the apartment, leaving her two kids with her father. The apartment is just a block away from the diner. The sun hasn't shown itself yet. The moon is still high in the night sky as she walks to the back of the diner.

Maria takes out her key and opens the door she just locked hours before. She turns the stoves on. Maria starts the burners for the flat grill. She pulls a couple of dozen eggs from the refrigerator. She goes out a backdoor, picks up two metal garbage cans, and brings them around front. She then walks over to a small box at the base of a flag pole. Maria pulls out the flag she put in the box the previous night. She attaches the flag to the pole then raises it.

Maria sees a pile of cigarette ashes and beer cans on the ground. Somebody dumped their garbage on the ground. Maria gets a shovel, scoops up the mess, and puts it in the trash can.

Maria walks back around the diner and goes to a sink to wash her hands. Maria goes over to the grill and put some bacon she cooked last night on the center to reheat it.

She then goes around to the front of the diner behind the counter. Maria fills the coffee machines with water then turns them on. Then she collects yesterday's paper from around the room. She walks over to the window that had the crossword puzzle. She is happy not to see the puzzle.

At or about a quarter to five, the first waitress comes in through the backdoor of the diner. At the age of forty, she is a mother of three boys. Sometimes she is late and on occasion has failed to show up. Maria would know if she would be out when the diner phone would ring early in the morning. Maria had Andy hire her.

The woman promised Maria that she was a hard worker. She also told Maria she needed the money to help send her boys to college. Maria found the woman to be a very hard worker and never asked to leave early. Her name is Sue.

Sue comes into the kitchen and yells out to Maria, "Good morning, Maria. I made it." Maria from where she is at the time would thank her for being here. Maria knew she could depend on Sue showing up for a day of work. Maria would go to the front door and turn the closed sign to the open sign and unlock the front door.

Sue would take the dishes, cups, and utensils out of the dishwasher. Then she would start to set up the four wood tables with dishes and cups the way Maria wants her table set. Then she would set some cups and dishes across the counter.

Currently till 6:00 AM, the women were the only two workers. Maria was the cook till Andy came down at 7:00 AM.

The morning coal train passes behind the diner. It is laboring, pulling its heavy load of coal to the city. The power of its engines and the heavy coal cars shake the diner. The glass and the dishes rattle as the vibrations from the train travel unobstructed up to then past the diner.

Maria is in the back-making egg sandwiches for the customers who are walking into the diner. Sue is taking the orders and putting them into the order window. Sue is making coffee and ringing people out and keeping the line moving.

At 7:00 AM, Andy comes downstairs. Maria fills him in on how many people are working that day. She also tells Andy what day before receipts were. Andy knows that this diner is making more money than anybody dreamed. Then Maria goes up front and joins Sue.

At 8:00 AM, a cook comes in. Andy and the other cook will be there all day till closing.

Sue goes over to Maria and tells her the toilet is backed up again. Maria gets the plunger and cleans the toilet. Then she goes in back and talks to Andy. Maria then goes to the phone.

Another waitress shows up at 8:30 AM. Her name is Samantha. Everybody calls her Sammy. She has her two grandkids and their parents living with her. Her son lost his job and had to move his family back with his mother. Sammy speaks a little Spanish. Maria likes the woman because of her tough take-no-crap attitude toward the customers.

At 9:00 AM, the paper is dropped off. Sue goes outside and brings in the ten English papers and the ten Spanish papers.

At 10:00 AM, one of the diner's venders pulls into the driveway and blocks some cars in. Maria seeing this happen and goes outside and starts ripping into the driver. She tells him that vendors are only allowed to make deliveries in the afternoon. The diner now being so busy, one call from Andy to the vendor's office would have the driver taken off the diner's route.

The driver apologizes to Maria and tells her he'll be back later. Maria tells him if he does it again, she will call the main office. Maria then works out a deal with him to bring it to the backdoor and she'll let him go this time.

At 10:30 AM, the first busboy comes in. He is a high school dropout who can't get out of bed sometimes. He was hired because Maria liked his mother. The busboy has days when he works very hard. Then he has days where he is just in the way. Everybody just calls him Junior.

At 1:00 PM, the diner is overflowing with customers. A truck driver comes inside and finds Maria. The two go out front. On the truck are two porta-johns. Maria instructs the driver where to put them. She goes back into the diner and locks the restroom, then she puts a sign on the door that reads "permanently closed."

Sue leaves the diner at 2:00 PM and goes home to her kids. Andy and the cook get a breather in the midafternoon.

Maria quietly goes upstairs to Andy's apartment and gets a second register drawer. She brings it downstairs and takes the morning drawer out that's stuffed with cash. She puts in the new drawer. Maria runs a report then takes it up to Andy's apartment. She learned to do this without any people noticing.

Up in Andy's apartment, she does a tally. She takes out the tally for the half day and leaves the drawer with one hundred dollars. Maria takes the morning cash then puts the money in one of Andy's socks. She puts the sock in the freezer with other frozen socks of cash. Andy or she would take it to the bank. Maria then goes downstairs and starts the prep for the dinner rush.

At 4:00 PM, another busboy comes in. His name is Paul. Two other waitresses come in. Three of them go to the same high school. Their names are Debbie and Patty. They will work after school till the diner closes. Sammy would leave now, the exact time of her departure depending on how she felt that day.

The dinner rush comes. Andy and the cook, the two busboys, and the waitresses win the war of the eat-and-run crowd.

It is closing time. A tired Maria walks to the front of the diner and turns the sign that reads closed in two languages. The cook, the waitresses, and the busboys leave for the night. The waitresses have a ride home from one of the parents. The two busboys will walk home.

It's just Andy and Maria left in the diner. Andy starts to clean the kitchen. Maria counts the drawer and brings it up to Andy's apartment. She takes the cash and puts it in a sock and puts it in his freezer. Then Maria brings the next day's drawer downstairs and puts it in the refrigerator.

Maria goes downstairs and cleans the diner. She walks over to the restroom with a mop and bucket and sees the sign she put on it. She unlocks the door and cleans it for the last time. She hopes.

Maria mops the floors, cleans the counters, and scrubs down all the counters, stools, and food bins. She starts to set the diner up the way she wants it for the next day. When Andy and Maria are finished with their nightly routine, they turn the lights off.

Andy walks Maria home. The two are just too tired to talk much. They save it for the next day.

Maria walks into her apartment and finds her two children in their bed. Maria talks to her kids for a while then kisses them good night. Maria then takes a shower and retires for the day.

On the next Friday, Andy pulls Maria outside. He tells her he is doing every other day deposit runs to the bank. Then he tells her that he would like to talk to her on Sunday. Whatever time that would be convenient. Maria agrees to meet him after she bring the kids to church. Three of them will come by then. Andy tells her that would be fine.

On Sunday, the one day the diner was closed,

Maria and her kids leave church and walk to the diner, the last place Maria wants to be on her one day off.

Maria and her kids walk through the diner's back door that is open. Then they walk into the diner. Maria sees Andy on a ladder putting the finishing touches on two wooden cubes hanging from the ceiling. The four-sided cubes are the diner's ten quick order meals. Two sides would be in English and two sides Spanish. Now anybody who comes into the diner could look up and see a menu that could be read quickly.

Andy sees Maria come in and look up at the sign. He tells her what a great idea she had. He's sorry it took him so long to figure it out.

Then tells her he doesn't understand how she knows so much about the food service business.

Andy gets off the ladder and walks over to Maria's two children. He shakes their hand then asks Maria if they would like some ice cream. The children scream yes. Maria says okay. Andy sets the children up at the counter with some ice-cream. Then he and Maria take a seat at a table by the front window.

Andy: "Maria I want to thank you for giving up some of your one day off for me. Since you been here, my job has gotten much easier, and I thank you for that."

Maria: "You're welcome, Andy. You know how much I need this job."

Andy: "Yea, I know, Maria. I can tell by how hard you work. The last person I saw work that hard was my father. My father loved the diner. He lived for it. I hated it for years.

"My parents came into some money illegally. They used it to buy this place. They had to spend the rest of the money they had just to keep it alive. My mother sometimes hated this place as much as me. My mother loved my father so much, she endured it for him. I never understood what this diner meant to them.

"Maria that was till I met you and your kids. I saw how hard you work here for them. Maria, my father worked at this diner for his family. His family was a twenty-four-hour life. To keep that life, he spent twenty-four hours here for his family. Thank you for that."

Maria: "Andy you're welcome, but I am just trying to keep what is left of my family safe and fed."

Andy: "Thanks to you and that chicken place behind us, this diner is rolling in cash. For the first time ever, I can tolerate this place."

Maria: That's nice, Andy. Are we done?"

Andy: "No, Maria. Your kids haven't finished the ice cream."

Maria: "Andy you gave them too much. I hope they don't get sick."

Andy: "Kids never get sick on ice cream."

Maria: "They do like the dessert you let me take home. Thank you for that."

Andy: Maria you are more than welcome. A diner always has food. Maria what I want to talk to you about is change."

Maria: "Andy you're not letting me go, are you?"

Andy: "Maria please don't think about that possibility. I want to change the diner to a twenty-four-hour diner. It was a dream my father had. We have people knocking on our front door at all hours of the night. So long as that chicken place is there, we're going to be printing cash."

Maria: "Andy I don't know if I can work anymore than I do."

Andy: "I know, Maria. That is part of the change I want to do. We can come up with a new schedule for you. I want you to have an office. You will oversee all the people who work at the diner. You will set their hours and work schedule. I will still order the food and be a cook."

Maria: "Andy you're assuming I can do it. I don't know if I can."

Andy: "Maria my mother couldn't do it because she wanted to rely on my father, then me. My wife didn't want to do it. You have the mindset to do it.

You can visualize how this diner should operate. That's what this place needs, Maria. It needs you."

Maria: "Andy I have to ask you; will I get a raise?"

Andy: "Yes, you will. Sometime this week, you and I will go down to the bank and do some paperwork. You're going to be able to sign some checks with limits for me. The bank is concerned about you, so they insist on a monthly audit of our banking. But you won't even know they are doing It, if the books balance."

Maria: "That's a lot to think about. Andy how much time do I have?"

Andy: "You don't have any time to think about it,

Maria. And there's more."

Maria: "More? What can be more?"

Andy: "That place you live in. The roach and mouse hotel."

Maria: "I know it's bad, but it's better than the back of that pickup for my kids."

Andy: "I know. My father lived in train boxcars. He lived on the streets for a while. Then he lived in an orphanage. Then he lived in a basement below a sewer pipe. So, I want to change how you live and how I live."

Maria: "I don't understand."

Maria: "Martin, the building he owns, is in tax trouble. He is going to lose that building. I made him an offer. I made the bank an offer. I made the IRS an offer. When you and I go to the bank this week, I will be the owner of the building.

"You and your kids will move into my place. I will move into that building while they renovate it. When the renovation is done, you and your kids will move back into the building. You will have the whole first floor with four bed rooms and two bathrooms. So, you get a bedroom. Your father the bull gets my old apartment upstairs. He can be my night watchman. Each of your kids gets a bedroom.

"My apartment over the diner will also be an office—one for me and one for you. I will have two restrooms built for the employees. Maria, I could only do this with your help. I want to live away from the diner.

"This is my only chance. I am going to live on the top floor of that building where I can see the diner.

"So, Maria, we have a lot of work ahead of us. I must spend a lot of money. I need your help to have the diner make even more money to pay for everything. I am not giving you anything for free here, Maria. If we fail to pull this off, you, your kids, and the old man could be in trouble again.

So, we need to hire more cooks and more waitresses. To go twenty-four hours, Maria."

Maria: "I will work so hard for you. I will work even more hours to make it work."

Andy: "Maria that's not what I want. That's not going to help me. That's what happen to your father. People worked him too hard. That's what he thought he had to do. I want you to work smart. We have employees to work the manual labor. I want you to give me a list of what you think we need to go twenty-four hours a day. I want you to set a schedule for yourself with set hours. I need you to cover when needed. You and I are the only ones who could do everything, Maria. Maria we both need to change. So, let's start working the change. It's time to change."

CHAPTER EIGHTEEN

Grinding

It is 1998. Maria is now running the twenty-four-hour diner. The day-to-day grind of her work schedule is taking a toll on her. She doesn't have time to listen to anybody's problem. The only problem that she could relate to is not having a job. This is an ongoing problem that Andy has talked to Maria about. Andy had asked Maria to show more patience with the workers and customers.

Andy is now living in Martin's old apartment building. He owns the building and resides on the top floor. His room has a view of the booming twenty-four-hour diner. Maria and her kids live on the bottom floor. Her father sleeps in Andy's old room and works on the maintenance of the diner.

On this early, clear, bright Texas morning, a twenty-four-hour diner is bustling. People are going in and coming out of the diner. In the parking lot are benches set up for people to eat on. Some cars are parked on the street. To the side of the diner are two plastic outhouses. The inside restroom was taken out to make room for more tables.

Maria shows up to work after dropping her two kids at school. She says hello to the three waitresses and two busboys who are working the morning shift. She goes behind the counter then into the kitchen to see the two cooks working with two new stainless-steel grills. Maria then takes the mail, time cards, and paperwork upstairs two her new office that is in Andy's old apartment.

It's 8:30 AM. Maria has counted the cash from yesterday. The cash and the credit cards add up. She takes the cash and puts it in one of Andy's old socks, then puts the sock with the cash into Andy's old freezer. Maria then takes the time cards and adds up the hours for the previous day. She notices her problem child, John, is punching in eight minutes early. John does this, so he gets payed for the full fifteen minutes.

Maria then adds up some invoices for the diner supplies. She writes out some checks to pay the vendors. She takes the checks and sets them aside for Andy to sign. Maria then starts to work on next week's schedule. One of the cooks will be out that week. Then it's a balancing act of waitresses and the time they want off to spend with their boyfriends.

It's now 11:00 AM. She has spent enough time doing paperwork. The midday lunch rush is about to start. Maria's Monday to Friday workday has just begun. She will be at the diner till needed, waiting and bussing tables.

When Maria comes down the stairs, she sees her problem child, John, talking to a new waitress. John has his arm blocking her path out of the kitchen.

Maria goes right up to the two. She clears her throat loudly to get John's attention. John moves his arm back then takes a step backward. The new waitress named Nancy looks at John and laughs. Maria takes a hard look at John and says, "I hired you because your mother said you were such a good boy. Just a little misunderstood. I think I understand the little boy in front of me.

"He likes pretty girls. He doesn't like work. He would like to impregnate my waitress. He doesn't like to pay for his child. He likes to have the state pay for his indiscretions. He doesn't know how to use a time clock. He likes to punch in early and steal time. He doesn't like to move fast. He likes his fast cars with the blue pin stripes. He has his father buy him a shiny new grill.

"So, Nancy, the new waitress who has a big boyfriend, I would not let this little boy be the father of my child. This little boy who spends more money on blue pins stripes than his baby. So, Nancy, if he tries to make time with you again, I'll spend some time telling your big boy friend about this sorry excuse of a male reproductive organ. Now please go back to work or I will fire the both of you."

Then Nancy walks out into the diner. John tells Maria he's sorry then heads out to the table.

Maria turns and goes to the cooks and goes over some of their working time. Then she talks to them about supplies. After about twenty minutes of Maria cleaning and thanking the cooks, she leaves and heads out to the tables.

Maria instantly scans the room. She sees tables that need to be bused. Chairs that are no longer with the table they are supposed to be with. The two bus-boys are on the same side of the room. She has repeatedly told them not to be together on one side of the diner. Nancy is spending too much time taking an order from one person at the counter. Then she sees the register drawer half open. This holds Maria's attention.

Maria walks over to the register first. She opens the draw. Maria can tell that the drawer looks okay by the way the cash is in its bins. Maria goes under the drawer and pulls out all the big bills. Then she removes half the twenty-dollar bills. Maria takes the cash and brings it back upstairs. She puts the cash into a sock then places it into the freezer.

Maria comes back downstairs and sees her two busboys are on different sides of the diner now. Nancy has moved on to another customer at the counter. Maria goes up to the busboy named Steve and asks him when the last time was that he checked the parking lot for garbage. Steve tells her about an hour ago. Maria pats him on the back and thanks him for doing it.

Maria then walks over to a table that four guys are sitting at. She asks them if they are ready to order. The four guys just order some drinks. Maria takes their drink order. Then she tells them that she will be right back to take their order, "So, have it ready." Two of the four just look up at her as Maria walks to the counter.

Maria goes to the counter, gets the drinks, and stops to talk to Jill, a waitress. She tells Jill to try and keep herself close to the counter. "All the walking is going to catch up to you and wear you out. Jill says okay and goes back to work.

Maria is back at the table with the four guys. Three of them have given Maria their order. A fourth guy is just looking up at the square menu board and whistling. Maria's legs are not moving now. She is just staring at the fourth guy, waiting for his order. Maria is just tapping her foot. Two minutes have gone by. One of the other guys have asked the fourth guy to stop playing and give her his order. The fourth guy says, "The bitch can wait. She just wants to rush us out of here, so she can have the table for the next customer. That is what she always does. She can wait."

Maria just says "fine," and walks off to the window and places the order of the other three guys. Then Maria goes to work another table.

The order for the table with the four guys is in the window. Maria walks over to it and takes it to their table. She places the food in front of the three guys who ordered it. She turns to the fourth guy and asks him if he was now ready to order.

He says yes and wastes more of her time changing his mind on what to order. After the changes his order five times, Maria just walks off. The man calls her "bitch" again. Ten minutes later, Maria brings the check to the table with the four guys.

Maria takes the cash for the order. Then she tells the fourth guy he is no longer welcome in the diner. If he shows up again, she'll call the police. The other three guys just laugh at him. Maria takes the cash, pays the tab, and brings the change back. Maria then goes on to other tables. Ten minutes later, the four guys leave the diner. There is no tip left for her. Maria has noticed that her tips are far less than the other waitress. She knows it is her fault, having to be the boss and be the most efficient employee.

Maria goes outside to check on the two outhouses. The toilet paper supply for them is never ending. Sometimes, she thinks people are stealing the paper and bringing it home. The two outhouses stink, but they are fine for now. She goes back inside. Maria washes her hands then goes out to the dining room.

The afternoon goes by with everybody in the diner working hard. Its 3:35 PM when Maria sees a big green car pull right up to the front door. The driver does this several times a week.

The driver is a state worker who is a clerk that gives the written test for the motor vehicle license department. The woman goes to work 9:00 AM and gets to leave at 3:00 PM just five days a week. Maria is afraid that a customer is going to get hit by the car parked so closed to the front door.

Maria watches the woman through the front door put a handicap tag on her rear-view mirror then gets out of the car. The woman is a big woman who has most of her fat on her stomach. The woman comes into the diner. She sees an empty table and walks up to it and sits in a chair. The woman is out of breath as she puts her over-sized laundry bag of a pocketbook down on a chair.

This one table Maria will be the waitress for. She knows she will have to go over there and address the woman's parking again. Then her taking a whole table and not a chair at the counter. The woman's name is Hana.

Maria: "Hello, Hana, how are you doing today?"

Hana: "Maria I am so hungry, I don't understand it. I am eating these protein shakes, but they are just a waste of time."

Maria: "I have asked you before not to park so close to the front door. You may hit somebody. Please don't do it anymore."

Hana: "Maria, like I told you before, I am handicapped. I have a handicap card. So I get to park in handicap accessible parking. This place is in violation of numerous laws, Maria. So I will park in a place that is easy for me to walk from."

Maria: "You are fat, Hana. You are a fat girl. Lose that fat around you, and your walking will get easier."

Hana: "Maria you just don't understand the handicap I have. There are laws to protect me. I wish I didn't have to be subjected to this harassment."

Maria: "You will find the door open, Hana.

There may be a big green car on the other side, but the door is open. Would you like me to show you to the door?"

Hana: "Maria please, you know what I want to have, so just be the dear and bring it to me. I am just too tired from work and not eating."

Maria: "Yes, the number three. The three-pound mushroom and beef omelet. A side of biscuits and gravy. Then a dish of mozzarella sticks and let's not forget the diet soda."

Hana: "Maria you don't have to say it so loudly, please."

Maria: "At one time, people used to come here as a stop while they cheated on someone they were married to. Now you stop here just to eat. I'll place the order. Then I'll go see where my waitress and the one-female-just-isn't enough busboy is."

Maria puts Hana's order in the order window.

A man comes into the diner and stops at the door. He looks around the diner. He has a motorcycle helmet in one hand and a backpack in the other. He walks up to the counter and takes a seat. He drops his backpack to the side of the stool then puts his helmet on the next stool.

He looks back over his shoulder to Hana eating at a table. Then he looks at all the people in the diner. Maria comes over and puts the menu in front of him. The man just asks for some apple pie, vanilla ice cream, and black coffee. Maria then calls back to the cook, "Hot apple pie," then she puts some vanilla ice cream in a bowl.

The man reaches down into his backpack and pulls out a large notebook. He puts the notebook down on the counter, opens it, and starts to write something inside. Maria comes over and puts the ice cream and pie in front of him. She pours him some coffee then asks him if he would like anything else. The man just shakes his head no and smiles at her. He starts to eat his ice cream and pie

Later, Maria finds John and Nancy by the dishwasher talking. Maria pulls Nancy off to the side.

Maria: "Nancy, as one woman to another, that boy is a loser. He has one kid by another woman. The only reason I don't fire him is his family sells us our bread. Andy would pay him to stay at home for the savings he gets from that company. Please stay away from him because I will fire you. Do I make myself clear?"

Nancy: "I am just playing with him, Maria."

Maria: "Playing? What's that playing? I don't understand playing?"

Nancy: "It's harmless, Maria. We're just talking."

Maria: "He is not harmless, Nancy. He wants to get in and out. That's what we do with customers. We get them in and we get them out and forget them. That is the playing he wants to do. In and out and you'll have a big belly and you will be playing with your baby. Then he will be playing with another girl who likes to just play. Wake up, playtime and recess is over. Now get back to work. The second girl is the dumber one."

Maria goes to the pick-up window and gets Hana's order. She picks it up and brings it to the table that Hana is at.

Hana: "Thank you, Maria. I hoped they cooked it all the way. Last time some of it wasn't cook all the way. My weakened immune system has a hard time digesting uncooked food."

Maria: It's cooked. Your weakened immune system is a joke. Stop eating so much and it wouldn't be so weakened. There is enough food on your order to feed a family for a day."

Hana: "Maria I don't understand why you don't understand my condition. I hope they didn't put any salt in this food. Your cooks should ask the customer if they have health issues that would limit salt intake."

Maria: "I don't believe my ears. You think your

fatness is a health condition. Lose some weight, fat girl."

Maria leaves Hana and goes to the counter to help Nancy who is backed up with customers. She sees the other two more experienced waitresses moving customers in and out of the diner.

Maria walks up to a repeat customer named Hector. Hector is a local car salesman. He set up a lot and is one of the new businesses that have started to find a growing market in this small town that is in a boom.

Maria: "Hello, Hector. How is the car business today?"

Hector: "I sold one car today, Maria. I lost my shirt. It was like I had to give the car away. I can't believe how much I am going to lose selling cars here."

Maria: "Hector you told me you lost your shirt yesterday. You must have a lot of shirts."

Hector: "Maria I have a lot of bills for all those cars you see on my lot. I need to sell a lot more to stay on that lot."

Maria: "You'll find a way. There are lot more people in this town that would like a car."

Hector: "How about you, Maria, would you like to buy a car? The manager of this diner shouldn't have to walk to work. Wouldn't you like to take your kids to school in a new car? Think about that, Maria—a new car. What color would you like?"

Maria: "You're so funny, Hector. What color would I like? I like green in a bank account for my kids. My kids and I can walk anywhere in this town. My kids are going to go to college, not to your lot of the latest and greatest junk car on four wheels heading to the next repair shop."

Hector: "Maria used cars lots have a bad name, I know it. My lot and cars are different. I want to change the way cars are sold. Any car that is sold from my lot will look just as new as a new car would look. I offer a maintenance package that is second to none.

"I had a big car lot in the city look at what I am doing, and they say I am crazy. They said when it gets out what I am doing for my customers, it would ruin me."

Maria: "I saw one of your cars broken down on the side of the road yesterday in the rain."

Hector: "I know who you are talking about. I paid for a tow truck to bring that car to me. I put in a new battery for my customer. No one can tell how long a battery will last. Now enough on cars. What should I have to eat?"

Maria: "How about some of our chili. But it's yesterday unsold hamburger. It's just a little false advertising. Maybe just a little lie. Little lies are okay in advertising. Everybody knows today's chili is really yesterday's unsold food. I'll be right back, Hector." Maria gets the chili and some crackers for Hector then she goes on to another customer.

Maria was working on some other customer when the man who ordered the pie and ice cream was at the register to pay his tab. Maria looks back over where he was sitting. The man left a paperback book on the counter. Maria tells him that he left a book there. The man pays his bill and tells Maria it is hers now. He leaves her a tip, puts his backpack on, and walks out of the diner. Maria watches him get on his bike and drive away.

She goes over to see what book he left. Maria picks up the book and reads the cover.

Maria then walks over to another customer. She asks the customer what they would like to order today.

A young man in his early twenties gives Maria the order, starting with the words, "Give me." Maria stops him before the next word.

Maria: "Give me. Give me what. I don't understand the words give me. Is it adjective? Is it a pronoun? Is it part of a sentence? Is it the beginning of a sentence? Can you tell me what give me those two simple words are for? Can you tell me why you must use those words when somebody is working to take an order for you? I think you were about to ask me to take an order for you. You could have started the sentence with please. Then follow that by can I have. Or please can you please take my order.

"I have two children at home. I try to teach them that the words give me when used like that are bad. There are so many other ways to start a request for something. I often wonder where people get the idea that any request needs to start with give me."

The young man just looks at Maria as she talks at him. When Maria is finished, the young man just says, "Grilled cheese on white bread and a soda."

Maria takes the order and puts it in the window and goes on to other customers. When the young man's order is up, Maria gets his order and gives it to him. Then Maria apologizes to him.

The afternoon passes, the dinner rush comes. After the dinner rush, Maria goes to the register and pulls out more cash. Maria takes it upstairs. She does some more paperwork. Before she comes back downstairs, Maria puts the cash in a sock and places it in the freezer.

Maria comes downstairs and one of the cooks starts to tell her one of the new stoves is not keeping its temperature. He wants to shut it off for the night and have a plumber look at it. He thinks one of the gas lines may be clogged. Maria tells him to wait till the next cook comes in.

Maria then hears a couple of loud cars out front of the diner. She walks to the front door and looks out the glass. It's a couple of young guys in some little sports cars with a loud exhaust. They started to hang out at the diner at night. The next day Maria would find beer cans and cigarette butts on the ground by where their cars were.

Maria walks out to the guys in the cars. She see one guy who looks like the leader. Maria goes up to him then tells him, "I just called the police department. I offered them free coffee and free donuts to any police officer who showed up tonight. So, you should leave before you see them speeding here with their lights on.

Anytime I see you or your friends in this lot, I will call them and do it again. Good night, guys." Then Maria walks back into the diner.

Maria gets on the phone and calls Andy. She tells him she sorry to bother him on his day off. Andy tells her she did the right thing and to call him anytime. Then Maria tells him about one of the new stoves having problems. She would like to have it fixed before the morning breakfast rush. Andy tells her he will come by and look at it. Maria apologizes again about bothering him.

It's 9:00 PM when Andy walks through the backdoor. He talks to the cook before that cook left for the night. The night cook comes in and gets an update on the stove. Andy thanks the cook who noticed the problem and tells him he should go home; he'll take care of it.

The diner is down to one cook for the night and two waitresses till morning. Andy finds Maria working the front and tells her he'll be here for a while to see if he can fix the stove. Maria again apologizes to Andy for not being able to solve this problem. Andy tells her nobody can solve all the problems.

One of the night waitress calls out sick. Maria knows she will be there all night. She could have gone home when her schedule ended. Her kids will not see their mother till tomorrow afternoon. It's sometime after midnight. The diner is slow enough for Maria to see how Andy is making out with the stove.

Andy has his head in the bottom of the stove. There are pliers, screwdrivers, yellow Teflon tape, and the smell of gas all around him.

Andy tells Maria he found the problem. One of the gas feed pipes had a clog in it. So he cleaned the pipe out. It will be about an hour before the stove is back together.

About two hours later, Andy has the stove back together. The night cook and Andy are satisfied the stove is right. They test for gas leaks with dishwashing soap and water.

When everything is okay, Andy goes up front and tells a tired Maria the stove is all set for tomorrow's breakfast.

Maria: "Andy it would have been crazy tomorrow without it. How did you fix it?"

Andy: "I am so used to fixing. One of the pipes had paper in it. I just blew it out. If I knew which pipe and what it was a couple hours ago, it would have been easier."

Maria: "Andy you look so tired. You need to go home and get some sleep."

Andy: "Maria if you like I can stay till the breakfast rush and you can go home to your kids. I still have the shower upstairs and some clean clothes."

Maria: "No, Andy, not a chance I would do that. I will see them later. My father will watch them like he always does."

Andy: "Yeah, that's what I knew you would say. If you like I can get them some ice cream, Maria?

Maria: No, Andy. My kids are eating too much ice cream and pie. They are going to get fat off what you are feeding them. I know you sneak them ice cream and don't tell me."

Andy: "Yeah, Maria, you caught me. I am guilty, but so is your father. I think he eats more of it than your kids."

Maria: "He is old, and I don't have to worry about him eating too much. But, Andy, I do worry about the weight you lost. What did the doctor say to you today?"

Andy: "You know what they do. Put you on a scale. They take blood, then they say they must run some tests. Then they take your cash. Maria, they said they will let me know."

Maria: "Okay, Andy, you go home now. Take a shower, get some rest, and I will see you later."

Maria updates Andy about some other things happening with the employees and diner.

It's 2:00 AM. Maria is outside at the outhouse trying to stand it back up. Somebody has tipped it over again. It's just too heavy for her.

She sees two big men eating an early breakfast. Maria goes over to them and offers them the breakfast for free if they would stand the outhouse back up. The two men look at each other. Then the bigger says "Deal." He gets up and walks outside with Maria.

The big man walks over to the plastic outhouse and lifts it back to a standing position. Then he bear hugs it and resets it on its stand. The man and Maria go back inside. Maria thanks him and the other man. Then Maria pays their bill. Maria took care of the waitress tip with her own tips.

About twenty miles south of a large city is a booming town. This small town has a set of old train tracks and a service road that run alongside of it. The town has the usual small local roads. The roads in this town have the same name other roads in small towns have, like Main Street, Bank Street, Park Street, and other familiar names.

The town has a new post office and police department. As the city to the north stagnated this small town grew with people and jobs.

On this service road that runs along the old train tracks is a small diner. The diner is now open twenty-four hours a day. Inside this diner is a young immigrant woman with two children and an old man to take care of it.

The young woman, Maria, has been up for twenty-four straight hours managing this twenty-four-hour diner. She had to make the right decisions on people, customers, and equipment.

The decisions she made has kept the diner open and the customers served.

It is five o'clock in the morning a very tired Maria goes outside to put up the flag. She walks the parking lot and doesn't see any beer cans or piles of cigarettes.

Maria goes back inside and helps the night cook start cooking the bacon for the Saturday morning breakfast rush.

The first morning cook comes in and takes the grill. At 6:00 AM, a tired-looking Andy comes in to do his twelve-hour shift. Andy finds Maria up front mopping the floor. The two talk about the stove and the people who are working the day. Maria tells Andy he's looking very pale. She asks Andy if he wants her to call a cook to see if they could take his shift. Andy tells her he'll be fine.

He also tells her he worked longer hours years ago cooking and working on the diner at night. Andy goes back into the kitchen and Maria goes back to mopping the floor.

The morning crew of waitresses and busboys come in on time. That gives Maria a sense of relief. The stream of customers come in all morning. So many people come in this Saturday morning, people are looking for the waitresses to serve them outside on the wood benches.

Maria tells the other waitresses that she'll cover the outside. She tells them to stay inside and do what they can.

Maria is running in and out, bringing food out to customers and bussing the tables herself. She has been keeping an eye on the two plastic outhouses, hoping they last the weekend. If she must call a truck to pump them out, it's going to stink the place up.

It's 10:00 AM. Maria has just a couple of people outside now. She tells the customers that they can go inside and pick up their food.

Maria goes inside, runs a tally on the register. She takes the money out and walks to Andy in the back cooking on one of the stoves. She talks to Andy about the big morning rush. Then she tells him about the thousands of dollars upstairs in his old freezer. She tells him he has a lot of checks to sign and he needs to stop and do a bank run. She suggests that he gets one of the local cops to give him a ride. Andy tells her he has already worked that out. He'll get the ride at 9:00 Monday. Maria goes upstairs, does more paperwork, and puts more money in the freezer.

Maria calls her kids and talks to them for a couple of minutes. Then Maria goes downstairs for the lunchtime rush.

Once again, Maria is outside running in and out of the diner. Bringing the food out and bussing the tables. For the afternoon, that's all she does.

At 5:00 PM, the next cook comes in to relive Andy. The afternoon and evening waitresses show up for work, and Maria can stop waiting tables.

Andy finds a very tired Maria upstairs doing paperwork. Andy tells her to go home. He'll be here all night upstairs if anything happens. That he'll be here all weekend helping and being the on-duty manager. Maria tells him if he needs her to call her. If she doesn't hear from him, she will be here for her Monday shift before he goes to the bank.

After Maria leaves, Andy takes a shower and changes into a clean set of clothes. He lies down on his old couch and falls asleep. At 12:00 AM Sunday morning, Andy wakes up and looks at the clock. He has overslept. No one has checked on the diner. This is the longest time that his father, mother, him, or Maria haven't been on the first floor.

He looks over to the freezer and sees the door open. He gets up and runs to the freezer.

It looks just like the way he last saw it before he fell asleep. He is relieved he just left the door open. Andy walks downstairs to the diner. He sees everybody serving customers or cleaning. He walks over to the head cook and tells her he fell asleep.

The cook said she understood, and everything is fine. Then she asks Andy to check the register.

Andy walks around to check on everything. He also talks to the head waitress. Andy walks back to the cook and asks her to wake him up at 5:00 AM tomorrow. Andy finishes the weekend. He ends up sleeping through Sunday night. At 5:00 Monday, Andy is bright and cheery when Maria comes in.

CHAPTER NINETEEN

Bye

In the year 1998, about twenty miles south of a large city, was a booming town. This small town has a set of old train tracks and a service road that run alongside of it. The town has the usual small local roads. The roads in this town has the same name other roads in small towns have, like Main Street, Bank Street, Park Street, and other familiar names.

The town has a new post office and police department. As the city to the north stagnated and this small town grew with people and jobs.

On this service road that runs along the old train tracks there once was a small diner.

The chicken processing plant was investigated by a group of animal rights activists. One of them noticed the chicken droppings being used as grass fertilizer. That person called the EPA.

The EPA came out and tested the ground water. The EPA found the ground water to be toxic. Years of creosote from the railroad tracks had leeched into the ground water. They also found lead contamination, benzene, arsenic, motor oil, and dozens of heavy metals neurotoxin.

The EPA closed the chicken plant and put it into a Superfund cleanup. They closed the diner down and labeled the land unsafe for any building ever.

When the diner was torn down, Andy showed up to see it come down. He later walked home with a smile on his face. The next day, the water tower came down. In the tower they found an old car battery, an old car headlight, and the skeletal remains of a young man who was later identified as Michelle's old boyfriend.

There were no signs of trauma to the body, so his death was ruled a possible drug overdose. Later that week, Michelle and her son buried him. Two days later, Andy is told that Dan the policeman whose wife died a year earlier from breast cancer shot himself in his front yard. It was ruled a suicide. The probable leading contributing factor was his wife's death.

It is the year 2001 on an early Sunday Texas morning. The sun is breaking over the horizon. An old man named Andy walks out of his apartment. On his way to church, he walks past a vacant lot that sits along a service road for an old railroad track. Andy is on his way to see a young man giving his first sermon.

Andy walks into the church and sees the preacher's mother and sister in the front row. Andy thinks of joining the two. He thinks to himself it is their moment to be proud of a boy that turned into a good man.

The young preacher walks up to the podium, watched by his mother and sister and a church full of people.

The sermon

"I would like to thank all the people who showed up on this wonderful Texas morning. There is something about a Texas morning. Sometimes, I think the world was created in Texas. This state that I call home may be big enough to be the birth place of the whole universe.

"As a young boy, you think such things would be possible. Then you go to school and learn such things are not reality. The things you learn in school just do not fit into the physics of a young boy's mind.

"I looked out the window and saw all the people come into this beautiful building. All the lovely women dressed in their Sunday outfits. All the men dressed in their Sunday outfits. Then I saw a little girl.

"This little girl was dressed up for something special. It was such a special day for her, she dressed herself. She picked out her two favorite dresses and put them both on. One over the other. Both were pink, so they didn't clash. Then the little girl put a tiara on her head. Alongside the tiara she put on a set of cat ears. Around her neck she had a necklace of plastic white pearls and two other shiny plastic necklaces.

"In one arm she had a large pink-and-white bag filled with stuff as her hand was holding her pocketbook. The other hand she had a death grip on two dolls. On her feet was a set of pink clogs.

"This little girl was all set for the day. I don't think anybody here was as prepared as that little girl. We should all think about that today. We should think about that every day. Are we prepared for what we may encounter or what we may need? That little girl did. She was prepared for the here and now.

"I often hear stories from adults on something that happened to them as a child. The adults would tell me it was a learning experience. The adults told me how it gave them experience. The experience was a teaching lesson for them.

"Some stories are just people talking about what they did five miles up a road where they lived their entire life. Or five miles down the road. The story of what they consider their biggest adventure or achievement. So, we listen in hopes it ends soon. Then we hear them tell that same story to a different person. Then we wonder how many times they tell that same story to themselves.

"Sometimes, I hear a story and I wonder how much of it is true or how much of it was just miss-remembered. I guess it makes no difference if it's just a story.

"We all have those stories of our younger self.

We all look to tell others of our past experiences. The story we think that relates to the moment that is at hand. Or the story we think that needs to be told.

"The story we want to tell most is that story we have of our most trying times. The times that we feel that almost broke us. The story of the hardest challenge. The stories of our hardest times. The stories of the times when we felt alone.

"Did you ever hear a story from a person and wish you were there to help them? Did someone tell you a story of such hardships it made you wonder if you could have endured their hardship?

"We hear stories of such hardships from the survivors of the genocide from the thirties and forties in Europe. The people trying to escape from a government that wanted to kill them and their children.

"Stories that make a person wonder why there is so much hate. Stories of people before the last great war looking for a safe place to exodus to. Then the story of how ships of people were turned away. How borders were closed to groups of people trying to flee an uncertain future.

"Those of you who were alive then you saw the stories happening, can you believe that today in, the present world, we still have people trying to escape? The borders, the nations, and the simple lines on the world map have changed.

"What hasn't changed is the want of people to seek out a land that offers a promise of freedom and the opportunity to their family and future generations.

"We still see people travel from the borders of many generation's homeland. They hope that their travels are the last borders that any future descendant will have to cross just to survive. Just to live on a land that their kids will have a stable shelter and the promises of the next meal.

"How about the story of our parents or grandparents that came to this great land? The story of the hardship they had to endure. Was it the new language they had to overcome and learn? Was there a more popular religion than theirs? Was it not knowing where they can find an honest day of pay for an honest day of work?

"Did your ancestors have to seek out places and people who were from the same religious backgrounds? At sometimes and in some places in this world that could have been dangerous.

"Do we tell stories of our travels? Do we tell stories of where and what you saw? Then you return home to that same place you know. The foundation of the way you live your life. The place that keeps you with the comfort of being secure.

"Well that little girl who came into church with all that she could carry, and wear must have felt secure this morning. Don't we wish we could make all the little girls and boys feel secure? I know we can't do that.

"Don't we wish we can go back and help those people who were turned away at borders before the last war in Europe? Don't we wish we could save those people from the death camps? I know we can't. Don't you wish you can go back and help your ancestors? Well, I know we can't. We can't go back and help anybody. We just can't do it.

"There are people living with the same life conditions and challenges that our ancestors had. I think that it would be easy for us to see. I think we would be able to help them with their challenges. We can help the here and now.

"We could look back with the life stories we were told. We could use those stories to solve any problem. We see it or heard it all before, didn't we? That is what those stories are for. We can help the here and now.

"In the papers today, in the papers of the past, it tells of groups of people seeking new lives for themselves and their kids. Papers tell of the cost to be paid if the wave of people were to be taken in by a community. We can help the here and now.

"The community that is already strained to be strained even more. The local population to bear the inconvenience of the unprepared new group of people.

"The local police force asked to police something that was not part of any of their training. The new fences that must be purchased. The meetings and the planning for the unplannable.

"Then the papers with the faces and stories of those people. The stories of people who put their life at risk to flee a land where life itself came into question. We can help the here and now.

"The pictures of children in dirty clothes. The pictures of mothers with their clinging children who can't understand the fight just to live that day of their life. We can help the here and now.

"The stories of the ones who died on the path taken by so many others. The story of the opportunist, who showed up on that path only to hide their faces as they help many others fall on the path. We can help the here and now.

"As you live your life, think of who is across from you. They may be the one who had to live the fight or fight to live.

"I heard a story of a young boy and girl who lived with an abusive father. A mother who tried to feed her kids. The woman who worked all night as a waitress in a bar that offered prostitution in the backrooms.

"She spoke English well enough for the management to keep her just as a waitress. From sundown to the hell of the sunup, she had to endure the sounds and profanity. A pornography play of dangerous people and the fear of a personal assault. Five years of a hell that was at work and home.

"Then into the unknown. Across borders went a woman without her husband with two kids. She went looking for her father. A father who had traveled to another land with the promise of opportunity.

"Across the border with little money. The woman found her father and an old pickup. The man with his daughter and two children took to the streets. The same streets that many before had heard the streets were paved with gold.

"They found the street once promised with gold blocked with borders. The street blocked with language barriers. The streets block with the saying 'There are too many of you now.'

"The old man, the young woman, and two kids end up alone one day with no money and no food. The two children in dirty clothes and dehydrated.

"With a prayer from a little girl to a god that she was hoping to be up one late night, the little girl asked for some water. That's all she wanted was water.

"The old man driving a truck that was on its last drop of gas saw a diner he found months ago. They found the water the little girl had prayed for. Then they found a police officer. Then they found the diner owner. Then they found a young woman who found no borders in her compassion for some people who needed compassion.

"I know that prayer happened because I was the little boy who was next to the little girl–my sister. My sister named Faith.

"The woman was my mother. We were at the end of everything that night.

"We were just migrants. We were just immigrants, that's all. Just a few from millions. It makes no difference who the people are. They could be on a boat seeking political asylum. They can be walking across the European continent trying to stay out of a death camp.

"It could be the migration of millions in Africa walking across the plains just looking for food.

"It could be people on boats fleeing a dictator that opened the prison doors. The mixture of the group of good and the bad will happen when both are forced to travel the same path.

"From the slaves of the cotton fields of the South to the cities that promise work and equality, we are all migrants.

"From the land of the green where a famine forced the migration of millions to this land, we are all immigrants.

"In the land where the fascist drove million from the Italian homeland, we are all immigrants.

"From the home land of the Indians to the Indian reservation. To the nation that now sits on the land they lived on. We are all migrants.

"The people in the ghettos who wish to travel to that street promised of gold. They are just a migrant from the poverty of the ghetto.

"That's what this country is: immigrants and migrants. At one time, this country was known as the melting pot. This country held its head in pride because of how diverse we once were.

"We had no walls on our boarders. The day we put up a wall, it's the beginning. It's the beginning of us becoming one of those countries that put up a wall to imprison its own people.

"To the children of the past the present and the future, you will find our borders always open to you.

"You will find an open path that leads to our land of the free. The path is what you will have to cross. Many children have come before you.

"Many children will find the cold of night and the thirst of the day. Look to a lady with a torch in her hand.

"The torch is a symbol of the light of hope. You need to have hope that your next step will be the step that crosses into our land of freedom

"Her book is the stories of those who came before you and are waiting for you.

"Her robe is made up of the fabric that is this great nation.

"Her arm has the strength that can carry the heaviest burden that is bought by any child of any nation.

"She is standing tall, looking out for the children of other nations to find her. Standing there, she waits to welcome you to this land.

My time is up for today. So, in closing, I go back to that little girl I saw with two dresses on.

"We live in the land of the free for this little girl to dress herself in two favorite dresses and put them both on. One over the other. Both were pink, so they didn't clash. Then the little girl put a tiara on her head. Alongside the tiara she put on a set of cat ears. Around her neck she had a necklace of plastic white pearls. And two other shiny plastic neckless.

"How close was she dressed today like the lady with the torch?

"Amen."

The preacher's mother and sister stand up and start to clap. Andy sees Michelle standing with her ten-year-old daughter. Next to Michelle is her husband and her son in a naval officer uniform.

It is the night before Thanksgiving 2001. Andy is up in his apartment alone. The doctors have told him he is going to die of cancer. The leading cause was drinking the groundwater at the diner for fifty years.

Andy hears a knock on his door. He gets up out of his chair by the window that has a view of the lot that was his diner. Andy opens the door and sees a man with a familiar face. It is Harper the newspaper reporter who used to visit his diner.

Harper and Andy say hello. Andy invites Harper into his apartment. Harper looks around the small room. A small TV and radio are in a corner, unplugged. The walls are all painted a flat-white. The two windows have white shades pulled down halfway. The floor is just a plain roll sheet of vinyl flooring. On the TV is an old picture of a baseball player.

There is a small kitchen and two doors, one door for a bathroom and one door for a bedroom. There are just a couch and a chair in Andy's living room. Andy asks Harper to have a seat on the couch.

Andy: "Harper is been a long time since I have seen you. How are the wife and kids?

Harper: "Kids are grown adults now. I am a grandfather with four grandkids. Andy there is nothing better than being a grandfather. My wife and I go and see the kids with the grandkids. It makes everything worth it."

Andy: "That is nice to hear you say that. You used to complain about the wife and kids all the time."

Harper: "I guess it is old age maybe. It has a way to mellow a person out. Or it was the passion my wife and I had for each other. It is what a real marriage needs "

Andy: "I never had kids, but I saw Michelle's boy grow up to be a fine man. I also got a chance to help a woman named Maria and her kids. Not having any kids of my own, I felt like I did the best I could for them."

Harper: "Andy I saw what you did for those people. You gave them the best chance at just living a decent life."

Andy: "Harper what brings you here? You didn't come to see me after all these years, just to tell me about your grandkids."

Harper: "Andy I never became the book writer I always thought I should have been. But I did find that I was a damn good investigator reporter. Whoever thought newspapers would die. Andy my job now is finding facts and details that are needed to report news stories. Andy it's all about computers now. The facts that a story need are out there. That's what I do. Andy, I do it very well."

Andy: "That's very good for you. Your old friend Haden would have been envious of you. That's kind of what he wanted to do. Only he wanted to be something in a movie."

Harper: "Before he died, he got to do it. He would stay up all night and watch old detective movies. What a way to go."

Andy: "I guess if it made him happy, so be it."

Harper: "Andy sometimes I come across some mysteries in my work that can't be solved. It's just the way it is. In my life, I have three of them that interest me more than any other. Andy you are in all three of them. All three of them are related. I don't know what I am going to do with them, Andy. I think you would like to know them."

Andy: "Harper I am dying as you probably know. What you don't know is I may not make it another month. There is nothing I fear or have any concern for. So please tell me what you came here for."

Harper: "Andy I have to know if I am right on what I have been trying to solve a good part of my life. Andy, I think you hold some pieces that go together."

Andy: "Okay, Harper, tell me what mysteries I know."

Harper: "I am going to work backward on this. The first one is Michelle's boyfriend being found in that old water tower behind your diner. The police think he wanted to get high and climbed into the tower to do it. Inside the tower was an old battery and headlight. The battery and headlight was from a car from the forties before that boy was born. Andy you had access to the tower and the old junkyard across the tracks.

"The last person known to see him a live was

Michelle. I talked to her after they autopsied what was left of him. She said that she was sure he was going to see you that night. He was asking her a lot of questions about the diner and you. That was the last time anybody saw him.

"Then for whatever coincidence this is, Dan shoots himself after they find his body. No suicide note. If he wanted to kill himself over his wife, he had plenty of chances to do it.

"Two days after he shoots himself, Michelle gets a letter from him. The letter tells Michelle he knew how Paul died. He apologizes for not telling her. He couldn't tell her because he was protecting someone. That was you, Andy.

"There were words solved in the puzzle. Your waitresses used to work on crossword puzzles and hang them up in the ordering window. I remember going in there on Friday nights and see them in that little window hanging up. Harley would work on them too.

"They found Dan had a crossword puzzle from the same day Michelle's boyfriend disappear. The words on the puzzle were door, path, tracks, coal, car, track, bridge, victim, antenna, and incriminate.

"I think Michelle's boyfriend was robbing your place. Dan, who was working that night, found him and shot him. You hid the body. Why, I don't know, but my guess is Dan saw the crossword puzzle in the diner. I placed you as a serial vigilante. The crime stopped around the same time. No one was ever arrested for the crime. No one ever confessed to it.

"It's just fits you. A Vietnam vet with the skill to do it. Then I went to your doctor. He couldn't tell me if you had a mental condition from the poisoned water you drank for all those years, but another doctor who study cases like yours said you fit the pattern of a serial killer. Andy what do you think so far?"

Andy: "You're close. Michelle's boyfriend shot himself by accident. Michelle's boyfriend fired a gun at Dan. Dan had threatened to kill him before. I got Dan to let me take care of the body and the car. I knew no one would go into the tower. I always thought I should have taken the body out and buried it. I drove his car across the tracks to the old junkyard. Dan found the crossword puzzle by mistake.

"I told him to go into the diner and wash his face. Then he must of saw the puzzle and connected the dots. It was my puzzle that day. I put those words in there. I was probably trying to get caught.

Harper: "I was close, Andy. I was close."

Andy: "So, Harper, what are you going to do with what you know?"

Harper: "Nothing, Andy. Nothing. Too many lives are already messed up. Why do more harm?"

Andy: "So you did all that work to do nothing with it?"

Harper: "Andy, there's more."

Andy : "What more?"

Harper: "Andy that's two mysteries. What happened to Michelle's boyfriend. You are the serial vigilante and Dan solved it. He would have been a legend in the police department. He couldn't say anything because that boy killed himself and him finding you and that puzzle that night. Two mysteries solved, Andy. Two out of three. And we know what the third murder mystery is."

Andy: "The third one is my father's murder, isn't it Harper?"

Harper "Yes, it is."

Andy: "You solved who killed my father, Harper?"

Harper: "No, Andy, I didn't. That is the one both Haden and I wanted to solve. We felt like we owed it to you to find who killed your father.

"In my field of investigative reporting we often find other things. Sometimes, while investigating one story, it may lead us to another story.

"I met an FBI agent on another investigation I was doing. We were talking about unsolved murder cases. I told him about your father's murder and how it was never solved. He promised me he would look at the case. I gave him the facts of the case as I knew them. I didn't expect anything to come from it.

"Then a month later he called me. He said he found something, and he was coming in from Washington. Then he would tell me what he found."

Andy: "They found who killed my father?"

Harper: "Sorry, Andy, no they didn't. What they found was a much bigger mystery to him. The FBI agent got your father's fingerprints and palm print from the state's unsolved murder cases. He loaded them to a new computer the FBI has.

"He hoped to find something that may help to solve the case I asked him about. The computer came back with something that no one could dream of.

"Andy, you know the story of the massacre on February fourteenth?"

Andy: "Yes, I heard of it. Everybody knows the story."

Harper: "Andy they found your father's palm print was a match on a shotgun. It was one of the weapons used that day. The weapons were found in an old speakeasy turned restaurant.

This building was burned to the ground on August 31, 1939. The next day the fire department found three burnt bodies. They also found an old grandfather clock, untouched by the fire, standing in the middle of a pile of ashes and bodies. One of the firefighters noticed the clock wasn't working, so he opened it up. Inside were two Thompson machine guns, two high-powered rifles, and one sawed-off shotgun. Under the guns was a bloodied police uniform.

"The police came and took it away. When the police received the weapons, they dusted it for fingerprints. They found only one palm print on a shotgun. The guns were put away and the palm print was later forgotten about.

"The world of computers came to be, Andy. All the old finger and palm prints got loaded into the world of binary numbers. Andy that means Big Brother is watching.

"When the FBI agent put your father's finger and palm prints into that computer, the computer found a perfect match to your father. Your father was probably ten years old at the time. The FBI doesn't think your father had anything to do with that famous massacre.

"They wanted information on your father. They had no information on your father from before 1945. They found no birth certificate on your father. They had a blank.

"They guessed who your mother may be. They guessed who her father may be. They guessed who her mother was.

"Andy, I had no idea that was her father. She never let anybody know did she."

Andy: "If they guessed Litti. Yes, it was Litti. She wanted no part of his legacy."

Harper: "I went to Chicago after I talked to the agent and found the place of the building that burnt down. There was no building there, just a graveyard. A dead-end street and a train station. I wanted to find someone who may remember that building and what your father may have been doing there. It was so long ago most of the people back then are long gone.

"I went to the local police station and asked them if anybody who may have known the restaurant was still alive. They gave me the number of an old woman who lived in the same building her whole life. She lived near the restaurant.

"The woman told me when she was a young girl her father took her picture in front of the place called Borders. She remembered a boy who would take the garbage out and get the papers in the morning.

Then she started to tell me a story about a big man called Raggedy."

Andy gets a big smile to his face.

Harper: "Andy that is the biggest smile I ever seen you have."

Harper stops and thinks about it for a moment.

Harper: "Oh. I got it. You are named after him, aren't you? She said the big man was a bodyguard for a little girl who lived at the speakeasy. Was that your mother, Andy? She didn't say much about her and couldn't remember her name. Andy, she said she had a picture of the building. In the background is the picture of the speakeasy with a fire escape."

Harper gives Andy a copy of the picture. Andy looks at it then gets up and walks to a table with a lamp on it. Andy opens the drawer and takes out a magnifying glass. He holds the picture under the lamp and looks at it with the magnifying glass. Andy starts to cry.

Andy: "It's them together sitting on the fire escape with a picnic basket."

Andy takes a minute looking at the picture then sits back down.

Andy: "You did a good job, Harper. That was my mother. That is where she lived. That man was her bodyguard. The young boy was my father."

Harper: "Your parents did such a good job of hiding who your mother was."

Andy: "My mother didn't want anybody to know."

Harper: "Andy what can you tell me about your father?"

Andy: "What I know I promised never to tell.

But I do think now may be the last time I get the chance. They may want me to do it now.

Harper I am going to give you the short version. After I die, my lawyer will send you my mother's diary. It has love letters written to my father. Cross-word puzzles she would send to my father as a young girl in love. She would just put the simplest letters to my father in those puzzles, so no one would know.

The complex story of a daughter and father who loved being with each other. But they couldn't live in the same house. It is what my mother wrote about her life. Please try and find a way for her story to be told.

"Harper it's a story of a love my mother had for my father. It's a story of a young boy that lost who he was. Harper, I think it's time I tell somebody the story of Nitti and Hayes. That was their names back then. My mother was named Nitti to have power over someone who had power.

"My father was called Hayes because of his loss of his memory and not knowing who he was. One day my father woke up and didn't know who he was or where he came from.

"He woke up years later and remembered his name. He remembered who his parents were. He remembered what he wished he didn't remember. He remembered how different he was from the others in the place he lived. My father couldn't tell anybody what he was. It was the 1930s and things were different back then.

"My mother told me she fell in love with my father the first time she saw him. At first, she couldn't understand my father being so quiet and shy.

"Then my mother realized my father lived in fear of the people around him. My father had a bigger fear of going back to the streets if he did something wrong.

"After a couple of years living under the same roof, the two started to talk sometimes.

"Then one day my grandmother died. My father with that man Raggedy went to the school to tell my mother. My father didn't understand why Raggedy wanted to take him along.

"After my mother was told she went to the young man, Hayes, my father, and cried on his shoulder. My father said his life changed at that moment in his life. For the first time that my father could remember, he was emotionally committed to someone.

"After my grandmother was laid to rest, my father went back to the reality of who he was. That was till August 31, 1939.

My mother's grandfather saw my parents holding hands and going into a movie theater. He went back and told my grandfather what he saw.

"After the movie, my mother confronted my father on why he didn't show the interest in her that she had for him. My father didn't want to tell her. My mother told him if she didn't tell her the truth, she would leave and live at the girls school in New York.

"My father, thinking there may not be a better opportunity, told my mother he remembered who he was, and his parent were a mixed race.

"My mother put her arms around my father and kissed him. It was their first kiss.

"Back at the restaurant, all hell broke loose that day. Nicholas Litti wanted to kill Hayes, my father. "Nicholas Litti's father-in-law wanted to kill my mother. So Raggedy had to kill both. Raggedy saved my parents. It cost Raggedy his life.

"When my parents got back to the building that day, they found what had happened. Raggedy gave my parents all the money he could find. He put it in a suitcase then told them to leave and hide.

"My mother and father made a plan that night. She would go to New York and live at the school for a while. My father would fake a name and join the Marines. Then after my father got out of the service, he would find my mother. She would be old enough to get married.

"The next day, Germany invaded Poland. Nicholas Litti's son was butchered with a razor. Five years later, my father leaves the military and finds my mother waiting for him. She has the money saved and hidden. They get married at Niagara Falls. Then they come to this town, buy an old building from the money Raggedy gave them, and make it into a diner.

"To get back to the gun, my father told me about it, but I didn't know he touched it. You can tell them that that young man's name was Luis Ross.

"That's why he is Luis Ross. My mother is Daisy Ross and I am Andy Ross. That is why the diner was called Daisy.

"The next day is Thanksgiving Day. The year is 2001. Andy gets up at 5:00 AM. He washes his face and brushes his teeth. He walks out of his apartment and down a set of stairs. He leaves his building.

Andy walks past a field of daisies. The field is by an old abandoned railroad track that once had a water tower, a service building, and a diner.

He walks up a couple of streets with some common street names. Andy walks into a hospital for his cancer treatment. He walks into the small luncheonette and takes a seat at a booth. A waitress comes over to Andy and takes his order for a coffee. The waitress brings Andy a cup of coffee. Andy thanks the waitress. Ten minutes later, the waitress looks over to her customer. He hasn't moved since last time she looked at him. She walks over to see the man has passed away.

On the other side of the hospital, Maria's daughter, Faith, has delivered a baby boy. Faith and her husband name the baby boy Andrew.

The End.

It is a year after Andy Ross has died. Harper has written a story about the young life of the long-lost daughter of Nicholas Litti.

One of the most known, powerful mobsters of the twenties and thirties did have a daughter. The myth of a young girl who had to live in the shadows. A young girl that was the last person who survived that world of murder for hire.

She survived a set of parents who had two lives together. One life that was hidden from this young girl. The early years her parents had together. The years her parents had together in England during the first world war.

After the war, her father went back to the life of loyalty to the power and money a poor man dream of. Her mother, the daughter of a general, returned to West Point. Her mother found a band leader years later who found an attractive woman who could sing.

One day in the early thirties, this band was in Chicago. A man named Nicholas and a woman named Sadie found each other again as adults. The stories had to change. The lies of a one-night stand were made.

The reputation of this young woman would always be the price she paid to protect her child and the child's father. No stories of two people who found the love of their life.

The safety of a deal that was made. The two people who gave up each other for their daughter.

The girl was Nitti. Yes, just Nitti. I found her and her life.

Nitti was a mother and the wife of a childhood love. She never thought to come forward and claim any title that was waiting for her. The people and organization that search for her in vain. How the day her father died was the last known day of her.

I found her. I found the greatest story I will ever have. I can't tell the tale. I can't tell the rest of the story. I can't tell you who she became.

The price paid by her husband and her child to hide her was greater than what the story would be worth.

I had letters and documents that would be a trophy in the world of what I do. I buried them about a year ago.

I will tell you Nitti was a sympathetic figure. I have somebody close to Nitti who let me publish the following letters.

There is no happily ever after for her. I will leave her and her family in peace. I hope these letters explain her early years.

Harper

CHAPTER TWENTY

Nitti letters

September 2, 1936

Hello, Hayes, my name is Nitti. Just Nitti. Yes, just Nitti. My mother gave me that name, so she would be able to have something on my father. Maybe I will explain that better later.

I am the girl you saw yesterday morning. I am a thirteen-year-old girl. This is my home. I lived here all my life. During the school year, I go to an all-girl school. During the summer, my father sends me to a summer camp for girls.

In the morning, I eat my breakfast at the bar. After school, I eat my dinner at the bar. That's funny when you think about it. A thirteen-year-old girl eating at a bar. At night, I sleep in my room. I have the biggest room in this place. I have my own bathroom. At night in my room I do my homework then go to bed.

On weekends, I get to spend some time with my father. I love my father. He is so good to me. He takes me to movies. He takes me out to eat. He buys me nice, pretty things. Girls like nice, pretty things.

Sometimes, he will have what he wants to give me when he picks me up. My father will have all it wrapped like a present. My mother… Maybe I will explain that better later.

Raggedy told me he took you out of an orphanage. Raggedy is a very scary person to everybody but me. He is my personal bodyguard. It's nice to have a personal bodyguard. Everybody should have one.

Raggedy had to get rid of that old, ugly-looking man for stealing. I never liked that ugly old man. I am glad he's gone. I don't care who killed him or who is responsible.

Please don't do anything to make Raggedy mad at you. He is a person that can hurt anybody. I did see him beat up three men at one time. Raggedy runs this place.

Raggedys mother is Rag. That's not her real name; it's just some disgusting name that found her. It is a name that does fit her. Please don't make her mad either. I saw her shoot a couple of people. She will shoot people in different body parts if they can't pay her the money, they owe her. The woman is crazy, if you ask me. I try to be as nice to her as I can be.

I don't know whose side Raggedy would be on. Would he be on my side or hers? I hope I never find out.

Raggedys father died years ago. Rag remarried Conversation. Yes, that is what he is called—Conversation.

He doesn't talk much, so he got the name attached to him of Conversation. If he talks to you, just say yes and do what he asked.

Tony runs the kitchen. He is just a normal person. He is the head of the other cooks and waitresses. They all must do things the way Tony wants it done. If they don't, Tony will tell Raggedy and things will get done Tony's way. Or somebody gets hurt. So please do what he wants you to do.

This hotel or restaurant you now live in his really owned by my father's father-in-law. I don't like him, and he doesn't like me. My father is married to his daughter. She is a fat cow who doesn't like me either. My father and her has a dopey son. He is a couple of years older than me. I guess that makes him your age. Nobody likes him.

This place used to be a speakeasy. A gambling nightclub. A place to drink in Prohibition. A train building or something. Now it's just our home. Welcome home, Hayes.

Hayes I am very lonely here. I have nowhere else to go. My father's wife doesn't want his mistake. My mother can't take care of herself much less a young girl. Hayes, I hope we can be friends.

Please for now don't try and talk to me. Raggedy will not like it. If you smile at me or wink your eye at me, that will make me happy. I understand you may be scared to talk to me. You don't have to worry about that. I will not tell anybody.

Raggedy drove me to school this morning after meeting you. I asked him who you were. He told me you were an orphan he got from an orphanage. He also said you lost some of your memory. I hope you get it back sometime, Hayes. Hayes, we have something in common.

I think of myself as an orphan who can't go live with her mother and father. This place we now both live in is an orphanage for the orphan who can't leave. Tony gets to come and go. He has a real family to go to.

I met his family. They get to come over here for Thanksgiving. But the rest of us—Raggedy, Rag, Conversation, you, and me—are here.

Hayes when I get older, I will leave this place and never come back. I am going to get away as far as I can. I am going to change my name and never tell anybody who my father his father-in-law was. One day, Raggedy caught a newspaper reporter following me. Raggedy buried him in the graveyard behind us.

Hayes you can write me back and no one will ever know. I promise no one will ever know. You can hide your notes to me in the paper you put by my door in the morning. You don't have to write me every day, just sometimes.

If you check the crossword puzzles, I will leave you notes hidden in the puzzles. No one will ever find them. Hayes that could be so much fun between me and you. It will be our secret.

It's getting late now, Hayes. I am too tired to write more. Please write me back. I am so lonely here in this place that has found us two orphans.

Nitti

Hayes

Hello, Hayes. I went and saw a movie called *Lost Horizon* the other day with my father. My father can be so nice to me. I guess every father is nice to their daughter. My father picked me up in a big, shiny new car. He had a couple of boxes of presents. They were wrapped up in different colored wrapping paper. Hayes, girls like to get presents wrapped up. Inside the boxes were some new dresses and a necklace. I wore the necklace all day. I bet it cost a lot of money. My father had to take it home with him to keep it safe. But he said I could get it anytime.

My father then took me out to brunch. That's a meal between breakfast and lunch. I just love that word brunch. It makes the time eating feel more special. Whenever I am with my father, I feel special. Hayes I am not supposed to say anything, but my father always has a bodyguard with him. He also has a couple more in a car close by. Please don't tell anybody.

My father orders me some French food. He said it was crepes suzette. It just sounds great, doesn't it? Brunch and crepes suzette. Girls love that kind of stuff, Hayes. When I get a boyfriend, he is going to take me out to places like this all the time.

My father asked me about you, Hayes. I told him you don't talk at all and you are always working. He likes that about you. Raggedy must tell him the same or you would be gone. Hayes, I hope you don't leave. I like seeing you every day. It would be nice if you write me back. I understand why you don't. Raggedy would not like it.

After we ate, my father had to stop by his father-in-law's barbershop. My father goes in by himself. Outside the barbershop is always some young men dressed up in business suits. Those young men are just dreaming that they hold any place around my father.

Those young men will not be able to hold the place where their two feet are standing today. Next month there will be a wannabe, with his feet where somebody else's feet were today. They are just like billiard balls on a pool table. My father is playing them against each other.

There is no loyalty in the work my father does. The wannabes are just temps. They are given promises of a future if they do certain tasks asked of them. If they are the lucky one, they may live to be asked to do another. Those young men get to dress up and be part of playtime. I will tell you what playtime is later.

Those young men are made to feel like part of an organization. It's a bad organization, Hayes. My father tells those young men the last workers he had couldn't do the jobs asked of them. The past workers weren't smart enough. The past workers had no patience for the big payoff that was coming. The next big job is where the money will be handed out to everybody.

My father tells that to all the want to-be-bad guys. Every time I come here and see those young men out front of the barbershop, I want to yell at them. I want to yell at them and tell them to go home and get a real job. Go home and take care of your family. I want to yell louder at the ones that have kids because my father is going to make their kids an orphan.

Then I look at those young men. Some good-looking young men with nice smiles. How they will try to use that smile to impress a girl. How those second-hand, hand-me-down suits and pretty smiles may be enough to impress a girl. If a girl falls for that, then the girl can have him.

One day last year, one of those young men started to wave at me as I sat in the car waiting for my father. I waved back at him, Hayes. Then he came over to the car and said hello to me. We talked a little. I think he liked me. I do look older and I think I am a pretty girl.

My father came out of the barbershop and saw him talking to me. My father took that young man back into the barbershop. A couple of minutes later my father came out of the barbershop with blood on his suit. He asked me not to talk to any of those men again. I think I know what my father did to him. I hope he wasn't married or had kids.

I am sorry, Hayes, I got off track. I want to tell you about the movie I saw.

My father and I got some popcorn and candy and took a seat in the balcony. My father could have any seat in the place because of who he is.

The movie had all old people in it. Not like *Romeo and Juliet*. There were five people escaping from China. They got on a plane and thought they were safe. Not so fast. The plane was highjacked and taken to a faraway place.

On the plane there five men and one pretty woman. The woman was blond and reminded me of my mother. She was sick and lost hope on finding a cure for herself. I thought she would be the female lead in this movie because she was a pretty woman with blond hair. Hollywood just loves pretty women with blond hair.

The man who is the star of the movie was too old. He had a nice British accent, but he was too old. He had an annoying little brother. He reminded me of my stepbrother, a crying, annoying wimp.

The other two men on the plane had no reason to be in this story or the movie. I don't know what the writer was thinking with the other two men.

The plane crashes in some mountains the no one knows about. Then the five are rescued and taken to a hidden paradise on top of a mountain. The five find themselves in the care of a man who wants to live in some utopia.

Well the lead man finally sees his love interests in the story. When the man sees this beautifully dressed woman in white, he falls in love at first sight. The woman is looking down from the stairs at him. You can tell that this is the part where boy meets girl and the story is supposed to be about that. Boy meets girl. Love at first sight.

It's supposed to be a love story. The story of the man will do anything to be with the woman. The story turned out to be about this so-called utopia of this lost place. They spent too much time on telling the story of the magic of this utopia.

There was one scene of the lead man and the beautiful woman on a horse ride having some fun. It was the woman wanting to be caught by the man. It was pretty good. I liked it.

Then the lead man and woman have their first kiss. It was good. The director did it right. The lead man catches her after some flirting. The man has her back up against a white wall. She has no place to escape. They look at each other, then the kiss. It worked. I felt like those two were in love. It was just those two in the world.

This magic utopian place did cure the pretty blond woman. I wish I could do that with my mother. I wish I could send her there and have her cured from what makes her sick. There is not much more with the pretty blond woman or the other two men. I just didn't understand their part in this story.

The lead's young brother finds another pretty girl who lived there. The girl is twenty, the age everybody in this movie should have been. The young brother talks his older brother into leaving the land and trying to get back home.

Why the lead man would leave the lead woman, I don't know, but he does. As the lead man's wimpy younger brother leaves the place, the lead woman tries to stop him. Well she doesn't, and her love is gone.

The three who left run into problems. The young brother dies, and the once-young girl turns old and dies. The lead man gets lost and goes crazy but gets rescued. He loses his memory like you, Hayes. When he gets it back, he goes to any lengths to get back to that lost land.

Hayes, he keeps trying with all his effort to get back. He does finally make it back. They should have had the woman, his love interest, at the entrance waiting for him. He went back for her. He went back just for her.

The last scene in the movie shows him looking at the land he left with his brother and girl. He wanted to get back for the beautiful woman. The story should have ended that way. That was the only way the movie should have ended. Him and her. The man and woman in each other's arms forever.

Nobody cares about the utopia that some dreamer wants to create. It's a love story, this movie was supposed to be. The movie should have ended with her in his arms. That's how this movie should have ended. Then you know that's how the rest of their life would be.

My father liked the movie. He told me if he was there, he would be running the lost utopia. He told me I would be the princess. If any young man wanted to win my hand, they would have to go through him first. Then that young man would have to beat up Raggedy. Then they would have to kiss Rag. Then I asked my father if he would ever let me get married.

He had to think for a moment, then he said no. I know he was just kidding.

He took me out for some ice cream after the movie and we talked about school. He had to get back home, so he took me home that day. I was so happy to have him to myself that day.

I must go and get ready for bed, Hayes.

Good night,
Nitti

Hayes

Hello, Hayes. I want to tell you about a movie I saw with my father. It was called *The Informer*.

I didn't think I would like it. It was about a man named Gypo Nolan who told the police were his best friend was hiding. Gypo's best friend did something wrong and the police put a bounty on his head. Gypo wanted the bounty money for his girl. Gypo's girl was a speakeasy girl.

Gypo. What a great name, don't you think? He reminds me of Raggedy but not as big. Everybody liked Gypo. Gypo drank too much the night he informed on his friend. The money he got for the bounty ended up buying him a good time. When he finally gets whatever money to his girlfriend, there wasn't enough to get her what she wanted.

There was no real love story here. There was no boy meets girl here. It's a story my father must face every day. I guess that is why he wanted to see it. The best part for him was when Gypo died the informer. He said Hollywood glamourized the informer. At the end I spent time with my father and I like that. After the movie, we went out to eat. My father said he was thinking of buying a real restaurant.

So, he took me there. What a nice place this was. There were boys your age to park cars. At the door was a doorman dressed in a funny suit. Everybody at this place was so nice to us. They called my father sir or by his name.

They gave us the best table. We had three waiters just for us. My father ordered my dinner and I loved it. My father had such a good time. He was telling me about all the important people he knew. Then he pointed out the people who were here trying to think they were important. My father is important.

I was having a good time with him when a man came over and asked my father if he wanted to see upstairs. My father told me he would be back in twenty minutes or so. He told me a woman was going to come over and sit with me while he was gone. He kissed me on my cheek. He got up and went right to the next table and tapped a beautiful young woman on the shoulder. He whispered in her ear. Then she came over and sat in my father's chair.

This woman was in a beautiful, long blue dress. She looked like something right out of Hollywood. Then I saw she had on the necklace my father gave me. The one he said he had to hold. She also had a pair of earrings to match that I didn't get. She sat down next to me and introduced herself as Ideas. She said that is what I should call her. Then she said sometimes names and people shouldn't go together. We talked for a bit.

Nitti: "It's nice to meet you."

Ideas: "Your father has told me what a beautiful young lady you are. You have your mother's looks, Nitti. Your mother was a very beautiful woman."

Nitti: "Thank you, Ideas, that's very nice of you to say that. My mother was very beautiful. Now she is very sick, and I hope she is trying to get sober."

Ideas: "Your father said you're no fool. That's hard for a daughter to say that about their mother. I give you a lot of credit for it."

Nitti: "Ideas did you know my mother?"

Ideas: "I heard her sing when I was very young. She had a great voice. She had a hold on everybody in the room when she sang. She had a voice Hollywood would have loved."

Nitti: "That's what my father's says. When I ask my mother about it, she just starts to drink more. So, I don't ask."

Ideas: "Yes, I understand. I am sorry to bring it up, Nitti."

Nitti: "It's okay. How do you know my father, Billy?"

Ideas: "Nitti I knew that question was coming. Could I just leave it with you we are friends, and leave it at that please?"

Nitti: "I understand, Ideas. My father has a lot of friends. Could we just leave it at that please?"

Ideas: "Sure, Nitti. I am just who I am. Nitti I am going to change the subject about us. I met Raggedy. He is just the most special person I ever met. You are so lucky to have him as a friend. Last week I had to go somewhere, so your father had him go with me for a couple of days. When you first see this giant of a scary man, it is very intimidating. But after a couple of minutes, you think of him as a fuzzy warm blanket. He is just too good to be true."

Nitti: "Yes, I like him. He is very nice to me. I sometimes think he is my only friend. But my father must pay him to do what he does. I don't think he would be around me for long if my father didn't pay him."

Ideas: "I don't know about that, Nitti. I wish I could tell you what you want to hear. I think you know the answer better than me."

Nitti: "I like that necklace you have on, Ideas. It looks very pretty on you."

Ideas: "Thank you, Nitti, I love this necklace. I know it's yours. I picked it out for you. I asked your father to buy it for you. I told him if I was a teenage girl, that's what I would like. After he gave it to you and took it back to keep it safe for you, he asked me to hold it, so his wife didn't see it. The earrings came with the necklace. Your father wanted you to have the necklace and me to have the earrings. Nitti your father wanted me and you to meet tonight and get to know each other. The necklace is his way to show me what he thinks of you. I am going to give you both the necklace and the earrings, Nitti. I want you to know that I do care for your father. He loves you, Nitti. One day he may, or we may, come for you. If that happens, Nitti, we will need to be friends. You think we could be friends, Nitti?"

Nitti doesn't answer Ideas right away. She looks around the room. Then she looks at Ideas.

Nitti: "Ideas look around the room. You see all the people in this room? There are a lot of people in this room. Somebody in this room would like to kill my father. That's his life and I know it. Someday, somebody is going to do it. He knows it. I don't have any real friends at school. They're all afraid of Raggedy. I can't go out like other kids do. If the day comes and my father and you come for me, he will be broke. He will be a man with a target on his head from his father-in-law. My father's wife, the cow that she is, is what keeps my father around beautiful women like you. You can keep the necklace and the earrings. I lied before. My father doesn't have a lot of friends like you. You must be very special to him. I bet he does really love you.

"That is why he wanted us to meet. It would be a nice dream, Ideas, the three of us. You two happily married. Me the happy daughter who lives with her father and stepmother. It's not going to happen.

"All you could do for me is get my father killed for me. I would like to keep him. As much of him to myself as possible for as long as I can. Your dream or his dream of the happily ever after is the graveyard, like the one behind the dump he has me live in. If I ever see you again, I am going to be thinking you want to get my father killed.

"You are such a beauty for a man not to like you. You can make a man do something he shouldn't do, and I do like you. You can keep the necklace and the earrings. You can have anything I have. But don't take my father from me please. I must live sometimes months without him. Coping with what I must cope with makes me so crazy. It must be having some effect on me. The relationship I have with my father the gangster. My father the killer. My father who isn't always mine. My father who isn't who you think he is. My father isn't in heaven.

"I am going out to the car to wait for my father.

When he comes back, tell him whatever you want. Bye, Ideas."

Nitti leaves Ideas at the table and goes out to the car. The doorman leaves the door and walks Nitti out to the car. Nitti is joined by her father later.

The doorman has waited outside the car for Nitti's father to come back. Out in the car, Nitti's father asks her what happened to Ideas. She was gone from the table. Nitti tells her father she wasn't feeling well so she told Billy she would be out in the car. Nitti sees Ideas in a movie a year later with a different name. The name of Daisy

Hayes that is what happened that night.

Good night,

Nitti

Hello, my friend Hayes.

My father took me to a movie. The movie is called *My Man Godfrey*. Hayes you would like this movie a lot. It reminds me of you and me. Pretty woman was looking for a forgotten man. Let me explain. A group of people were playing a game to find a man down on his luck. The game she was playing called for her to find a man down on his luck. She finds a man; he is somebody very special. That is so much like you, Hayes. I wish I found you. Hayes. I see how very special you are. The man becomes her family butler. The pretty woman falls for the man.

The woman sees what a good person he is. The man accepted her and her family for who they were. The man could have left the job of just being a butler, but he didn't. The man wanted to stay and find himself. The woman and her crazy family let him find himself.

The place where the woman and her family live is like a castle. You can see the woman falls for the man who is now her family's butler. She tries to get close to him. She wants to see the man show her some affection. He has a job with the family that calls on him to know his place. He does his job every day and carries himself with a pride of a good man. Like you.

The man is set up by an evil sister of the woman. The evil sister hides a piece of expensive jewelry in the man's bedroom. When the police are called to the scene of the crime, the smart man, Godfrey, had removed the piece of jewelry. At the end of the movie, Godfrey gives the evil sister her jewelry back. Godfrey also gives the family a lot of money he made from having to hold the piece of jewelry.

Godfrey finds what he wants to do in this time with the pretty woman and the crazy family. He wants to help as many people who came from where he lived at one time. Godfrey opens a restaurant on a river. The pretty woman goes down to the restaurant at the river to marry the man she loves.

I think when the pretty woman sees the restaurant, she thinks that is what he wanted. It's not the restaurant he wanted. The restaurant was just a vehicle he uses to help who he can help.

Hayes, they get married at the end. In the movies, you want to think they live happily ever after. I don't know about this one. She just wants him. He wants his life of work. He falls for the pretty woman enough to marry her. I think some time in the future she is going to find that Godfrey is more committed to something else but her. That would break her. She wouldn't leave him. She couldn't leave the man she loved. The years she would spend with him wouldn't be fair to her. It would be the price she pays to love someone who loved something more than her.

My father is like the movie. He asked me if I wanted Raggedy to dress up like a butler. My father thought that was funny. He should be careful with Raggedy. Sometimes, I think Raggedy would like to walk away and forget my father. My father has asked Raggedy to do things that I know Raggedy didn't want to do. Raggedy has the same loyalty that Godfrey has in the movie.

My father promises to take me to New York City someday. I would like to see the city but maybe with someone else. When I get married, I want to go to New York and see the falls. Then spend some time in the city with my husband visiting the sites and dining out every night.

The dreams of a young girl, Hayes. We see movies and start to imagine ourselves in the roles of a young woman. We imagine who we want to marry. We start to the process of constructing what we want him to be. I can picture the person I want to marry.

I may tell him at first that I may not like him. That his efforts are in vain. That's what girls can do. We do that because we want the young man to want us. We want to see that want from them. We will be the ones who will decides if the young man's effort will be rewarded. Or we will be the ones who will see the young man's effort go to waste. That he is left with only the dream of the pretty girl. God, I want to be his dream, I love him so much. Please be kind to me in this way and bring him to me. Please God, that young man is the person who waits for me. He is the one who will be what I lost with my father and mother.

Bye, my very dear friend Hayes. Nitti

A love affair

Hayes

I saw a movie with a boy today. I think this was my first date. I don't know for sure because I spent time alone with you before. I really didn't care for him. If you want to know about the boy I was with. He had greasy hair. All he could think of was my father. He never stopped asking about him. Then he wanted to meet him. I went on this date for two reasons: a girl in school needed another girl for a double date, and I wanted to see if you cared if I went out on a date, Hayes. I care what you think of me.

The movie was a boy meets girl. It was the simplest of movies. Most of the early part of the movie the man and woman tried to avoid each other. The man was somebody the press liked to follow. The woman was looking for Mr. Right.

Somehow, on this big boat, they run into each other over and over. When they did run into each other, not much was made of it. I kept waiting for something. They had a drink of pink champagne. It remined me of you and me with ice cream and apple pie.

The two find themselves on an island visiting the man's mother, I think. The people who made the movie had to think of something that meant something. So, they came up with a scene where his mother gives the woman a white shawl. Well, she promised to mail it to her.

At the end of their boat trip, the man and the woman agree to meet in six months. The six months would give each of them time think about if they wanted to see the other person.

Both the man and woman couldn't wait to see the other. The movie was about the woman getting in an accident. It left her a crippled and she couldn't make the date that was planned for the six months.

Anyway, at the end of the movie the man finds the woman and sees that she is a cripple. He loves her so much that he will spend the rest of his life devoted to her.

It made me think of us, Hayes. Every time I go away, I think of you. I think of you waiting for me. Would you wait for me, Hayes? If I was to go away for a longer time, would you wait for me? Then when you found me, if I needed help, would you help me?

If I was that crippled woman with little hope of a healthy life, that would be asking a lot of you, Hayes.

I think we have something between us. The way we came together, you and me. The place we are in. This isn't any place for a boy to meet a girl and fall in love. Hayes, I fell in love with you in this place. This place that I hated for years has brought you to me. I regretted it for years, putting the poker money in the old man's coat. I had no idea they would kill him. Hayes please believe me that I am sorry.

No one saw anybody else do it because I used the dumbwaiter that goes into your room. When all the men playing cards left the room to take a break, I took the dumbwaiter into the room. I took all the money on the table and put it in the old man's coat. The next day, Raggedy told me that one of the men shot him. I was going to tell Raggedy what I did, but it would have been too late anyway. He wasn't nice to me anyway, Hayes.

Then I saw you, Hayes. I would dream of a young prince that would come and find me. You were my prince, Hayes. The timing of the old man being killed, Raggedy finding you at the orphanage, you not remembering who you were. It all came together to bring you to me.

I said sometimes I don't get to spend time with you, but like the movie, we must wait for the right time for us. The right time for us to be together forever.

There is a future for us together. Somewhere, you and I will live as a real family. We will have kids. You will be the devoted father who comes home at night. The father who never finds another woman or a one-night stand. You will love only me and our children.

I will be the loving mother that cares for her family. A mother who spends time with her children. A mother who reads them stories. A mother who talks to her children about their day at school.

We will be done with diners or restaurants. Your life as a person who works so much will end. You'll get a job somewhere that will take care of us and our kids. Hayes, I want to give that to you.

Hayes I was talking to my father about me going away to college. He gives me the father talk about boys. He told me I shouldn't go on too many dates and stay away from older boys. He went on for a while and I lost track of time. When he finished, I told him I would do as he wanted me to do.

Hayes my father asked me what I wanted for my sweet sixteen birthday. Hayes, I asked my father if he, me, and you can have dinner together before I left. I could read my father pretty good sometimes. But this time I couldn't do it. He looked at me for a minute then looked at his watch and then he said he had to make a call.

I sat there wondering if I made a mistake asking him that. My father has asked me about you. I tell him you're very nice to me and you are always working.

When he came back from the phone call, my father told me he would think about the three of us having dinner together. He tried to tell me the time that it's just him and me is so special to him. Having another person would take away from our time.

Then he told me something that I didn't want to hear. He told me that you may leave when I am gone. My father told me you could get a better paying job because you were so good at what you do. He said I would probably forget you with all the other boys a girl meets at college.

A couple of minutes before he was telling me to stay away from all the boys in college. Hayes, I think my father should be given a book on how to raise a daughter.

Then my father changes the subject to money. He said he is going to give me some money for spending and he'll send more to me.

Hayes I never had money. I never had to hold it. Isn't that strange? Whenever I wanted something, Raggedy bought it for me. I never had to pay a bill. Hayes I never had to work for anything. I don't even know how to cook. I can reheat apple pie. I hope college teaches me what I need to know.

You know what I would like, Hayes? I would like it if you came up and visited me. Then I could show all the other girls what a good-looking friend I have. I could dream of that now. You, my tall, dark-skinned, black, curly-haired, green-eyed young man.

We are more than friends, Hayes. We may not act like boyfriend and girlfriend, but we are friends. In the story of *Romeo and Juliet,* it was their parents who kept the two apart. We are so much like those two, Hayes. What brings us together is keeping us apart. I don't want to end up like those two. I want to be with the one I love forever.

Hayes on the way home my father said you would probably find a girl soon because that is what young men do at that age. I know you work with a lot of pretty waitresses. That last two you hired are very pretty and older than me. They probably had a lot of older boyfriends. I guess the nice word for that is experience. Hayes please wait for me. I'll be sixteen going on seventeen when I come back next summer to see you.

Hayes my father had girls that were friends behind his wife's back. She must know that my father is unfaithful to her. My father is a good-looking man with money and power. I know a lot of women like that in a man. My father told me a long time ago why he had to marry her. It was to show his now father-in-law a commitment to him.

My mother was my father's first affair behind his wife's back. He had to show his father-in-law how sorry he was for the mistake. My father was told to kill the mother of an informer. My father killed her and her husband. That's the two people and Val in the cemetery we saw that night.

The informer is buried with the old man that was killed for stealing the money at the poker game.

That's four people that are dead. That's four people murdered because I was born.

You're forever mine, Hayes.

Nitti

End

ABOUT THE AUTHOR

I don't claim anything in this story is correct. I don't have a side on any side that may be taken by this story.

The only part I like writing was Rag. If you relate yourself to any part of my story, you're trying too hard. The only common factor between you and a person in this story could be if you are a female or male. I made it all up. It is not you or anybody you may know or ever dreamed of.

If you see a name in here and it looks familiar, it is not. I have met a lot of people. I've seen a lot of names in movies. Get yourself out of my story.

Some things I have written may be mean to some people. I am bald and missing most of my teeth. On Sunday, I wash my clothes and separate my black T-shirts. I get up at 5:00 AM Monday- Saturday. I must work six days a week. So, you can make fun of me.

I am a loser who lost.

A wise person once said, and I quote,

"It's always funny till it's about you."

No matter what side of the fence you want to be on.

I am on the other side. I am on the other side not wanting to be on your side.

Edward Licciardello